One Carefree Day

One Carefree Day

a novel

Whitney Amazeen

SWAN PAGES
PUBLISHING

One Carefree Day

For information address Swan Pages Publishing, 100 Maple Street PO Box 1568, Hollister, CA 95023.

This book is a work of fiction. Names, characters, locations, and incidents are products of the authors' imaginations. Any resemblance to actual persons, things, living or dead, locales, or events is entirely coincidental.

The author acknowledges the copyright or trademarked status and trademark owners of the following wordmarks mentioned in this work of fiction: Disney, Harry Potter, In-N-Out, *Everytime You Go*, Ellie Goulding, Phoenix, *My Cherie Amor*, Stevie Wonder.

Cover Design by Murphy Rae and Ashley Quick
Printed in the United States of America

ISBN
978-1-7348997-7-1 (hardcover) | ISBN 978-1-7348997-0-2 (paperback) | ISBN: 978-1-7348997-3-3 (e-book)
10 9 8 7 6 5 4
3 2 1
***
First Edition: February 2021

For Ashley—
the jelly to my peanut butter, my other half, my person, my
parabatai.

AUTHOR'S NOTE

Dear Reader,

The book you just picked up spawned from my feelings of loneliness.

Loneliness, in terms of the state of my mind. I've always been a huge reader, but growing up, I'd never read a book told from the perspective of a character who thought the way I did. Not even close. In fact, I remember thinking there was something specifically wrong with me, because every book I read contained characters who thought so—for lack of a better word—*clean*. And while my mind was a mess of intrusive thoughts and a tangled web of urges to perform rituals, reading books about "normal" people made for a somewhat refreshing experience. I got to take a break from my own head. But at the same time, it made me feel lonely. Like I was the only person in the world who thought the way I did. Which isn't true, of course.

As a result, I created a character who thinks in a similar fashion to the way I did—a character who also struggles with OCD, and I put her in situations that would trigger her, thus, creating this book and its protagonist, Willow.

Growing up, if I'd read a book about a character like her, I probably wouldn't have felt so lonely and strange. I hope anyone who thinks they're strange because of something they can't control realizes they aren't. You're not alone. I'm here too, along with so many others who are doing the exact same thing as everyone else: playing at being "normal".

You've got this. I promise.

Lots of sincere love,

Whitney Amazeen

One
Carefree
Day

One

I'd like to think I'm in control of my life, which is why today is such a problem.

It's the first day of cosmetology school, so it makes sense that I'm more on edge than usual. Today is the start of something new, which makes it unpredictable and uncontrollable.

Even for me.

My cousin Ash sits on my bed, waiting for me to get dressed. I've been staring into my closet for far too long now. Deciding what to wear is an important decision. Opening a salon together has been our dream since we were kids, so I don't want to do anything to mess this day up for either of us, like choosing the wrong thing to wear on our first day.

"Hurry up," Ash says, gesturing towards my closet. "Just pick something."

I sigh and scan the neutral-toned display.

The clothes in my closet are perfectly arranged: first by color, then by type. I bite my lip, scanning everything I have in white. I move on to gray, but my mind remains as blank as the moment before. These choices are part of the butterfly effect of my life, whether I like it or not. If I make the wrong decision, it will affect the rest of my day. It sounds crazy, but I know from experience the complete and utter devastation caused by one misplaced judgment.

Ash glances up from her phone and catches me still staring at my clothes. She stands up from where she was lounging on my bed and nudges me gently aside. "Move, babe," she says. "You're taking too long."

Getting dressed in the morning is never easy for me, but it usually doesn't take me this long. There have been too many changes lately. They're throwing me off.

Starting a new school is one thing. It's always been just the two of us, me and Ash, doing things together. And that's how I like it. That's what works. But now the guest house has a new tenant. The damn guest house that's mere yards from my bedroom window. It used to be my grandma's dwelling until she passed away almost a decade ago. It's been empty all this time—but last night someone moved in.

Ash rummages through my closet, her back facing me,

and I admire the contrast between her blond hair and black romper. She pauses and pulls a tank top off its hanger. "Everything in your closet looks so similar." She re-hangs it the wrong way though, causing my heart to race.

"You are underestimating the value of basics. And you hung up that top the wrong way," I tell her. "It's not facing the same direction as the others."

Ash ignores me and continues her search, probably hoping to find something trendy in which to clad me. Her simple error aggravates me so much more than it should. She's completely oblivious to what's happening inside me. The way my heart is racing, and how my senses feel heightened. The sound of her in my closet rings in my ears: the way she mutters impatiently to herself when each garment lets her down, the jangling of the hangers as they're shoved aside. I think my palms might even be sweating. Disgusting.

I'm not going to be able to focus on anything else until that damn shirt is fixed. It's like a curse. But my attention to such detail is mandatory, because as soon as one thing in my life goes wrong, everything else tends to follow suit. If I don't turn that stupid tank top in the right direction, how can anything else go right from here on out?

I slide past Ash and grab the shirt off the hanger.

She huffs. "It's fine, babe."

"It's not fine." I ignore her tapping foot and her taut, impatient posture and do what needs to be done.

"We have to hurry, or we'll be late," she warns.

American River College has the best cosmetology program in town. It's affordable, with a great passing rate. But according to the introduction pamphlet, tardiness is their equivalent to first-degree murder.

I can't focus on Ash's words because I'm still bothered after fixing the top, so I remove it and hang it back up again. I do this until my anxiety ebbs, which turns out to be five times. I exhale sharply.

"What the hell are you doing?" Ash eyes me. When I don't say anything, understanding crosses her features. "It's getting worse, isn't it?"

I nod but don't meet her inquisitive glance. I've had OCD for a long time, but it's been progressively intensifying for about three years. My compulsions used to be limited to small rituals that weren't so outwardly apparent, like obsessive thoughts. I still have those thoughts, in addition to a complicated mess of other issues that decided to join the party. These past years have proved my problem is only getting worse. Some days, I can barely function. I've never told anyone this, but I'm afraid someday I'll become a shut-in, so absorbed in my compulsions and rituals that I won't have enough time to ever leave the house.

Ash resumes going through my closet, her concern palpable. She eventually settles on a lilac shirt—one of the only colorful pieces I own—and a denim miniskirt. "This will have to do," she sighs. "But shopping is happening this weekend." She throws the outfit at me.

"As fun as that sounds, why even bother?" I ask her. "We'll be wearing scrubs the rest of the semester anyway." Since scrubs are the default uniform at American River Cosmetology, we can only wear regular clothes on the first day—today—and on holidays.

She grins at me. Her usually pale skin has a healthy tan glow. Despite us being nearly the same height, her inherent confidence makes her seem so much taller than me somehow.

"Because I drank too many Mai Tais in Hawaii. All my pants are getting tight," she says.

I let out a breathy laugh. "You're so lucky. I wish I could spend a week in Hawaii with my mom, just because. Just the two of us."

Ash's little brothers were supposed to go along too, but it was their dad's week, and he refused to budge on their court-enforced schedule.

I take the outfit from her and hold it to my body, facing the mirror. "Don't you think this is a bit revealing?" I ask, staring at my reflection. "What if I get sent home?"

She laughs. "It's a beauty school, not a convent." I start to protest but she shakes her head. "I'll be damned if you're going dressed as a nun." Her tone is final, but I swap the skirt for a pair of less-revealing shorts when she's not looking.

"Babe." Ash stands next to me in the mirror and frowns. "What the fuck happened to your hair?"

"I know." I sheepishly try to smooth down my frizzing

hair. My long curls are damp, pulled back in a low ponytail, tickling my elbows when I turn my head from side to side. I take it down, hoping to somehow improve whatever Ash is commenting on, but she only bites her lip.

"Your hair makes Medusa's look tame," Ash informs me.

I smooth it down with my hands again. I should have just straightened it. It would have been easier.

My doorknob turns without a knock and my mom peeks inside. "Willow," she says. Her cheeks are slightly flushed and she's wearing her nurse scrubs, the blue ones with pink flowers on them. She worked the night shift at the hospital last night, so she'll probably head straight to bed after we go to school. "Good. You haven't left yet." She doesn't react to Ash's presence, primarily because Ash, as both my cousin and best friend, is here all the time.

My mom looks me over from top to bottom and offers me a tight smile that doesn't reach her eyes. I know what she's seeing: me, still in my pajamas, my long curly hair a complete mess, and my dark face, taut with nerves.

I look nothing like her. And though Ash and I are cousins, I hold no resemblance to her, either. In fact, Ash looks more like my own mother than I do. They both have the same shade of white skin and hair a similar shade of blond, but their resemblance ends in their eyes. Where Ash's eyes are a warm brown that can see right through anyone, my mom's are the blue ocean of the beach she left behind in South Africa. The beach she'd spent her days surfing and petting penguins before she became a mom.

My mom clears her throat. "Don't forget, Mildred's son moved into the guest house last night," she states.

I shake my head. As if I could forget the fact that we have a new neighbor. Especially since that neighbor happens to be my mom's dead best friend's son. "I haven't."

"And I know it's late notice, but he's going to need a ride to school today."

I blink. "What? Who is going to need a ride to school today?"

"Mildred's *son*," says my mom, bordering on impatience. "Theodore."

I blink again, sure I missed something. I knew Theo moved in. But I must not have heard my mom tell me he's going to college here. "He's in school? College?"

"Yeah. He offered to ride the bus, but obviously I can't allow that."

Of course not. Mildred was my mom's friend for longer than I've been alive. She lived in London so I never got to see her much, but my mom used to visit her at least once a year. They would constantly talk on the phone together; time differences be damned. For as long as I can remember, talking on the phone with Mildred was my mom's default state of being. Four months ago, Mildred committed suicide. She didn't leave a note, and as far as my mom knows, the reason she took her life is a complete mystery to everyone.

I throw my hands up, unable to ignore my frustration.

"I wish you would have asked me before this morning, right before we need to walk out the door."

My mom frowns. "I'm sure I mentioned it to you before."

I laugh humorlessly. "Definitely not. This is a huge change of plans. I wouldn't forget something like this, Mom." I huff. "It's going to influence the rest of my day now."

My mom raises her eyebrows at me. "Are you serious, Willow? The poor boy lost his mother. I lost my best friend. You're being ridiculous."

My cheeks burn. A wave of sympathy mixed with chagrin crash into me, sympathy for my mom, losing her best friend so unexpectedly, and chagrin for my inconsideration.

I glance at the guest house through my bedroom window. No new cars are parked in the driveway. No sign of life is visible next door at all.

I never actually met Mildred or her family as an adult but know what they look like from a Christmas card she sent a few years ago. They were the stereotypical picture of a happy family. One mom, one dad, one son. All three of them attractive. All that was missing was a sibling for Mildred's son, Theo.

"You're right," I say, eyes cast downward. "I'm sorry."

It was considerate of my mom to reach out to Theo last month, offering to let him come stay with us if he wanted to for any reason. I must admit, I was surprised he took her up on the offer. He hardly knows us, after all. To him, my mom is probably nothing more than a phone call and an occasional visit from America, regardless of how close she was to Mildred.

"How's he doing?" Ash asks my mom.

She purses her lips. "He hasn't spoken much since he arrived, so please be sensitive. And nice." For some reason, my mom narrows her eyes at me when she says this. "He just lost his mother." Her voice cracks on the last word.

I suppress a sigh. How am I supposed to be mad, or even express my annoyance, when she's clearly still grieving? "He's going to American River, at least, right? I don't need to make a detour to drop him off somewhere else?"

"American River College, Willow," my mom confirms in a tight voice. "He's doing cosmetology school, like you."

Perfect. Even better.

Ash tilts her head. "Is he gay?"

I shake my head. "Really, Ash?"

"What?" She holds up her hands. "He's going to *beauty* school."

I frown at her. "So? What does that matter?"

Ash shrugs, but the mischievous glint in her eye suggests she's probably considering trying to hook up with him. I hope she does. Maybe if Theo has Ash as a distraction, he'll focus on something other than ruining my plans in the future.

I arrange my expression into one that resembles benevolence. I need to muster up a polite demeaner for Theo, in order to please my mom. I also need to try not to focus on the possibility of him potentially ruining my life by throwing this unexpected curveball into my morning. I know my reasoning seems harsh and insensitive, but schedules and advance notices exist for a reason. Then again, it's probably my fault for not interrogating my mom more thoroughly when she told me Theo was moving in.

My mom sighs and rubs one of her temples. "I don't know if he's gay. I haven't seen him since he was a kid. Even when I used to fly out to see Mildred, he'd never hang out with us much. But he'll be over here any minute."

Any minute? The thought of it instantly makes me break out in a cold sweat, like I do every time I'm forced into an interaction I'm not prepared for.

"Theo is lucky he got a spot on such short notice, Aunt Charlize," Ash tells my mom. "Cosmetology fills up fast."

"Mom," I interrupt, realizing in horror that we'll all three have to squeeze into my car. "Mitten Chip isn't exactly spacious," I say, referring to my Volkswagen Beetle. Ash can't stand when I refer to my car by the name I gave it, but I can't stand not to.

"We can take my Mustang," Ash offers.

I groan internally. That's an even worse option than us crowding into my Bug, because sitting in the passenger seat of a car is the greatest source of my anxiety. If I'm not driving, I can't stand the fact that I'm not in control. That my safety is in someone else's hands. That I'm forced to perform a ritual that consists of imagining us crashing over and over, because doing so is like playing reverse psychology with life. Kind of like how expecting a specific scenario to play out according to your predictions almost always guarantees that it won't. I do the same with my ritual. I imagine the worst possible thing happening, over and over again, until it feels like I've done it enough. I tempt life, daring it to make the living hell inside my head a reality.

It never does.

No rituals are necessary when I drive because I'm in control.

"I suppose we can make it work in Mitten Chip," I whisper.

Ash reaches for my hand and squeezes it gently. She's one of the only people I confide in when it comes to my OCD. She's also the only one who knows how to help me lighten up when I'm on the brink of an anxiety attack. "If you name one more of your inanimate objects," she tells me, "I'll disown you."

A laugh escapes me just as the doorbell rings.

"That must be him," my mom says. I dress quickly, and we follow her down the hall and past the kitchen. She walks briskly to the front door and unlocks the handle.

When the door opens, I do a double take because

standing on the porch isn't the boy I remember from the Christmas card a few years back. In his place is a tall man who looks about my age, maybe a few years older. My skin tingles when I take in his dark hair, stark blue eyes and strong, elegant jaw lined with stubble.

"Theo!" My mom exclaims. "You're here. My daughter is going to give you a ride to school."

Theo smiles at her, though it doesn't quite reach his eyes.

"I have to go to bed, but I wanted to introduce you to Willow first." My mom yawns and stretches before shuffling down the hallway. "Text me if you need anything, and I'll read it as soon as I'm up."

We all watch her disappear down the hall. When her bedroom door closes, Theo glances at Ash. My mom never actually pointed me out as her daughter, so Theo probably assumes by Ash's resemblance to my mom that she's me.

"*I'm* Willow," I preemptively clarify. Theo frowns at me as soon as I speak, and there's a beat of awkward silence. His eyes are startling, pale blue without flecks interrupting the color's steady consistency. There's a subtle dimple in his chin beneath the stubble, and his dark hair is thick, professionally cut and only long enough on top to reveal its wavy texture. Though he's tall and slender, I notice the bulge of muscle on his arms beneath his green long-sleeved shirt.

"So, I take it you need a ride," Ash says, breaking the ice. The way she says it makes me blush. There's clearly a double meaning in her words. "Your car didn't make the trip here?"

Theo arches an eyebrow. "Last time I checked, vehicles don't make great carry-ons." He smirks. "Not to mention, everyone in London either walks or rides the tube." His voice is deep and indifferent, yet surprisingly soft and thick with a British accent.

Ash snorts. "As much as I'd like to ride shotgun, you're way too tall to sit in the back of Willow's Bug. And I don't do back seats." She pauses, reconsidering her words. "Well, not as a passenger, that is. If you know what I mean."

I blink in confusion when she makes for the front door. "Wait, where are you going?"

"See you there, babe," she tells me nonchalantly, ignoring the murderous glare I send her way.

There's no way Ash is going to leave me alone to carpool with a total stranger on our first day of school. She wouldn't.

I watch in complete and utter disbelief as she actually leaves. It takes me a moment to turn back around, and when I do, I stare at Theo blankly, at a total loss for words.

His lips twitch with the effort not to laugh, though I can't imagine what he possibly finds humorous about this situation. "Shall we?" he asks wryly. "I hear this school has a rather strict late policy."

"Very strict," I snap. "And if I get in trouble, I'm blaming it on you." I grind my teeth. This entire morning has already fallen apart. The rest of the day isn't looking good at this rate. And all because of my mom, infringing on my carefully structured plans.

"Is that so?" he says with raised brows, amusement in his voice. "And why me?"

"Because *you* are a last-minute change of plans." I snap, knowing that if my mom heard me, I'd be in a world of trouble. I turn to him, ready to take it back and apologize, but stop at his expression.

Theo's mouth is in a half-grin. "I am known for my impeccable timing."

I watch him walk out the door, unable to think of a response.

We get inside Mitten Chip. Theo's head almost touches the top of the car, just as Ash predicted.

There are several moments of complete silence as I start the car and drive. I'm filled with dread knowing I'm really going to have to sit here with him and make small talk the entire fifteen minutes to school. I hardly know anything about him. For all I know, Theo could be a serial killer. I can't believe my mom let him move in.

Tapping the steering wheel to ease some of my anxiety, I wrack my brain for something to say, anything to eliminate the painful silence. "So, how are you liking America?"

"Well," says Theo. "I haven't been here long, but my expectations are high."

"Really?" I ask. "Why?"

He smiles blandly at me. "Haven't you heard? It's the land of opportunity."

I exhale a reluctant laugh. "So they say."

It's already starting to get warm outside. I consider rolling the windows down but doing so will probably cause my hair to dry even frizzier. I play with the lanyard dangling from my keys. It's Harry Potter themed, sporting my Hogwarts house, Ravenclaw.

Theo glances at my nervous hands playing with the lanyard. "You like Harry Potter?"

I flick my eyes at him. "*Like* is such an understatement."

He chuckles. "Really?" It sounds like a challenge. "Have you read the books?"

"Yep. I'm currently reading the series for the seventeenth time."

Theo gives me a withering look. "Right."

I frown. "Right, what?"

"You haven't read the series sixteen-going-on-seventeen times."

"You don't believe me?"

He arches one of his brows at me. "It's a bit hard to believe that someone like you would spend so much time reading."

My body tenses. "Someone like me?" I demand. "What's that supposed to mean?"

My first thought is that he's making some kind of crack at my intelligence level, but then I notice the way he's taking me in slowly. From top to bottom. He presses his lips together. "I think you know what I mean."

A flush creeps across my entire face, and I try to find a

way to change the subject. "What—what Hogwarts house are you in?" I sputter.

Theo's lips twitch, and he half-shrugs. "Hufflepuff? Gryffindor? To be honest, I'm not quite sure."

"Probably Slytherin," I suggest, shrugging innocently.

Theo's mouth falls open. He presses his hand to his chest. "I can't believe you'd assume such a thing," he says, sounding not at all indignant. "And either you've chosen the wrong colors, or you're a Ravenclaw." He nods toward my lanyard, and I have to admit that I'm surprised he even knows that much.

"I am. You know what they say. 'Wit beyond measure is man's greatest treasure.'"

Theo attempts to disguise his laugh as a cough. He probably thinks I'm a complete dork, which is totally fine with me. Anyone who thinks someone attractive wouldn't bother reading books isn't worth my time anyway.

Theo examines his fingernails. "Why did your friend lie about hating the back seat?"

It takes me a moment to realize he's referring to Ash. I clear my throat. "She wasn't lying. She really does hate sitting in the back. She would kill me for telling you this, but she gets carsick." Theo doesn't react, so I add, "And we're *cousins*."

That gets his attention. He turns to look at me, his brow furrowed. I'm used to the surprised or even confounded expressions that people wear every time they discover my relation to Ash, but what interests me is that Theo doesn't exclaim the almost guaranteed follow up statement: "But you're black!"

As if I'm unaware.

"Our moms are sisters," I tell him, though he didn't ask. "And I'm half black, from my dad's side."

Theo says something just as a cat runs across the road, and I slam on my brakes. Missing its death by a hair, the cat darts away, unscathed. I take a steadying breath to calm myself.

"Stupid animal," I gasp. "I don't even like cats. I should have run the damn thing over." My voice is weak. I feel like I'm going to faint. None of this would have happened if my mom hadn't infringed on the order of the day.

Theo laughs unsteadily. "I'm sure it's much obliged."

"Shut up." My heart is racing. Though I'm trying desperately, I can't calm myself. I'm breathing hard like the oxygen I'm inhaling isn't working.

"Me? I'm not the one with the tapping problem," Theo comments, oblivious to the heavy panic sloshing in my veins. "This isn't a musical. We don't need a constant beat."

My cheeks burn. If I were more self-aware, I would have tried to hide the tapping, or made it subtler somehow. But some rituals are so ingrained that I don't even notice when I perform them. And I definitely didn't realize how much I was tapping.

"But I've hardly said a word. You're the one who won't stop talking," I say through gritted teeth.

"You're doing it again. You're tapping right now," he says cheerfully, flustering me beyond belief.

"I'm going to leave you on the side of the road if you don't shut up," I warn him.

He laughs. "I could probably walk faster than you're driving."

"I almost hit a cat! What do you expect?" My hand twitches. I want to smack that unperturbed, mildly entertained look right off his face.

"Relax, love." He reclines his seat, resting his arms behind his head and shutting his eyes. "Untie your knickers." He speaks with the kind of confidence I've never known. As if there's nowhere this conversation could take him that would make him uncomfortable.

I wonder if he would continue to treat my stress with such irreverence if he knew how impossible it is for me to truly relax. But there's no way I'm going to fill him in. I hate telling people I have OCD, because they always feel the need to reciprocate by saying they do too. A lot of people assume that having OCD means liking things organized or hating germs. It tends to be treated like a quirk or an endearing trait. But it's so much more than that. It's the one thing that prohibits me from being free of myself.

So instead I say, "Believe me, if I could I would."

There must be something of my inner turmoil in my voice because Theo doesn't come back with something witty or smart-assed to say. He only opens his eyes to stare at me for a brief moment before glancing away.

The school building looms in front of us on the street, and anxiety enters my veins yet again. Theo sighs deeply, his eyes still closed. Even in his relaxed position, he somehow looks troubled, and I wonder for the first time if maybe he feels it too. If maybe, like me, he isn't a stranger to the feelings that linger after the horrors of the past. If he too feels that those horrors hold no fault in anyone but himself.

Two

Ash is waiting for us in the parking lot. She marches over to my car as soon as we park and grabs my hand when I get out. "Come on," she says. "I want to find Joseph. I'm pretty sure his statistics class doesn't start for another half hour."

I glare at Ash, but she smiles back at me with faux innocence, as if she didn't abandon me. Especially to someone as insufferable as Theo. I can't help but glance over my shoulder to look at him.

"Thanks for the ride, love," Theo says, displaying a wide grin. As he passes me, he pats me on the head like I'm some sort of pet. I try not to let the gesture get under my skin, but irritation is already clinging to me like a wet blanket.

As soon as he walks away, I frown at my cousin. "I can't believe you left me alone with *him!*"

She has the nerve to laugh. "Calm down, babe."

"You wouldn't have gotten *that* car sick if you'd come along and sat in the back! Besides, I bet Theo wouldn't have minded giving you shotgun."

She laughs. "Please tell me you aren't complaining about being alone with him. He's hot!"

"I don't care," I practically yell. "Don't you ever do that to me again!"

"Do what?" She holds up her hands.

"Throw a curveball at me like that!"

Ash rolls her eyes. "Fine. Sorry, babe." She is so not sorry. The smile she presses between her lips proves it.

"Do we even have time to look for Joseph right now?" I cross my arms.

The parking lot is practically full at this point. Cars are circling around, trying to find a spot, and several have already paused near me and Ash, probably hoping we're about to leave so they can snag mine.

"We have plenty of time," she says. "Let's go."

Plenty of time.

A completely ridiculous concept.

Every second that passes leaves us with less time than before.

Eventually, we'll completely run out.

Just the thought of it makes me feel like there are hands wrapped around my throat. I try to focus on something else, anything else, but now that time passing is at the forefront of my attention, it's all I can think about.

I feel compelled to tap because somehow doing so feels like I'm setting things right. So I tap my fingers against the side of my leg like I did on the steering wheel of my car on the way here. I tap until my anxiety doesn't suffocate me anymore.

Tap, tap, tap, tap, tap. Repeatedly, even as we walk toward the opposite end of campus to look for Joseph, Ash's on-and-off friend-with-benefits. They recently became off during her trip to Hawaii, but I'm sure they'll be back on now that she's returned.

I trail behind Ash reluctantly. We're only halfway there and once we get to his classroom, he might not even be there yet. Even Ash seems to be losing momentum, her stride slowing with each step away from our side of campus.

"Let's just go back. Otherwise we'll be late," I say. "We can find him later."

Ash exhales sharply. I wonder if she expected his classroom to be closer. "Fine." She runs a hand through her blond hair, eyes darting around wildly as if hoping to catch him at the last second.

We make our way back to our side of campus. The cosmetology building is the largest department by far. The tall building looms in front of us the closer we get, and the floor-to-ceiling glass windows reflect the sun like diamonds.

When we reach the doors, a hollow feeling invades my stomach. Ash and I have wanted to be hairstylists our entire lives, so it's hard to believe the start of our journey is today. There's a sudden shakiness in my limbs. The possibility of all the ways the day could go wrong nearly sends me running. Especially since we already started off the day unplanned. As if Ash can sense my apprehension, she narrows her eyes at me and threads her arm in mine, leading us inside.

The walls are painted a cool gray, and the smell of hair products wafts through the room. The front desk at the entrance displays a selection of hard plastic nametags. I quickly find the nametags labeled *Willow B.* and *Ashton M.* and we fasten them to our shirts.

The chatter of students fills the room, sending my stomach plummeting as we turn the corner. There are girls everywhere, mostly our age, but some that look a bit older than the rest. There seem to be only three males, including Theo. He's talking to the instructor, Mrs. Harrison, who I recognize from her picture in the introductory pamphlet.

The desks are large, and one girl opens the top of hers like the hood of a car, or the lid of a piano, to reveal an area to keep cosmetology tools. The room has a traditional classroom setup, aside from the twelve hair dryers and six shampoo bowls lining the walls. The numbers in this room drive me crazy, because they're all even. I hate even numbers because none of them have a middle, a center.

Twelve hair dryers.

Six shampoo bowls.

Twelve.

Six.

I discreetly tap five times to make it better, because five is an odd number.

Tap, tap, tap, tap, tap.

1, 2, 3, 4, 5.

I exhale slowly to relieve the tightness in my chest.

I glance around the room. The class is mostly seated now, apart from a few girls nervously scanning the now-packed aisles. Mrs. Harrison turns away from Theo to write her name on the board. Her hair is golden blond and cut into a sharp bob, and though her face is lined with age, her eyes are alert and darting. The room echoes the hushed conversations of the girls around us, and I try to look inconspicuous as we find seats near the middle of the room.

"Damn, girl. That's a tight romper," snickers the girl sitting behind us.

I glance at Ash, realizing with dawning horror that the girl is talking about *her*.

Ash catches on much more quickly than I do, turning around and smiling at the girl. "Is that a problem?"

"Ash," I whisper. "Just let it go." This poor girl has no idea who she's messing with. Ash has never lost a fight in her entire life. I would know, because I've been the one to soften the blow for her mom every time she got suspended in high school for breaking someone's face. If we get kicked out today, there's no way we'll be allowed back. Considering how strict this school is when it comes to things like tardiness and the dress code, I doubt they'll be lenient if Ash gets in a fistfight on the very first day.

"No," the girl replies, clearly surprised at being confronted. She holds up her hands. I glance at her nametag. *Destiny L.* "No, girl. You work it!" She smiles like she's joking, but there's a sour edge to her voice. "How much do you charge for an hour? Or . . . is it free?"

My mouth falls open. Destiny's brashness is more than I know how to handle. I can't believe she would say something so rude to a complete stranger.

Ash's smile widens, but her eyes are hard as stone. That smile is more dangerous than any other expression she could make. This is a disaster waiting to happen. I belatedly realize we have attracted the attention of some of the girls sitting around us.

Ash uncrosses her legs, leaning in toward Destiny. "That depends . . . " she says, her voice low. "How much are you willing to pay for that comment?"

I knew giving Theo a ride to school would mess with the order of the entire day. That's the only explanation for something like this happening, and I need to fix it. I must correct the situation, and somehow save us.

To create some sense of order, of rightness, I reach into my bag and grab three fountain pens from my personal collection, arranging them on my desk until they're lined up perfectly and symmetrically with one another.

I will the situation into feeling right. As I arrange the pens, I think, *I will not let us get in trouble. I will not let us get in trouble. I will not let us get in trouble.* The words are almost like a prayer in my mind.

Theo sits down next to me, sandwiching me between him and Ash. He leans back in his chair languidly, until the back of the chair touches Destiny's desk. A waft of Theo's cologne stirs my senses. Expensive. That's the only way to describe it. I hadn't noticed before.

"As much as I enjoy a good catfight," he drawls, "perhaps this is not the time nor the place, ladies." He glances from Ash to Destiny, who seems struck at Theo's intervention. She goggles at him for a moment before pasting a saccharine smile on her face.

"Are you British?" she asks. She leans forward without seeming to even realize it.

"Very," Theo answers, his voice low and tantalizing. It's almost as if he's intentionally making his accent more prominent, just for her.

I roll my eyes and scoff. Leave it to Theo to make it his goal to seduce someone the first chance he gets. But despite my irritation, I can't help but notice that he's successfully distracted her. Whether or not it was intentional, Theo prevented a fight between Destiny and Ash from transpiring.

Or maybe, it was the ritual.

Mrs. Harrison clears her throat, and everyone faces the front of the classroom.

"Good morning, class. My name is Mrs. Harrison. But those of you who read the registration packet know that already." She goes through a standard outline of our syllabus and cost of materials. My eyes feel like they're going to fall out of my face when I see the total cost of our beauty kit. The very idea of my mom having to pay for most of this fills my stomach with knots.

I'm fortunate that she makes pretty good money as a nurse, but I still can't deny that as an adult, I should be paying for this. The problem is that I've never been able to keep a normal job because of my OCD. Whether it be clocking in at only certain times to avoid even numbers, arranging items where they aren't supposed to go, spending an hour locking and unlocking a door, or simply not showing up on Fridays, it's always been my fault. I make a small amount of money walking the dogs in my neighborhood, because it's hard to mess that up. But it really doesn't pay much.

As a result, my mom pays for almost everything. She's never made me feel bad about it, but the deal has always been that I can live with her rent-free as long as I'm going to school. I won't have to move out until I get my cosmetology license. *If* I can manage to pass state board.

Mrs. Harrison drones on, outlining prison-like rules about clocking in on time, and her hopes that the class will have a successful semester. It all takes over two hours. It's amazing that there's even enough content on the first day for her to cover.

When it's break time, I grab Ash's arm and pull her from her seat. She tilts her head to the side but follows me past Theo and out the building. There are benches outside the door, but we don't sit.

"Just this once," I plead, "could you try not to get yourself in trouble?"

She raises one perfectly groomed eyebrow. "What are you talking about? That bitch was asking for it."

I place my hands on her shoulders, hoping to somehow make her see reason. "She totally was." I take a deep breath. "But we're going to be spending a lot of time around these girls before we graduate and get our licenses. So can we please just try to make more friends than enemies around here?"

Ash shakes her head. "If she opens her mouth again, I'll remove her teeth one by one."

I sigh. "Fine. As long as it's not on campus."

She laughs. "Stop worrying so much, babe." She links her arm through mine. "Let's go to the bathroom. I want to check my face."

There's a bathroom in our building, so we go back inside. We pass the main room, and I glance at our desks to find Destiny still talking gregariously to Theo. I suppress a large eye roll.

In front of the bathroom mirror, Ash seems to come down from her high. To her, that little tiff was her espresso shot for the day. She fixes her hair and wipes non-existent eyeliner smudges from beneath her eyes. I decide to wash my hands, even though they aren't dirty. I scrub my skin raw, letting the hot water run over my hands until they burn.

When I was younger, my skin used to crack and blister because of how often I'd wash myself. I would try with all my might to wash the darkness on my skin away, if only so I could more resemble my mom, the only parent I had.

A memory flashes through my mind as I stare at my long, dark fingers under the stream of water. My mom, saying to one of her friends when she thought I couldn't hear, "God, she looks so much like *him*. I'd hate her if I didn't love her so much." Their smothered laughs. My even expression afterwards, revealing nothing.

My mom never told me the exact reason why she hated my dad, but I'd always assumed it was for cheating and leaving her before he died. And though I had some of her facial features, I knew all she saw was my color. My dad's color. To her, I looked like him, and it pained her enough that she could hardly stand the sight of me.

I'd try and try and try to wash him away. In the sink. In the shower, hoping to reveal any traces of *her* underneath so she'd have no reason to hate me. But I finally stopped trying when I realized the stain of my father's betrayal— and his color—weren't going anywhere.

I leave my hands under the water, unmoving.

When I dry them, I always use three paper towels.

Even numbers are favored by most people because there's never a straggler. No one is left out. Everyone gets a partner. But I can't stand that even numbers can never be centered, only divided. To me, there must be a middle.

1, 2, 3.

I dry my hands with one paper towel at a time. One towel is never enough to dry every single last drop of water. But two would probably suffice. Three paper towels, if I'm being honest, is one too many. Even for long-fingered hands like mine. But there's no way I'm using an even number of paper towels, and I'm not leaving a trace of water on my hands to potentially attract dirt and other germs. So I use three paper towels, every time.

When we sit back down, Ash makes a point to ignore Destiny. I'm so grateful I could cry.

The bell rings, signaling the end of break, and Mrs. Harrison begins passing out more forms for us to sign.

"Feeling better, love?" Theo murmurs softly, without looking at me.

I frown at him. "Who says there was anything wrong?"

He faces me then to arch a brow at me, which I choose to ignore. There's no way he could have sensed my distress at the almost-fight Ash got into. And even if he had, why would he care?

As Mrs. Harrison lectures on and on about the importance of sanitation and electricity safety, I let my mind wander from the room. In one hour and thirty-five minutes I'll be able to go home and read.

It's one of things that helps, reading. It allows me to take my focus off the mess in my mind that constantly burdens me. I've had moderate OCD since I was young. I was officially diagnosed at twelve, progressively getting worse year after year. I always try find ways to cope, because doing so is my only hope of living day to day without crumbling from the inside out. Even though my doctor has told me my condition can easily be managed with meds, I can't take them. I won't.

Mrs. Harrison passes out an information packet about all the different services we'll be learning to perform this semester, and I begin reading.

Theo pokes me with his pen.

I ignore him.

He clears his throat.

I turn and face him, already scowling.

Theo is frowning, as if deep in thought. "Do you have any idea," he says, low and quiet, like he's letting me in on a secret, "how long my mum knew yours?"

I shrug lightly, surprised at the question. This is the first time Theo has mentioned his mom to me, and I'm not exactly sure how to respond. "They were friends for years," I tell him. "Your mom apparently had a travel year in Cape Town at the same time my mom lived there."

"Your mum is from South Africa?"

I nod. "She was born there but came here when she married my dad. He was American," I add, trying to keep my tone chatty, light, and appropriate for the classroom setting. But I see when Theo's attention lingers on that word. *Was.* Even though I say it casually, he catches it, and his eyes soften a fraction.

He doesn't remark on it though, and instead asks, "So, in all the time our mothers were best mates, she never brought you with her to visit?"

I press my lips together. Even though most of the class is talking to one another right now instead of reading, I'd rather be reading the packet on my desk.

"Not that I can remember. I usually stayed with my aunt, Ash's mom, the few times my mom went to London." I frown. "Why?"

"Just wondering why I've never met you. It's rather strange, don't you think?" Theo stares at me for a moment too long, and I look away, pretending to pick my nails.

"Not really," I say. "Just because our moms were friends doesn't mean we need to be."

Theo laughs. "You say that like being my friend would be such a terrible thing."

I roll my eyes. "I don't need any more friends."

Ash chooses this moment to break away from her reading to chime in. "Oh, yeah. Because you have so many besides me."

Theo chuckles, earning a death glare from me. "Oh, shut up," I say.

"You can always be best mates with Destiny," he whispers in my ear, sending chills racing down my spine. "If you're desperate."

"The only thing I'm *desperate* for is solitude, at the

moment." I snap.

Ash leans over my desk to talk to Theo. "By the way," she says, "thanks for stepping in with the bitch behind me. If you hadn't, I would have beat her ass and Willow would have had a conniption."

I shake my head. "*No,* I wouldn't have."

"I know." Theo smirks, ignoring me. "It was clear."

The bell rings, and I stand up and march out of the classroom, not waiting for either Theo or Ash. If they want to talk about me like I'm not even there, then I might as well not even be there.

I'm half tempted to leave without him. He should just ride home with Ash at this point. She's the one who thinks he's so irresistibly hot anyway.

But Theo walks over to my car, to my great dismay.

I don't say a word as we get in and I turn up a random radio station to keep him from speaking to me.

We've been driving for mere seconds when Theo turns the music down.

I turn it back up.

He turns it down again. "Trying to drown me out there, are you, love?"

"I was trying so hard to hide it."

He grins. "The least you can do is thank me, like your cousin did."

The nerve of this guy. It's like his sole purpose in life is to annoy me beyond belief. "Thank you? What on earth for?"

"Well, seeing as I prevented you from having a breakdown in class today, it seems like some gratitude could be in order." He folds his arms behind his head, relaxing into his seat.

My cheeks burn with rage. "Gratitude?" I can't believe my distress at the situation was so blatant. Who else had noticed? Was it really that obvious? "I didn't ask you to step in. In fact, I had everything under control on my own."

"Control? That's what you call it, is it?"

I take my eyes off the road to shoot Theo a glare but catch him staring at my mouth. Something unfamiliar burns deep inside me, and I quickly turn away.

Thank goodness we're home. I pull into the driveway. "Get out."

"Don't you want to keep chatting?" Theo teases. "Or would you rather go inside and read?"

"That's not what I'm going to do," I sputter, though doing so was my exact intention.

"Little Willow, comfy in her bed, not a care in the world," he murmurs. He studies me, like he's trying to imagine it.

I hold his gaze defiantly, despite the flutters that course through me at his unguarded eye contact. His blue gaze sears through me, making me feel slightly dizzy.

I have absolutely nothing to say to that, so I get out of the car, leaving him alone inside. He frowns at me through the windshield, like I'm being rude for ending our conversation without his permission, but I just turn on my heel and walk up the driveway without looking back at him.

I unlock the front door. I'm about to make straight for my room, but do a double take when I see my mom sitting at the kitchen table.

With a guy.

"Mom?" I backtrack until I'm within full view of them both. "Shouldn't you be asleep?"

My mom's smile is strained. "Hi, sweetie. I couldn't sleep, so I decided to wait up and find out how your day went. I also wanted to introduce you to one of my friends."

I take in the man's plain but pleasant face, his short red hair, and glasses with square frames. He's clad in scrubs, similar to the kind my mom wears to work.

"Hi," I say. I hold up my hand in an awkward wave and let it fall back down to my side. The man smiles at me.

"This is Gus Badgley," my mom says.

I glance at his scrubs again, wondering if he's a doctor, or maybe a nurse like my mom.

Gus stands and reaches his hand out, a warm smile on his face. I shake it, and immediately wipe my palm on my shorts. His eyes follow the gesture, and as he sits back down with my mom, his smile fades.

This isn't the first time my mom has done this. Introducing me to doctor friends of hers is one of her favorite pastimes. While the meetings may start out innocently, they almost always transition into me politely turning down advice and medication recommendations.

"She's just as cute and quirky as you described, hun," Gus says to my mom. The look in his eyes catches me off guard, the way he barely masks his adoration and reaches over to brush my mom's hand with his own.

Hun?

"Do you two work together?" I ask. There has to be some code of conduct against them dating if they work at the same hospital. "Are you a doctor?" I ask Gus.

Gus's face reddens. "I—no," he stammers.

"He's a pharmacist," my mom answers sharply, probably catching on to where my questions are leading.

A pharmacist? Not a doctor? Either way, I suspect there's more to this visit than what they're letting on. Gus's hand, still resting atop my mother's, tells me as much.

I have difficulty swallowing as I take it all in. His short red hair, combed neatly back, his tall, hefty frame and round green eyes.

"I've been wanting to introduce the two of you for some time now," my mom says in a rush, surely aware of the dread weighing down my stomach. Her voice is light and soft. She's starting to lose her South African accent because of how long she's been in America. Ever since my dad died, she's only dated three men, all of whom couldn't be more physically different than him.

I back away, toward the kitchen sink. I need to wash my hands, especially the one that Gus shook. I immediately turn the faucet on and start scrubbing. My mom clears her throat behind me, but I don't care if I'm being rude. I dry my hands with three separate paper towels and throw them away, one at a time.

Why did she bring him here? I can't breathe. I can't see straight, and there's a tight pain in my chest. I stare at the trash can. My skin begins to tingle. My heart starts to race as the familiar wave of anxiety crashes over my body. I get down on my knees, removing everything from the trash can, one by one.

"Willow!" My mom rises from her chair. "What on earth are you doing?" Her voice is full of false obliviousness. She knows exactly what I'm doing, but she doesn't want Gus to realize that this behavior isn't at all out of the ordinary for me.

"They're uncomfortable," I mutter aloud, mostly for Gus's benefit. "I need to fix it." As soon as all the trash is out of the can and on our kitchen floor, I begin putting it back in, arranging each piece of waste meticulously, so it sits right. My breathing slows as I make progress, the pounding in my heart ceasing.

"Willow Daphne Bates." My mom's voice is a deadly calm. "May I speak to you privately?"

I sigh, but not because of the talk I'm about to have with my mom. I'm relieved that the anxiety is mollified, for now. I get up and wash my hands again, ignoring the deafening silence and tension coursing off my mom's body as I do. I dry my hands on my shirt to avoid repeating that whole ordeal again, and follow my mom to my room.

"I'll meet you in the car, Gus," my mom says sweetly,

over her shoulder. She closes my door behind me as soon as I'm inside.

"I'm sorry Mom—" I begin, but she cuts me off.

"What the hell is wrong with you? You couldn't control yourself for a few goddamn minutes while I introduced you to my new boyfriend?" Her voice quivers, and even though this isn't the first time I've embarrassed my mom with my rituals, I've never seen her so mad before.

"So, you are dating," I say quietly. "I thought you said he was your *friend*."

Her nostrils flare. "That is not the point, and you know it." Her eyes are so wide, I can actually see the whites surrounding them on all sides. "You will get your issues under control, Willow. I mean it this time. I can't live like this anymore."

My eyes well up with tears at her words. I've always worried that at some point, my OCD would become too much for her. It hurts more than I expected to know that time has finally come. I inhale sharply. "I'm trying, Mom. Really, I am."

She shakes her head. "Then why have you only gotten worse since the accident?"

I swallow. My heart comes to a complete stop. "You know why," I breathe. It's something we don't talk about, ever, and she knows better than to bring it up.

My mom deflates, though only by a millimeter. "You need to get on meds, Willow."

"No!" I breathe rapidly again, fear threatening to suffocate me. "I can't even take painkillers, Mom. I refuse."

This sets her off again. "This fear of yours doesn't make any sense! In fact, it's downright ridiculous. Taking medicine isn't going to kill you."

But I shake my head, over and over. Ever since having an allergic reaction to a medication as a child, I've never touched it again. I can't. "I won't," I say.

My mom stares at me for a long moment. "Then you need to find somewhere else to live, because I'm done."

My head spins. I gape at her, unable to make sense of her words. She knows I couldn't bear to live on my own, that I'm terrified doing so would cause me to become a slave to my compulsive thoughts. And a roommate would be done with me the first day. Not to mention, my part-time job walking dogs in our neighborhood isn't going to cover paying rent somewhere, on top of my cosmetology expenses. She's left me no choice, and she knows it. "But you're my mom," I say, my voice cracking. "You can't be done."

She covers her face with her hand. "It's because I'm your mom," she says, "that I care enough to help you. You have three months to get your rituals under control, enough that you can go at least a day without performing one. Otherwise, you will get on meds, or you will find a place to live and move out."

As if she can't bear to look at me, she removes her hand from her face only after she turns around. Before I can say another word, she's out the door.

Three

I stare at my dusty-blue colored bedroom walls for ten minutes after my mom and Gus leave. Blue is supposed to be a calming color, which is part of the reason every shade of it is my favorite. But I feel anything but calm right now.

The tears won't stop spilling down my face. I'm not normally a crier, but my mom's ultimatum hasn't left me with a choice. I'm even more trapped than I was before. My phobia of consuming any type of medication isn't one I'm ready to face. I don't know if I ever will be ready, in all honesty.

I walk out the front door, not even sure where I plan on going. I'm not ready to call Ash and tell her what just happened. I need to get ahold of myself first. There isn't a bone in my body that doubts my mom is serious. Everything

I've put her through for the last three years has been leading up to this moment. It was only a matter of time before she got sick of me. Regardless, it hurts to know I was right.

I sit down on the front porch steps and cover my face with my hands. It feels good to ugly-cry when I know no one can see me.

"Tired of reading already?" a teasing voice calls from outside the guest house.

Oh, no. No, no, no. The last thing I need right now is Theo's antagonism. But sure enough, he makes his way over anyway, his graceful walk and glinting blue eyes making my stomach flip.

"Go away," I croak.

Theo sits down right next to me, resting his elbows on his knees. Again, I'm struck by that intoxicating scent of his, even though we're outside. I bury my face back into my hands, hoping he'll somehow mistake my sadness for exhaustion. Or maybe he'll think it's just sweat. It's warm enough outside for it to be a plausible idea.

"Are you crying?" he asks me, sounding genuinely shocked.

"Just leave me alone."

He scoots a bit closer. "Not while you're upset." There's a softness in his voice now, one I've never heard from him before. It's enough to make me peek up at him. His brows are furrowed in concern, his dark hair falling a bit into his eyes. "What's wrong, love?"

I sniffle. "Nothing. I'm fine. Go torment someone else." My voice is muffled in my hands.

He chuckles softly. "You can't possibly think I'd torment you right now." Ever so lightly, he brushes a strand of tear-dampened hair away from the side of my face. "Now tell me what happened, Willow." His voice is firm.

I glance at him again. That's the first time he's called me by my name. It startles me enough when he says it that I drop my hands and face him. "My mom is kicking me out in three months." I wipe my eyes.

His frown deepens. "Why?"

I swallow back another sob. "What you saw in the class-room today . . . you were right." At the moment, I no longer care what Theo thinks of me. Seeing me crying on my porch like a lunatic has probably already permanently altered his perception of me anyway, so what does it matter if he knows the truth at this point? "I would have lost it if Ash had gotten in trouble. I have really bad OCD and my mom . . . she can't stand my rituals. Living with a daughter like me has finally become too much." My throat tightens, and to my annoyance, more tears well up. They spill over when I blink at him.

"That can't possibly be true," he says.

"It is. Unless I go on medication, I have to find some-where else to live." I expect him to question why I won't take the meds, or to call me ridiculous for making a big deal out of something there's a clear solution to.

Theo shakes his head at that. "Why is medication the only way?"

I frown. "What do you mean?"

Theo turns his palms up. "Haven't either of you heard of ERP?"

"No." I bring myself into a straighter sitting position. "What's that?"

"*Exposure and Response Prevention.* It's a type of cognitive behavioral therapy," he states. "It's highly effective in treating OCD."

I stare at him. "How do you even know that?"

"Why?" He arches a brow. "Has my bounty of knowledge actually impressed you?"

I scoff. "No."

He laughs. "Of course not. But if you must know, little Willow, I used to assist my father at his practice. He's a psychologist. I'd take notes for him, aid in group therapy sessions and the such, while I attended university to earn a degree in the same field."

My mouth falls open a little, but I close it, trying hard not to show that now I am pretty impressed. "So, if you know so much about psychology, why are you in cosmetology school?"

"Because I want to be a hairstylist now," he says.

"You do? Really?" I can't help but find that surprising for some reason. I take in Theo's appearance. The way his arm muscles bulge from beneath his shirt, despite his tall, lean frame. His dark hair, the perfect length, falling from its combed style into his unnerving blue eyes. His skin is smooth and pale.

With a jolt I realize he's watching me check him out. His eyes are heavy with something that makes the pit of my stomach burn. "Is it so hard to believe?" he murmurs. I stare at my feet, remembering my indignance when he'd wrongly stereotyped me, insinuating that someone he found attractive couldn't possibly enjoy something as intellectual as reading. "Besides," he continues, "you should see what I pay *my* barber, or the money my mum used to spend on her hair extensions. Not to mention, I know how to give a mean fade."

I try to picture it now, Theo in an apron with a pair of clippers in his hand, spinning a swivel chair around to trim the edges of his client's hairline. I can't help it; I smile. "You're right," I say. "I guess I can *kinda* see it."

"No need to be modest." Theo waves at me dismissively. "I'm going to be amazing. That is, if I can pass the bloody test at the end of all this. Right?" When he laughs, it's the first time I've ever heard anything but the highest quality of confidence come out of him.

I frown. "The test? It will be easy. I've been studying for it since high school. It mainly consists of questions regarding sanitation, electrical safety, and bacteriology. There's actually hardly anything about hair on the written test."

He watches my mouth as I speak. When he looks at me, I can't tell if he wants to laugh or not. "Is that so?"

"Yes," I confirm. "That's so."

"Well, then." Theo stands up, brushing off his pants. "It appears I have a proposition for you, weeping Willow."

"You did *not* just call me that," I say. "I'm not even crying anymore."

He smiles brilliantly. "Thanks to me distracting you from your problem at hand. Which brings me back to my proposition."

Though I hate to admit it, he's right. He did distract me. I fold my arms across my chest. "What is it?"

His smile grows. "You help me study for state board, which without your help will surely be the death of me." He pauses thoughtfully. "I'm much more of a hands-on kind of guy."

"Imagine that," I mutter. "Go on."

"And in return, I'll teach you everything I know about ERP, free of charge."

I straighten my back completely. "Do you think it would get rid of my compulsions? Enough to prove to my mom I'm cured? She wants me to go an entire day without performing any rituals."

"Your compulsions will likely never *go away*." Theo crosses his arms. "But if you give it your best efforts, anything is possible. You could make that your incentive. An entire carefree day all to yourself, little Willow."

I snort. "Yeah, right. You think that's actually possible for someone as messed up as me?"

"You're not messed up," he states. "Believe me." The

way he meets my eyes when he says it makes me think he's telling the truth. I wonder what kind of clients his dad treats, and what Theo has seen to make him believe I'm not too hopeless to help.

Either way, if this ERP thing he's talking about can keep me from performing rituals, helping him pass the test will be a cake walk. I really have nothing to lose.

Except everything.

If his technique doesn't work, I'll be homeless before the semester ends. Either that, or on meds. Both of which are equally terrifying to me. I sigh. "You've got yourself a deal."

He smirks, back to his annoying self, and reaches a hand down to help me up, which I choose to ignore. "Brilliant. Now let's grab a bite somewhere."

I bristle. "What?" I have to admit, food does sound good right now. But I don't necessarily want to eat with Theo, even if he did just agree to help me with the biggest problem I've ever had.

He throws his arm around my shoulders. "Come on, little Willow. You can read a book any old day. But right now, you need comfort food. Know any good places?"

I shrug his arm off my shoulders plainly. "There's always In-N-Out," I suggest.

"*In-N-Out?*" He laughs. "Sounds vulgar."

I roll my eyes. "Don't get your hopes up."

Four

Ash texts me in the morning: *Running late. Not coming over this morning. Just going straight to school.*

On my way to the kitchen, I face the mirror in the hallway. Whenever I see my reflection, I always have to smile at it before I look away. For some reason, the idea of parting with my reflection wearing any expression other than a smile leaves me unsettled. I think it's because I'm not sure if it's the last time I'll ever see myself again. I could cease to exist at any moment, so if this is the last time I'll see my face, I at least want to look happy.

Even if I'm not.

When I enter the kitchen, the smell of French toast surrounds me, making my stomach growl. With my lips slightly parted, I watch my mom flip a cinnamon-coated slice of bread onto a plate, spatula in hand.

"Mom?" I walk closer, puzzled as I take in her work clothes. Why is she still awake? She hardly ever has time to make breakfast in the morning—which is technically dinnertime for her—and neither do I. It's the reason we have such an embarrassingly plentiful selection of cereal in the cupboard.

"Hi honey," she says, sounding a little like a zombie. After skipping out on sleep to hang out with Gus yesterday, she probably had a brutal shift at work last night. I'm surprised she didn't go straight to bed when she got home this morning. As soon as the last piece of bread is on the plate, she holds it out to me like an offering.

"What's this for?" I ask.

She sighs, shutting her eyes and wrinkling her nose a bit. "I'm sorry about yesterday."

I inhale deeply. Has she changed her mind? Maybe there's a chance she was just overreacting. Maybe she doesn't want me to move out, or to medicate me anymore. If that's the case, I won't need Theo's help after all, and I can go back to barely tolerating him instead of playing civil. "You are?"

"Yes," she says. "I shouldn't have yelled at you like that. I still meant everything I said, but I could have been a tad nicer if I had taken a deep breath or two first."

My heart sinks along with my appetite, but I take the plate anyway. "Oh."

Her lips turn downward. "I know you'll make the right decision, Willow. Starting medication is the right thing to do. If you just use these three months to mentally prepare yourself—"

"Mom, stop. I'm not getting on meds." I set the plate down on the table. "I'm going to handle this my own way."

Her lips thin into a straight line. "I'm sorry you can't see reason when it comes to this, Willow." Rubbing her forehead, she starts to head toward her bedroom. "No matter what you end up deciding, I love you."

I don't reply. I just take a seat and poke at my French toast with a fork.

"Don't let it get cold," she adds before disappearing down the hall, and the sound of her door shutting behind her follows.

I watch the steam rise and evaporate above the breakfast she made. She must feel at least a little guilty, to go out of her way to do this. But not guilty enough to change her mind.

With some effort, I cut myself a piece of toast with the edge of my fork and take a bite. It tastes like cardboard in my mouth.

"Get in," I say, patting the seat next to me. "Or I'm leaving without you."

Theo takes his time opening the car door and buckling himself in. He throws his navy blue backpack on the seat behind me. "So impatient, little Willow."

"You have no idea." I rev the engine.

"Tell me," he says, that annoying amusement already lighting up his expression. "Are you this pleasant with everyone? Or do you save this particular mood of yours for me alone?"

"You're awfully brazen for someone who relies on me to get to school."

He reclines his seat, propping his feet up on the dashboard. "You know very well that taking me to school is the only thing you look forward to when you wake up in the morning."

"It is *not*." I grip the steering wheel tight enough to pinch my fingers. "Not even close."

"You probably write all about it in your diary," he adds, displaying a wide grin.

I roll my eyes. "If I had a diary, which I don't, the only thing I'd write is how much I'd like to throw you out on the street while going top speed."

He laughs. "You have quite the imagination, love. It's probably from all that reading."

I sigh. "Are you going to talk the entire way?"

Theo waggles his eyebrows at me. "If you insist." He's wearing blue scrubs today, and so am I, but he has a denim jacket over his. He's used to London weather. But I don't bother telling him how warm it's going to be today here in Carmichael, California. He'll find out soon enough.

"In that case . . ." I bite my bottom lip. The conversation with my mom this morning has me on edge. Although I didn't expect it, part of me thought she really might change her mind about everything she said. It hurts to know she hasn't, even after sleeping on it for the night. Knowing I only have three months to eliminate my rituals enough to please her is more than I can bear. "Perhaps you could give me my first lesson on ERP therapy?" I glance at him, trying to make my expression pleasant. His dark blue scrubs make his eyes stand out, impossibly brighter than they already were against his pale skin.

Theo laughs. "We don't have enough time now. And I doubt you'd want to do something like that moments before walking into a classroom. You'd likely become all riled up from facing your compulsions. It isn't going to be easy."

I shrug. "I know that." It's a lie. I know absolutely nothing about ERP, but he's probably right about now being a bad time. Still, I can't help my urgency to get started. If I'm going to even have a chance of curing myself so I don't have to move out, I want that chance to be a good one. "I just meant," I continue, "maybe you could tell me what the process is like. What's the first step going to be?"

"You'll have to tell me all about yourself first, love." Theo says. He glances at me, still in his relaxed position. "Something I'm sure you're highly comfortable with and won't have any trouble doing at all."

I swat his arm without taking my eyes off the road, trying not to wince when I hit his hard muscle. "Shut up."

He laughs. "I'm serious, little Willow. You'll have to

open up for this to work." His voice deepens. "I know it won't be easy. But you're going to have to trust me if you want me to show you the techniques I know. If you can't do that, but still want to learn, I highly recommend seeing an actual therapist. Keep in mind that I'm not a true professional, just an ex-assistant."

I raise an eyebrow. "Are you sure you know what you're doing?"

Theo smirks. "My dad was successful with almost all his clients. And I know what he did. Take it or leave it, little Willow. It's no matter to me."

"Don't forget," I say through gritted teeth. "You need me too if you want to pass state board. I hear the questions are getting harder each year." That's a lie, too. The questions are almost exactly the same every year, as far as I know. But if Theo finds out I need him more than he needs me, I'm worried he won't help me.

Theo presses his lips together. "Right. Well, that's the first step. Opening up."

I inhale slowly. He's right—opening up about my OCD isn't something that's easy for me. Only Ash and my mom are aware of the extent of it, and I constantly worry that if anyone else learns what goes on in my head, they'll never let me live it down.

"Is there anything," Theo says quietly, all traces of teasing suspended, "you can think of that would make that easier for you to do?"

My eyes flicker toward him and then back to the road.

"You could tell me some things about yourself first," I suggest. "You know, considering I hardly know anything about you."

He smiles, but the seriousness in his eyes lingers. "What do you want to know?"

The question that's been weighing on me the longest comes out before I have a chance to think it through. "Did you . . . did you have any idea your mom was going to kill herself before it happened?"

He's silent for a moment, and I worry I've gone too far. I'm about to mentally berate myself for being so careless, for asking something so personal, when he answers me.

"My dad was physically, emotionally and mentally abusive," Theo tells me plainly. "So, I suppose I probably should have suspected it."

I can't help it; I glance over at him. His eyes meet mine, unwavering. That hadn't been something I was expecting at all. But then again, why does anyone make the choice to end their own life? I'm certainly no expert.

"I'm sorry," I whisper, and the silence stretches on, so I voice the only other thing that comes into my mind. "And he's a psychologist?"

Theo smiles bitterly. "You'd be amazed how convincing a face can be when it's worn for a stranger. And often, the people who give the most excellent advice fail to take it themselves."

Somehow, I can believe that.

"Is there anything else you want to know?" Theo asks.

I consider for a moment. "What's your middle name?"

He laughs, shaking his head a little. "Oh, now you've gone too far."

I laugh. "Names are important. They can tell you a lot about a person." I raise my eyebrows at him. "If you won't tell me, then I'll assume it's something terrible."

"Relax, little Willow. I'll tell you," he says. "It's William."

"Theodore William Tate," I say aloud, testing the way it sounds.

When Theo speaks, his voice sounds husky. "Have the depths of my secrets been uncovered with that revelation, love?"

I roll my eyes. "It's a gentlemanly name. It means you're probably not as much of an ass as you let on."

He smirks. "I don't think gentlemanly is a word." Theo places a hand on his chest. "And I'm wounded by that backhanded compliment. Now you have to tell me your middle name so I can have my turn psychoanalyzing you."

"Of course gentlemanly is a word. And my middle name is Daphne."

"Daphne?" His eyebrows fly up. "That's not at all what I was expecting. But Willow Daphne Bates suits you somehow."

"Thanks," I say. Warmth floods my cheeks. The exit for American River College comes up, the buildings already visible from the highway.

Theo raises an eyebrow at me. "If you're really set on starting ERP today—"

"I am." My tone is firm. If there's any way I'm going to be able to live with my mom and keep attending cosmetology school, then I really need to get started with this therapy he's been hyping. "Can you come over after school? I'll give you the bacteriology cheat-sheet I created. It has all the questions and answers on the topics that will be on the state board test."

He smirks. "If by that you mean, can I walk a few yards from your mum's in-law quarters to her actual house, then I'll try to find time to pencil it in." Theo frowns. "How on earth do you have a cheat-sheet with all the questions and answers about bacteriology?"

"Research," I state. "People who took the test post things like that online all the time. I just took the time to collect and organize it all." I pull into a school parking spot, turning off the engine. "I have cheat sheets for every subject on the test. Not just bacteriology."

Theo stares at me. "You're a bit frightening, little Willow."

* * *

We clock in with seconds to spare. Apparently, at this school, we lose fifteen minutes of our completed labor time for every minute we're late. How that calculation is supposed to make sense or be fair in any way, I'm not sure. Maybe they're just telling us that so we'll come on time. Either way, I'm not willing to test out the theory.

Ash is sitting at her station when we get there. She's talking to one of the only two other guys in our class. He has mousy brown hair with a blond stripe in the front, brown eyes, and skin that looks permanently pink. When Theo and I walk up, Ash smiles. "Charlie, this is my cousin, Willow." She gestures to me.

Charlie raises his eyebrows. "Wait, you guys are cousins? But you're white and she's black. How does that work?"

Ash looks irritated. "I'm adopted," she lies.

Charlie's face softens into a combination of understanding and pity. "Ah." He nods and wanders back to his station on the other side of the room.

As I take my seat between Ash and Theo, he disguises his laugh as a cough, but I wonder if he would have believed Ash, had I not explained the situation to him yesterday. He hangs his backpack on the back of his chair and starts texting someone, so I turn to my right.

"Ash," I whisper. "You'll never believe what happened after school."

She leans toward me, mouth open and eyebrows raised, and I launch into my version of what happened after I embarrassed my mom in front of Gus.

"What the fuck?" She frowns. "I can't believe your mom. Gus Badgley must be amazing in bed or some shit for her to care so much what he thinks."

I try not to gag at the image of them having sex. "I don't think it's because of him," I whisper. "She's been fed up

56

with me for so long now that it was only a matter of time. This was just the perfect opportunity for her to act on her feelings."

Ash shakes her head. "Just come live with me. You know my mom won't care."

I stare at my hands. "Thanks, but I don't think my mom would appreciate her younger sister taking in her daughter. I don't want to bring all this drama into your house." Not to mention, my aunt already has three kids, including Ash. The boys share a room, and despite Ash's offer, I know how much she likes her space. Becoming Aunt Christie's charity case would bring me more than shame than comfort.

Ash opens her mouth to say something, but Mrs. Harrison tells everyone to take their seats and quiet down. The volume of chatter lowers significantly, and Mrs. Harrison clears her throat. "Our spring fashion show begins in March," she announces. "And I know it's a little early, but I want all of you to start thinking of themes for the show. The nominations will be voted on at the end of the month, but first, everyone will be paired into a stylist-model team."

Ash raises her hand but doesn't wait to be called on. "Can we pick our partners?"

Mrs. Harrison pretends she doesn't hear Ash's question. "We'll be watching videos of past performances so you can get an idea of what to expect. They are also indicative of our standards for the show." Mrs. Harrison glances at a girl who has been raising her hand. "Yes, Daisy?"

"Can we at least choose whether we want to be the stylist or the model?"

"Yes." Mrs. Harrison smiles. "You may choose your partner as well. Anyone who can't make up their mind will be paired by me. You may also bring in a personal model from outside school if you want to. But there can't be two models or stylists in one pair, obviously. There has to be one of each."

Ash squeezes my hand. "You're my model," she whispers.

Mrs. Harrison has us work on our mannequins until break time. I give my dark-haired, heavily made up doll head a voluminous blow-out, taking care to hairspray it so it will still look good after break. That way I'll get more points when I show it to Mrs. Harrison. Theo wrestles with his mannequin, trying to keep it upright on its stand, muttering "Bloody hell" every time it falls off from his running a brush through the strands. A small giggle escapes me. Ash doesn't work on her doll head, opting to paint her own nails pastel green instead.

Charlie comes over to our stations, a pack of Marlboros in hand. "Wanna smoke?" he asks Ash.

"I'll bum one of yours," she says, blowing on her nails. "But we're going to go find my boyfriend after."

Charlie nods. He eyes me, like he knows not to offer me a cigarette. Like he knows I'm not cool enough for one. What I don't tell him is that Ash rarely smokes, usually only when she's extremely stressed out. It probably has something to do with her and Joseph, but I know better than to ask her right now.

"Come on, babe." Ash flips her hair and links her arm through mine.

"Want to come?" Charlie asks Theo.

He shrugs, his blue eyes flickering to me briefly. "Why not?"

The three of us follow Charlie to the smoking section. It must be break time for at least some of the rest of campus as well because hordes of students make their way past our department toward the cafeteria at a rapid pace.

When we reach the smoking-approved section of the parking lot, Charlie hands a cigarette to Ash and then offers one to Theo.

"No thanks, mate," he says. He removes his denim jacket now that we're outside, away from the classroom's air conditioning. When he does, I notice he has tattoos on his forearms. Theo gets a text and pulls out his phone, which vibrates excessively. At least five messages come through. Theo sighs and runs a hand through his dark hair, causing it to come out of its neatly combed style and fall into his face.

Ash lights her cigarette, and I sit on the curb, waiting for her to be done. What a fantastic way to spend our break, inhaling chemicals that will contribute to the decline of our health. Every breath I take while I'm sitting here is bringing me closer and closer and closer to lung cancer.

I shut my eyes, but that only exacerbates the scent. I'm aware of Charlie and Ash going on about something, but it's hard to focus when I'm surrounded by so many chemicals. Maybe if I fix the way my shoes are tied, I'll feel better. Or maybe I should just go inside.

"Well, Willow . . . ?" Ash waits.

I blink. "What?" I wasn't aware her conversation with Charlie included me.

"Do you want to come to his back-to-school party?"

I glance at Charlie. He puts a hand on his hip, his cigarette almost down to the butt. "When is it?" I ask.

He takes a long drag. "Next Friday." He says it without letting his breath go. When he finally does exhale, he says, "On Valentine's Day."

Friday.

My body races with adrenaline. "Oh," I say. "Thank you for inviting me. But I can't."

Charlie gives me an incredulous look. A look that says he knows I have nothing going on that day. "Why not?"

Ash sighs. "Because she has a date with her bed and a *Harry Potter* book." Her eyes flicker around the campus, looking for Joseph the way a hawk searches for field mice.

Charlie frowns. "Sounds . . . fun?"

Even though Ash is lying to Charlie for me, it allows me to breathe a little more easily. At least now he won't know the real reason I won't be attending his party. Or any others on a Friday for that matter.

Ash stiffens. She lets her cigarette fall to the ground and

doesn't bother stomping it out. Without a word, she darts away from the rest of us and heads in the direction of three people chatting as they walk to class. I stand up and follow her. It's Joseph, flanked by two girls who look identical.

I remain a safe distance away, not wanting to eavesdrop, as Ash finally catches up to him.

She grabs Joseph's arm, turning him to face her, and his green eyes widen. With Ash's back to me I'm unable to see her expression, but Joseph stares at the ground, rubbing his hand across the top of his shortly cropped brown hair. I can only imagine what she's saying and feel a very small stab of sympathy for him. I can't imagine being on Ash's shit-list is pleasant by any stretch of the imagination. I don't feel too bad for him, though, because if he is on her shit-list, he probably deserves it. Ash doesn't hold meaningless grudges.

Ash points a finger at him, and though I can hear the sharp tone of her voice, I can't discern any of the words she's saying. Joseph frowns, and the gorgeous twins he's with linger behind him awkwardly. One of them whispers something to the other, and they walk off without him.

We only have three minutes left before it's time to clock in from break. I'm about to interrupt Ash to let her know when she abruptly turns and walks away from Joseph.

"Ashton!" he calls, cupping his hands around his mouth. When she reaches me she says nothing, just keeps walking toward the cosmetology building. He holds his hands up in exasperation, and as I catch up with her I get a glimpse of Ash's red-rimmed eyes. Suddenly I want to punch Joseph for whatever he did to put her in such a state.

"What happened?" I ask her softly. But she doesn't look at me, doesn't answer me, doesn't acknowledge me. I follow her inside and we grab our timesheets. Clock in. We are just shy of being late.

We find our seats, Theo at his desk already. He raises his eyebrows at me, but I shake my head lightly. I don't know what's going on with Joseph and my cousin any more than he does.

Ash doesn't say anything as we take notes on sanitary maintenance areas—SMAs for short—or when we demonstrate our understanding of the set-up. I try to catch her eye a few times, but she studiously ignores all forms of communication. When Mrs. Harrison checks Ash's SMA, she doesn't say a word. My heart clenches. I want so badly to ask her what's going on, but I know she won't tell me yet. When the bell rings at three o'clock, dismissing us for the day, Ash shoulders past me without a word. I bite my lip as I watch her. If she doesn't text me when she gets home, I'm going to show up at her house and demand to know what's wrong.

Theo pokes me on the shoulder. I blink away my reverie and find him watching me. "Shall we stay here and people-watch?"

I roll my eyes and stand follow him. As we walk to my car, I glance at his hands, hanging loosely at his sides, and feel a jolt of nerves race through me.

"Do you need to do anything at your place before you come over?" I ask him when we reach Mitten Chip, mostly to have something to say.

"Oh no," Theo says, already reclining the passenger seat and propping up his feet. "I don't need you getting cold feet on me. We're starting right away, little Willow."

I swallow. "Okay, then."

"Just remember. You're going to be very uncomfortable," he says, a little too cheerfully. "I hope you're ready."

I start the engine, scaring away a flock of birds searching for food in the parking space next to us. "So do I."

Five

I send Ash a text before I start driving, still wondering if she's okay.

Want to talk?

Her response is almost instant, as if she's been waiting for my text, or maybe waiting for one from Joseph.

Tomorrow. I'll tell you everything. I just want to be alone right now.

I toss my phone onto the dashboard. I'm not going to push her as long as she really intends to talk to me tomorrow. Otherwise, I'm going to start demanding answers.

"I'm curious," Theo says evenly. "Did your mum ever take you to therapy in the past?"

I sigh. "Of course. I went once as a kid, and again more recently, about six months ago. It wasn't the greatest experience."

"Why not?"

"Because as soon as I opened up to her, she prescribed me Anafranil and called it a day. I refused to go back after that. If my therapist had any intention to try ERP with me, she didn't say so." At least I know Theo doesn't have the authority to prescribe me anything at all. He'll have to rely solely on cognitive behavioral therapy to make any progress with me.

"You should consider giving it another shot."

I roll my eyes. "Trying to get out of helping me already?"

He laughs. "No. But your experience isn't the norm. Therapy was the best thing that ever happened to me."

I look him over. "I didn't know you needed it."

He gives me a humorless smile. "Yes, well. Growing up with a dad like mine wasn't easy. I probably wouldn't be quite as *all right* as I am now if it weren't for my therapist. It was him who inspired me to start working with my dad in the first place. I know how messed up he really is, but if I could somehow help his patients the way my therapist helped me, I knew it would be worth it."

I'm silent. I don't know what to say, and I certainly hadn't been expecting him to say that. I'd always thought therapists existed solely for parents to force their children to go to them when they didn't know how to parent anymore. Had I really had such a bad experience, or was it that I'd never really been open to learning in the first place?

"I have to admit," I tell Theo, "I never really tried in

therapy. I've never wanted to give up my rituals and risk everything falling apart. I didn't want to get better, but instead somehow find a way to both live with having OCD and still somehow make my mom happy."

"Have you ever tried to stop reacting to your compulsions?"

I laugh. "I've never tried. To be honest, I'm not sure I'll ever be able to." My voice sounds shaky, nervous even to my own ears.

Theo arches an eyebrow at me. "Are you doubting my skills, little Willow?"

I huff. "You have no idea what you're getting yourself into, Theo." I shake my head, unable to meet his eyes. "I'm a hopeless case."

"No you aren't." His voice is so firm, I turn to look at him. Traffic is heavy and we're at a complete stop for the moment. Theo's expression is steady. When he speaks, his voice is low. "I've seen hopeless, and believe me, love, you aren't it."

I laugh without humor. "If this ERP thing works, I may give therapy another shot."

The car behind us sounds their horn, signaling us to move forward and making me jump.

"Ignore their hooting," Theo insists.

"Hooting?" I can't help but laugh in spite of the tone of our conversation. "What are you, an owl?"

Theo squints at me. "And what," he asks, "would you have me call it?"

"Um, I don't know. Honking, like a normal person?" My voice is teasing.

"Honking? What are you, a goose?" Theo displays a wide grin. I gape at him, at a loss for a witty comeback. He has me there.

"Beeping?" I suggest.

"Beeping," he agrees.

I fight the urge to smile. We're silent for a moment, and when the traffic causes us to stop again I glance at his forearms, taking in the swirls and patterns decorating them, like illustrations on a page, a tangible piece of a story.

"I didn't know you had a tattoo," I remark. "I noticed one earlier at school."

He glances at his arms. "I have several. Would you like to see?"

I lean over the center console to study his skin, my curiosity getting the best of me. "What are they?" I resist the urge to trace the images with my fingertips. My eyes linger on a small scar on his right wrist. It's shaped like a circle, and I can't help but notice how similar in size it is to the end of a cigarette. I don't comment on it, and instead study the tattoo next to it. It's an outline of a small hand, with a name in cursive underneath. *Lucy.* "Who's Lucy?" I ask, wondering briefly if it's his girlfriend back home.

Theo glances down, and then out the window. He places his palms flat against his thighs, obscuring my view of his tattoos. "My sister." His voice is quiet, resigned. My eyes flicker to his face. He doesn't look upset, but he's not smiling either. My mom never mentioned him having a sister, nor did I see one in that old Christmas card. In fact, I remember thinking that another child was the only thing missing in his perfect little family.

Well, perfect at the time. Or so I'd thought.

I decide this subject might be sensitive, so I don't ask him any more questions, though my curiosity is anything but satisfied.

"And we're here." I pull Mitten Chip into my mom's driveway. "Are you sure you want to do this?"

Theo offers me a humorless half-smile. "Are you?"

I sigh. "I don't have a choice." I shut the engine off and grab my stuff. "Let the torture commence."

At that he laughs. He grabs his jacket and backpack from the backseat of the car and follows me inside the house. "Spending time with me could never be torture."

I roll my eyes. "That is yet to be determined."

Once we're inside my bedroom, Theo looks around. I wonder what he thinks of my cool, dusty-blue walls, white curtains, white furniture, and white bedding.

"Your room is interesting. Not quite what I expected."

I frown. It bothers me that my room gave him expectations at all. "What do you mean?"

He stands and walks around, surveying my personal objects. "I don't know. I suppose I assumed everything would be ridiculously clean. Sterile, even. But it's not *that* clean."

I laugh. "Why did you expect it to be clean? Because I

have OCD? That doesn't necessarily mean I like everything like the inside of a doctor's office, you know." Despite my room not being *clean*, it's arranged exactly how I like it. Not a single object is out of place. Yes, there are dust motes in the corners of the ceiling. My surfaces aren't shining from being wiped down, but *everything* is where it belongs. I know most people would be baffled that I don't spend my free time as a maid, but that's only because of the way society tends to portray OCD. As a quirk for cleanliness rather than a debilitating disorder.

He faces me, his blue eyes searching mine. "How do you like everything, then?" His voice is soft, quiet.

"Are you always this nosy?" I ask, annoyed by the thrumming in my veins. But then I remember that part of him helping me involves telling him all about exactly what I try to hide on a daily basis.

I point to the right corner of my dresser, where a pen and paper rest at a perfect angle. "See that pen?" I ask. "Notice anything particular about it?"

He studies it intently before glancing at me. "It's black." He sounds proud of his observation.

I roll my eyes. "It's in a certain position. The clip attached to the cap is on the left side."

Theo frowns and looks at the pen again. He lightly touches it with his index finger, just enough that it rolls. The clip is now on the right side.

I inhale sharply. *"Don't."* I roll the pen back to how it was before.

I tap my finger against my dresser repeatedly until my anxiety ebbs. Theo doesn't miss a thing. He watches me tap the dresser, but he doesn't acknowledge it.

"Why? What's wrong with the pen facing the other way?" His voice is gentle now. I'm surprised he's not laughing. Most people would. He could readjust the pen to aggravate me, so he can watch me fix it over and over again, but he doesn't.

I shrug. "It just bothers me. I can't explain why. It's like, I get this feeling of dread. Like something terrible will happen if certain things aren't positioned the right way."

He nods like he understands. Maybe he does. Maybe he's worked with people like me before at his dad's practice.

"Does your cousin know you have OCD?"

"Ash? Yes. She's known forever."

He raises his eyebrows. "Forever? How long have you had it?"

My cheeks heat. "Since I was really young, but I wasn't diagnosed until about thirteen." This is a lie. I was actually diagnosed at twelve, but the fact that I was an even-numbered age kills me. So, I lie to everyone. I lie to myself. Thirteen.

I cough into the silence that has filled the room. It's not an awkward silence. More like a thoughtful silence. It makes me uncomfortable, regardless. "Do you still want to help me?" I ask. "Or are you secretly planning to have me committed to a rubber room instead?"

He laughs, his face lighting up with an impossibly

bright grin. "You're a funny one, love." He grabs the notebook and pen from my dresser. "First things first. Are the majority of your compulsions mental, or physical?"

I shrug. "Both, probably." I've never taken the time to consider such a thing. "How can I find out?"

"A crucial part of this will be creating a complete inventory of your compulsions," he says more to himself than me. "That's going to be your homework for tonight, little Willow."

I huff loudly. "Yeah, except I don't even know what half of them *are*. I've been like this for so long, I don't even notice some of my compulsions anymore."

He nods. "Learning what they are along the way and catching them before you have a chance to respond to them will be a huge part of this. Like the pen thing." He sits down on my bed. "For example, does my sitting here bother you? If so, how would you react to make yourself feel better?"

It's a mystery to me how he knows his messing up my perfectly made bed makes me feel like my blood is rushing at top speed. But my reaction to it is a second nature. "I would tap," I say, my voice sounding strained. "Until I felt better."

Theo nods again, his gaze like hard blue ice on mine. "Don't."

I laugh, but humor is the last emotion I feel. It's an uncomfortable, anxiety-driven laugh, and Theo must know it, because he takes one of my pillows from the head of the bed and holds it on his lap without looking away from me.

"This is a really nice pillowcase," he comments. "So smooth."

"It's satin, if you must know," I huff. "It keeps my hair from drying out."

Theo eyes the pillow with renewed interest. "Perhaps I should get one."

"I mean, if you're worried about premature aging, then sure. But trust me, you don't have the kind of hair that needs it."

Theo runs his fingers along the shiny material, and I resist the urge to cry out, to tap the walls or my leg, to rush over and stop him. But I can't help it. I can't breathe. I can't see straight. I can't think properly. I might even faint. Tears well up in my eyes, obscuring my already distracted vision. "I can't do this," I whisper. "Stop. You have to stop."

Theo's voice is low and steady. "I know it's uncomfortable, Willow. But you *can* do this. Breathe. Let this pass and you'll see that nothing terrible is going to happen."

I breathe rapidly, short and angry spurts of air inhaling and exhaling. My brain feels foggy and I'm hot all over. My throat is thick with tears. "You can't possibly know that. Has this ever actually worked for anyone?"

"Yes," Theo says evenly. "I've seen it with several patients."

I shut my eyes. "I don't think I can be one of them."

"Of course you can." Theo's voice is closer than I expect,

so I open my eyes. He's no longer sprawled across my bed but standing right in front of me. A piece of his dark hair falls into his eyes, steady and blue and staring into mine.

I blink rapidly. "I—"

"Don't *have* to participate in this," he finishes for me. "You have other options. You simply must decide which option you can live with."

I inhale. He's right. I know without hesitation I can't live with any of the options my mom gave me.

My bedroom is silent save for the sound of our breathing; mine uneven, his relaxed. I meet his gaze, blinking back the remaining tears I've conjured. "Okay." I glance over his shoulder at my bed, which is still in complete disarray. "Let's try again."

Theo holds up a finger. "First," he says, "I think it might be best for you to create that list of your compulsions. That way we can start conquering them from smallest to largest. We need to build your confidence as you tackle each of your fears so that you can move forward in a systematic way."

I exhale deeply. The idea of continuing what I just endured is too much to handle. Making a list, however, I can do. I eye my comforter. "I'm going to make my bed first." I start toward it, but Theo's hand on my shoulder stops me.

"I think," he says, "that if you can make the list while sitting on your unmade bed, we can call your first attempt a success."

I sigh, my blood still racing. "Fine. As long as I can fix it *right* after."

The list doesn't take me long to create, which surprises me. The hardest part is placing the compulsions in the correct order and making sure there isn't an even amount of them. When I've done the best I can, I wave the sheet of paper in the air like a white flag. "Done."

The corner of his mouth turns up. He walks over and takes the list from me, reading it over. "Brilliant. Now what I want you to do is write next to each compulsion, in parentheses, how you would react to it with a ritual, whether mental or physical."

I glare at him. "I thought I was done. I want to make my bed."

He chuckles. "You're nearly done, little Willow. You can make your bed right after this."

I scowl and return to my list.

	WILLOW'S TOP 11 COMPULSIONS/FEARS THAT COME TO MIND (IN DESCENDING ORDER)— AND THEIR RITUALS:
11.	Contamination (washing the contaminated area repeatedly)
10.	Conflict (tapping and imagining the worst-case scenario so it doesn't happen)
9.	Not being in control (tapping, or finding little things to control to prove I am in control)
8.	Not being happy (most of my rituals, like smiling at my reflection, serve as a way to prevent this from happening. If I find myself unhappy, I will sometimes think of my happy place)
7.	Objects in an "uncomfortable" position or in the wrong place (readjusting the object repeatedly)
6.	Losing time (tapping, arranging objects, anything involving odd numbers)
5.	Even numbers (tapping my fingers an odd amount of times)
4.	Going out on a Friday (there is no ritual for this because I would NEVER do it!)
3.	Sitting in the passenger seat of a car while someone else drives (see above parenthetical comment)
2.	Taking medicine (forcing myself to vomit until all the medicine has been expelled. But again, taking medicine is not something I would ever do unless my life depended on it)
1.	The idea of a loved one dying (the last time this happened, all my rituals were collectively exacerbated)

"You're tapping again," Theo tells me, breaking my concentration. "Why are you doing it right now?"

I glance up at him, and then at my left hand, on my comforter. He's right. My fingers are moving without my awareness, the other hand gripping the pen.

I breathe in. "I don't know," I say. "It helps me calm down. It helps me *stay* calm."

"What's bothering you right now that you feel the need to tap?"

I shake my head. "This list, obviously."

His lips thin. "Perhaps we should take a break, then. Get some fresh air." Theo takes the paper from me and folds it into a square. He puts it in his pocket and gives me a small smile. "I know just the place."

Six

When I park the car, American River—not the college, but the actual river—is nowhere in sight, hidden beneath the surrounding trails and tall brown grass mixed with threads of green. I carefully roll up the black leggings I changed into before we left, grateful for the feeling of warmth on my skin. I hope Theo didn't come to California expecting actual seasons, because we don't get them here. It's mid-January, but instead of snow melting into spring, it's merely cold in the morning before warming up in the afternoon. My hair is in a thick braid, allowing the warm breeze to caress my neck.

I've come here before, but I have no idea how Theo knows this place exists. When I ask him about it, he looks at me like I'm crazy and replies, "Google, of course."

Theo walks ahead of me, and the wind blows his scent

in my direction. It reminds me of expensive stores at the mall that make you want to eat the clothes because of how enticing they smell. I don't dare tell him he smells nice, though. His ego wouldn't be able to handle the compliment.

Instead, I opt for small talk. "I hope Ash is okay. I know she's only pretending to be right now."

He laughs. "Ah, yes. The famous language of women. Saying the opposite of what you actually want."

I scoff. "That is an unfair stereotype. And an untrue one, at that."

Theo holds his hands up. "Fine, little Willow. You know her best."

Our footsteps are the only sounds, crunching through the maze of grass until the trail opens up, revealing the river. The wind feels amazing, slightly warm, and a chorus of birds tweet from their nests, creating an ambiance I wouldn't be opposed to napping in, had I the chance. Theo takes it in for a moment, staring at the small waves rippling under the bright sun. The pebbled shore glistens with moisture, its array of colored rocks begging to be plucked up and examined. I give him a sideways glance. "Haven't you ever had a best friend?"

Theo laughs softly, bitterly. "None worth mentioning. In fact, the only that *is* . . . I can't even recall what her name was. Some details from my childhood are a bit spotty. I've been told it's a symptom of PTSD."

I don't know how to respond at first, because I don't

want Theo to think I pity him, but I kind of do. The fact that his dad is probably the reason he has PTSD, and memory problems, makes me unexpectedly angry. But then his earlier words catch up to my train of thought. His only friend was a girl? For some reason this surprises me. I'd pictured Theo to be the kind of guy with lots of other guy friends, or *mates* as he would say.

"Tell me about her," I insist, hoping to satisfy my curiosity and keep from saying something stupid. "Why was she such a good friend?" We walk closer to the water. It's clear as day, empty save for two or three paddle boats floating atop its surface.

Theo smiles without mirth. "I think I must have been seven years old the last time I saw her. We used to play in my tree house." He smiles faintly. "One time my dad was watching us, and while we were playing king and queen together, I fell straight out of the tree house and broke my arm."

My eyes widen. "You what?"

"I know," he continues. "And when I went to my father for help, he told me to stop whining like a girl."

His story stirs my mind like a stone tossed into a stagnant pond, resurfacing memories I had no idea I'd even repressed. The tree house, his dad, the fake plastic crowns. The king and queen game. I feel like I can't move. My eyes are wide as saucers. It can't be. "Go on," I whisper.

He frowns at my expression. "After that, she . . . " He runs a hand through his dark hair, shining under the sun's rays. "It was so long ago, yet it remains one of my fondest memories. She told my father that if he expected me to act like a grown up, he should probably start setting an example of one." A smile tugs at his lips. His impossibly blue eyes seem far away. "He'd never heard a child speak to him like that before."

"Theo," I say, my voice urgent. "Did your tree house have a pink flamingo curtain for a door? With a red and blue striped rug inside?"

Theo meets my gaze. "How did you know that? Did your mum tell you?"

"And the inside of your house had pale wood floors that smelled like Pine-Sol . . . " I trail off, trying to recall every detail. "Your dad had a room with a pool table and a cart for drinks, and your room was blue, with a brown carpet. Your closet door was broken, so it only slid open halfway . . . "

"It was you," Theo states. "All this time, it was you, wasn't it?"

We stare at each other for a long moment, both of us in complete and utter shock.

And then Theo laughs, loud and unconfined. It feels like my entire life is a dream, or maybe a joke. Of course it would be me, this person Theo remembers talking back to his dad for him.

It's hard to believe fate would bring us back together after all these years, after I've lost my mind and he's grown out of his awkward, juvenile appearance. It's no wonder I didn't recognize him. In fact, I'd managed to forget about him completely. But the memory of his scrawny frame flashes behind my vision, the way his dark hair used to be cut short, how his wide blue eyes were like gaping holes that led straight to the ocean. I take in his lean yet muscular frame, his neatly combed hair. His eyes narrowed in on me. I shiver.

My phone rings, breaking me out of my trance. I glance at the name on the screen and answer. "Mom?" I say, my voice cracking. "Hello?" I pull it away from my face just as the screen turns black. I cringe internally when I realize I never charged it after school. Anything could happen right now, and I won't have a way to contact the police in an emergency. "It just died," I tell Theo. "I'm going to let it charge in the car. I'll be right back."

Theo holds out his hand, still seeming dazed. "Allow me."

"What? No," I protest, but he snatches my phone from me before I can stop him.

"Get your hands dirty. I'll be right back."

"What?" My eyes widen. "Why?"

"It's number eleven on your list."

"You said we were done for the day!"

Theo smiles slowly. "I lied."

I gape at him.

"If your fingers aren't quivering from not tapping by the time I return, I'll toss you straight into the river." He offers me a serious stare before heading back to the car.

I roll my eyes as I approach the water and take deep, calming breaths.

I'm still reeling at the sudden reappearance of memories from a house where I played as a child, at vaguely remembering the face of the kid who lived there but having the recollections end there. I also recall asking my mom why we stopped playing there all of a sudden, but not receiving an answer.

Those memories lived in such a small, fleeting part of my mind, I never thought in a million years they would someday be pieced together.

He is the boy. The one I played king and queen with. The one who read me classic stories before I knew how to. His mom used to make us ham and cheese platters, fruit salad, and mac n' cheese. But her face, like the rest of what I remember about that time, is as foggy as a steamed window.

I don't know how to treat Theo now. Especially after finding out that I was the only friend from his childhood that mattered to him. I don't know how I managed to make such an impression on him, what I did to deserve that title.

Other than stand up to his abusive father for him.

I still need time to reconcile this very grown up Theo with the Teddy I used to play with when I was five.

Teddy. That's what I used to call him. It's no wonder I never made the connection. I can't believe my mom never brought it up.

I dip my hands in the water and pick up the dirtiest

rock I can find. I rub the dirt into my palms, pressing with more force than necessary. I don't know why the idea of my mom keeping my childhood friendship with Theo a secret makes me so angry. Maybe she simply forgot.

Or maybe I'm mad that I'm being forced to face my compulsions in the first place, and all because of her. Her and *Gus Badgley*. I rub the rock into my palm with even more vigor, my anger fueling me. It alarms me how much the pain of it pleases me.

"Hey!" A guy in a red shirt from the paddle boat waves at me. "How about you lose some of those layers!"

I glance around, assuming I'm hearing things, but the guy in the red shirt is staring directly at me. I look down at my loose, flowy top and then back up at him. The paddle boat is close enough to the shore that I know I heard him correctly. Another one of them catcalls at me, and I cross my arms defensively.

"Come on," a brown-haired one shouts. "Just for a minute!"

"Flash us!" Red Shirt waves his beer can in the air. "And we'll send some beers your way!"

I stare at my hands, caked in dirt. This is happening because of my hands. They're dirty, and I need to wash them. But if I bend down and rinse them in the water, Theo will know I failed. I breathe in and out rapidly. I have no idea what to do right now.

"Don't make us come over there. I don't think you'd like that, baby," one of them cackles. He makes a vulgar gesture, and chills travel down my spine. I'm frozen in place, terrified to run, and terrified to say anything in response.

Theo approaches me, his eyebrows narrowed in concern. "Are you all right?"

I look at him, my heart still racing. I can't even answer because I'm so shaken.

When I don't respond, he glances back and forth between me and the men on the boat.

"Come on, don't be a buzzkill," Red Shirt shouts. "He can join too."

Theo's expression sets in anger, his eyes blazing like blue fire. A moment later, his shoes are fully submerged in the water as he makes for the boat.

"What are you doing?" I gasp.

"Going to teach those bastards a lesson." Theo's voice is dangerously low, and I grip his arm before he can go any farther.

"Theo, stop. I'm fine." I tug, but his pulse thrums beneath my fingertips. The sensation calms me a little, almost as if I were tapping.

His gaze slices through me like shards of glass. "You're trembling," he informs me. He looks pointedly at the hand restraining him, and I follow his gaze, only then noticing the shaking of my fingers, still caked with dirt.

I swallow hard. I'm worried that if I release him, he'll confront those men. If he does, things might escalate from there, and someone could get hurt. Even though confrontation is a fear I will eventually have to face, I'm not ready yet.

I've already endured too much today. And with the way Theo's eyes gleam with barely concealed intentions of murder, I can't leave him to his own devices right now. "Please, just come sit down with me," I plead.

Theo takes a deep breath, and I can't help but wonder why those guys' comments bothered him so much. They bothered me too, but his reaction hardly seems warranted.

I take his other hand, tugging him towards the rocks farther back from the water. I'm hyper aware of the feeling of his skin on mine, but I try not to dwell on it. We sit on the pebbled ground, and Theo glares at the men on the boat, who are laughing at us for retreating.

"Don't pay attention to them," I say softly. "Just look at me." I wipe off the dirt on my pants and rest my hand hesitantly on his cheek. His lips look impossibly soft, despite the scowl they're set into. I think about the way I stood up to Theo's dad when we were kids, how much of an impression it had apparently made on him. He'd been willing to do the same for me right now.

"Thank you for wanting to defend me too," I say evenly. "But I'm fine."

"It's more than that." Theo's cheeks are heated, as if he's been lightly slapped. "I won't stand for men disrespecting women like that. It's over the line."

I stare at him, wondering if his feelings come from having to watch his dad treat his mom similarly, disrespectfully.

The fury in his expression ebbs a little more the longer

I force him to hold my gaze. His hair has completely forgone its perfect style, the wind parting it every which way and forcing it in and out of his face. I can't help but stare at the dimple in his chin, covered in light stubble. With my hand still touching his cheek, I've never been more tempted to inch my way closer and press my finger against the divot under his mouth. Theo lifts his hand, like he's about to touch me back, and my heart races in response.

"We should go," I say.

Theo glances at the pebbles on the ground. "Right. Your mother will be worried."

I blink rapidly, imagining him recounting today's events to her. "You're not going to tell her, are you?"

At this, he smiles. "Of course not, little Willow. I only meant because your phone's not working. She's probably still trying to reach you."

I relax a little. The last thing I need is my mom questioning me endlessly in a way that will make me feel three years old. "You're right. Let's go."

My mom is sitting at the kitchen table when I walk in the door alone. I figured it would probably be better if Theo wasn't with me when I came inside. Whenever my mom is worried, she's completely unreasonable. I have a feeling she's on that level today, and I doubt Theo would appreciate having to witness it.

My mom is in her pajamas—beige sweatpants and a white tank top, her blond hair pulled up into a high bun.

"Trouble sleeping?" I ask by way of greeting.

She glances up. "Where have you been?" Her cheeks look slightly flushed, and I notice her phone sitting on the table in front of her, face-up. Like she's waiting for it to ring.

A pang of guilt shoots through me. I hadn't thought to tell her where I'd be because she's usually asleep at this time. Of course the one time I'm not home she wakes up to find me gone. "I'm sorry I never called you back. My phone died while I was at the river with Theo."

She frowns at me. "Why were you at the river with him?"

"It doesn't matter." I pull out a chair and sit across from her, frowning right back. "But what does matter is why you never told me he and I used to be really good friends as kids."

She shakes her head like she doesn't understand. "What do you mean? Of course you two were friends."

I scoff at her dismissive tone. "Well, I didn't know that. Why didn't you tell me?"

She sighs. "Why would I need to tell you? What did you think? That I'd been friends with Mildred all those years and we never let our kids play together? Theodore is only a few years older than you."

I study my mom as she stands up and grabs a water

glass from the cupboard. Something is off about the way she's acting. She's trying to calm me down, though for what I have no idea.

"That doesn't make sense." I furrow my brows, still watching her. "If that's the case, why did you stop bringing me to visit?"

My mom doesn't move from her position staring into the cupboard. I doubt she's actually looking for something to eat but rather trying to find a way to avoid eye contact with me. I don't speak, hoping the silence will make her tell me whatever she's hoping to avoid. She exhales deeply before finally turning to look at me.

"Because of Rob," she tells me. Her voice is so quiet, almost like she hopes I'll miss her words.

"Rob?"

"Theodore's dad," she explains. "When you were little, I used to take you to London a lot to play with Theo, while Mildred and I hung out." My mom shuts the cupboard door, fills her glass with water, and sits back down across from me. She doesn't take a sip.

"And?" I prod.

She pauses to search my face. "One time, Mildred and I went out to get our nails done. Rob stayed behind to babysit. When we came back, he had ..." Her lip quivers. "He was removing his leather belt. He had locked you in his room and was going to whip you with it." My mom can't quite meet my eyes, so she takes a drink of water instead.

My stomach flips. "What? Why was he going to hit me?"

As I ask the question, it feels like my mind has somehow formed cracks, letting flashes of memories leak out like water behind a loose dam.

I recall the way the yellow bedroom felt horrendously wrong, the happy color almost mocking my fear and my tears as I wiggled the handle to no avail. The unnerving feeling of having no control over the situation. Hearing Theo's pleads for his dad to let me out, to whip him instead of me, even though his arm was already broken. The same sickness in my stomach that I felt then presents itself to me now, clawing its way up my throat.

Theo's words from the river echo in my mind. *Some details from my childhood are a bit spotty. I've been told it's a symptom of PTSD.*

"Apparently you had *disrespected* him." My mom says the word like it holds no meaning. Her voice is so low, it frightens me a little. "And so, I never took you back. Obviously, it wasn't Mildred's fault, but I told her that as long as Rob was around, we would mostly have to keep in touch over the phone."

I swallow hard. "So, that instance was the last time Theo and I saw each other?"

My mom gives me a tight-lipped nod. "I visited her alone a few times, but never stayed in their home. And Rob would never let Mildred come visit here. I don't think he knew I was trying to get her to leave him, but I obviously wasn't a fan of his, especially after what he tried to do to you," she says. "I promised Mildred, all those years ago, that my doors would be open to her if she ever wanted to leave him."

I stare at the table. "Wow."

My mom reaches across the table and smooths down my hair, forcing me to meet her gaze. "As much as I care about Mildred's son," she says, "be careful around him, Willow. Rob is not a good man. And Theo was raised by him."

I nod at my mom, but this time, it's me who can't quite make eye contact.

I take the neighborhood dogs around the block, mulling over my mom's words.

Rob is not a good man. And Theo was raised by him.

"Isn't that nice, Darleen?" I ask the rat terrier that won't stop pulling on her leash. "Isn't that just peachy?"

One of my favorite things about walking dogs is that it gives me time to think. Not in an obsessive way, but a rational one. Walking around my neighborhood, glimpsing the gardens people have put so much care into, the clay pots bright with the season's annuals, is strangely therapeutic. After I drop off Darleen and Tido—the only dogs scheduled for today—I head back home. The sun is just starting to retreat beneath the hills, dimming the street enough to make me rub my eyes.

When I enter my bedroom, I do a double take. Ash is

sitting on my bed. "What are you doing here?" My voice is hushed so I won't wake my mom. "Your car wasn't parked outside."

"I came in through the window about an hour ago," says Ash. "You were talking to your mom."

The conversation flashes through my mind, along with that moment with Theo at American River, my hand on his face, staring into his blue gaze, my heart thumping unevenly as a result.

Rob is not a good man. And Theo was raised by him.

I have so much to tell her.

"I could really use a girls' night," she says, her voice cracking. She's holding a bottle of Captain Morgan, and her eyes are red and swollen. Maybe she's still upset that Joseph was walking with those girls on his way to class today. I don't ask her, though, because I know she'll tell me when she's ready. If she knows her distress is obvious, it will only embarrass her. Whatever it is, my heart aches for her. Ash hardly ever cries. I want to hurt Joseph as badly as he's hurt her.

Instead, I sit down on my bed. She doesn't have to say anything else; just like that, we're taking shots.

Seven

My head throbs. My stomach churns. Sick. I'm going to be sick.

"Ash?" I glance around, but my room is spinning. I can't see straight. "Ash?"

No answer.

I stand up, fall down, and stand back up again. I stumble out of my room and open my mom's door. I peek inside, but she's already gone to work. The clock on her bedside table tells me it's three in the morning. I tiptoe down the hall and glance around the living room, but I don't see Ash. She could be anywhere. Knowing her, she probably left after getting drunk. I imagine her passed out in the middle of the street and slip on my shoes to check outside. I bump into the walls a few times on my way out. I scan the street, but there's no one in sight. The neighborhood is dead silent, the streetlights illuminating parked cars and shadows of trees in the darkness.

I start calling for Ash, my voice a harsh whisper, and then I imagine how I must look right now, drunk in the streets at such a late hour.

I start laughing hysterically. I have to tell someone. I have to tell someone how funny this is, how hilarious it is that I've somehow lost my cousin. Lost her like she's a pet. I tiptoe across the front lawn until I reach the guest house Theo is inhabiting. Even while under the influence of alcohol, my rituals take precedence in my mind.

1, 2, 3 knocks.

Theo will laugh. He will think this is funny. And then we will laugh together. We will laugh until we have to hold our stomachs, until tears stream down our faces.

Theo opens the door a crack. When he sees it's me, he opens it all the way. He's not wearing a shirt. I stare at his chest. The muscles are defined, his skin smooth and free of tattoos, with the exception of his arms. My eyes snag for longer than necessary on the fine trail of hair leading from his belly button to below the band of his sweats.

"Willow. What the bloody hell are you doing here?" Theo's eyes are squinting, like he's still half-asleep. His hair is ruffled, a dark ocean of waves. He rubs a hand down his face.

I giggle. I can't help it. I'm aware of how rude I'm being. I haven't even told him the joke yet, and he probably wants to laugh with me. "You're so British," I inform him.

He squints at me for a moment before sighing. "You're pissed. Get inside." He gestures for me to come into the living room.

I wobble through the threshold. "I'm not angry," I tell him. "Just a little wasted."

I'm surprised when he chuckles. "Yes. I know, love."

I glance around. "It's been so long since I've been in here." I wave my hand around. The place is still furnished the way my mom left it for guests—plainly. There aren't any decorations, but the small house is filled with bare, modern necessities. A TV is mounted on the wall, and a glass coffee table and black leather couch sit in front of it. The kitchen is visible from where I'm standing, and there's a stainless-steel kettle on the stove. "It's like you didn't even bring anything with you."

Theo ignores me as he situates me on the couch. The leather is cold through my leggings.

"Wait here." He goes off and rummages around in the kitchen for a moment. The cabinets open and close, and the faucet turns on. When Theo comes back, he's holding a glass of water. "Drink this," he orders. "All of it."

I take the water from him, but don't drink yet. First, I have to tell him my story. "Ash disappeared," I tell him. My voice slurs, and it makes me giggle. "She's a goner."

Theo frowns. "What do you mean?" His blue eyes are no longer hazy with sleep.

I pat his hand. "No, no. It's supposed to be funny. You don't need to be upset."

Theo glances at my hand on his but doesn't move it away. "Were you both drinking?" he asks.

I nod. Smile.

He stares at me. "Wait right here, Willow. I mean it." He heads for the door, looking over his shoulder at me once more, like he thinks I'll join Ash in whatever abyss I lost her in.

When he leaves, I set the glass of water on the coffee table. I look around, trying to figure out how a room can feel completely different with nothing more than a new person living inside. Theo is the only new addition, but the house has a wholly different vibe from when my grandma used to live in it. There is, however, a picture of Theo and Mildred on the wall. She's smiling in the photo, but Theo's eyes look troubled. I wonder how long ago it was taken, and why his dad isn't in it.

I head for the kitchen, rifling through the cupboards, and find a bottle of vodka. I sniff it but can't smell the alcohol. Frowning, I take a swig to see if it's really water in disguise. It tastes like nothing. I take another sip, and this time I feel the burn when it goes down. I'm about to put the bottle back when I realize I took *two gulps*.

I have to end it on an odd number.

I really shouldn't. I'm already dizzy. But I can't leave it on an even number, so I bring the bottle back to my lips.

* * *

When I open my eyes, it's far too bright and I don't know where I am. I'm in someone's bed, and it's definitely not mine. A grey flannel comforter is draped around the bottom half of my body. I glance underneath it, exhaling deeply when I see that I'm still fully clothed from yesterday. The walls in the room are beige with white crown molding. The same as the guest house. My heart races when I realize that's exactly where I am. The bedroom in the guest house. What the hell am I doing here?

I sit up, but my head starts spinning, so I lie back down. Just as I'm about to try again, Theo opens the door and walks in, his normally perfect hair slightly rumpled.

"Why am I in your room?" I ask him, though the events of last night are already starting to come back to me.

Those last three shots.

Theo coming back to me puking in the bathroom.

Theo holding my hair back. Me crying.

Telling him way too much.

No, no, no, no, no.

He smiles blandly. "Good morning to you too, little Willow."

I try to come up with something to say to him—try and fail miserably. His face is three emotions, somehow. Exhausted, concerned, and amused, all at once. He must think I'm some kind of nutcase now if he didn't already. Me showing up here last night, completely plastered, muttering a bunch of nonsense. Telling him about something I never should have. About *someone* I never should have.

"I'm sorry." It's all I can manage.

His chuckle is low. "You're lucky I woke up on time this morning, after the night we had. In fact, I may go back to bed."

I blink. "Where did you sleep?" My cheeks burn. If he slept in his bed with me, I hope he lies and says he didn't. Makes something up. Or maybe he didn't sleep at all. Either way, I won't be able to look him in the eye if he tells me we shared a bed last night.

He looks confused. "On the sofa." He watches me sigh in relief and glances at my loose shirt, wrinkled and worn. "Do you want to go home and get ready? We don't have to leave for a few more minutes."

I nod, pushing away the covers and slowly getting out of his bed. I search his room for anything I might be forgetting, noting how surprisingly neat he keeps his things. There is, however, one unpacked box shoved into a corner that could send me into a frenzy if I let it.

"Who is Daniel?" Theo asks.

All the blood drains from my face. Damn it. He remembered. A knot forms in my throat. "Daniel," I breathe. I can't remember the last time I said it aloud. "Where—why are you asking me that?"

Theo crosses his arms, but his voice is soft. "You said it last night. When you were crying."

When I was crying. When I was drunk. When Theo

was holding my hair back while I vomited my insides into his toilet. I am beyond mortified.

I double over, holding my hands over my mouth. Theo makes a startled noise and grips my elbow to hold me up. His other hand lands lightly on my waist. "Are you unwell?" he asks.

I inhale through my teeth. "It doesn't matter. I can't ruin my attendance. Or yours."

"I don't give a damn about my attendance," Theo informs me. "Sit back down, Willow."

"No," I groan. "There's no way I'm missing school today." But then it hits me how hungover I actually am. There's no way I'll be able to drive us to school. Not if I can barely hold my head up. I can't even stand without wanting to empty whatever is left in my stomach.

I weigh my options. There are only two that I can think of, both of which give me enough my anxiety as it is. I tap my fingers while I contemplate them.

1. Miss school
2. Let Theo drive us to school—aka sit in the passenger seat of the car while it's in motion.

My eyes fill with tears. Not only are there only two options instead of three, but neither of them is endurable. Regardless, I still need to decide. I glance up at Theo. His eyes are blazing with concern for me, his lips pulled down into a slight frown.

Rob is not a good man. And Theo was raised by him.

Damn it all to hell. I take a deep breath, ignoring the way my stomach churns with acid in response. "Do you know how to drive a stick?" I ask him.

* * *

Theo adjusts the side- and rear-view mirrors, which is almost enough to make me tell him to forget it. To say I'm not going to school today and neither is he.

Deep breath deep breath deep breath—

I don't like letting people drive me as it is. Even sitting beside Ash is hard for me, letting her make the turns on a road full of gas-filled machinery that could end us if she's not careful enough. Allowing someone else to drive Mitten Chip is unbearable. I haven't sat in the passenger seat of my own car since the accident.

"Could you please . . ." My voice is hoarse. "Can you try not to adjust anything too much? Please?" And then I realize that him not making necessary adjustments to the mirrors could very well result in what I fear. "Actually, go ahead." I wave my hand at him and close my eyes.

I count in increments of three. I tap my fingers. I try to breathe, but it feels like hands are gripping my neck too tightly for air to flow through.

"Are you sure you're all right?" Theo glances at me. "This is an advanced step, love. And you look like you're about to faint."

My skin prickles. I need him to stop trying to dissuade me, because if he continues I might actually back out. I'm not sure if it's because of the mention of Daniel this morning or my fear of failure in general that I'm so determined to make it to school today. Either way, Theo is only making me want to pinch him. "Will you shut up and hit the gas pedal? And stop calling me that. I have a name, you know."

His concern melts into amusement. I want to slap the smirk off his face. Part of me knows it's not Theo's fault I'm about to have a mental breakdown but at the moment, I can't think straight. Not after him bringing up Daniel. Not with him in the driver's seat of my car.

His smile is arrogant, teetering on the edge of triumphant. "My apologies, *Willow*. I've never known the word to miff a lady before."

I roll my eyes. "Yeah, well, not everyone is as charmed by you as you think." I'm lying through my teeth. Theo is completely charming, and his accent really doesn't help. "Take us to school, before we're late. And don't forget that in America, we drive on the right side of the road."

Theo laughs, and I vow to leave without him tomorrow morning.

When he starts driving, a wave of dizziness crashes into me, drowning me in panic. Dread weighs my stomach down like an anchor to a ship. I need to shake the feeling off me. I need to escape from my own body. I long to shed my skin like a snake.

I close my eyes the entire way. I keep my head down. I cry a little.

And I count.

When we pull into the parking lot, I'm still sobbing quietly. Theo hasn't spoken a word to me, probably completely freaked out by my reaction to being driven. I can't hold myself together. I should have stayed home. I should have never come to school today. I should have taken my chances behind the wheel instead of letting Theo drive.

My face is dripping with tears. My heart is pounding so loudly, I'm sure Theo can hear it.

The passenger seat of a car. Not just any car—Mitten Chip.

Tap, tap, tap. Tap, tap, tap. Tap, tap, tap.

I want to leave my body. I want to rip my veins out. My chest hurts. My blood is racing. I can't pull myself together. I can't remember the last time I've had a meltdown like this, the last time my anxiety literally attacked me. I can hardly breathe. My rituals are barely even helping.

We sit in the silent car. The ignition is off, and the only sound is my rapid breathing, interrupted by small sobs.

In, out. In, out. In, out—

It's over.

We're here.

We made it.

We survived.

My breathing slows, but I shut my eyes even more tightly. Tapping isn't helping, so I imagine my happy place.

Lying on a field of grass, beneath the shade of a tree. A book in my hand and my little black dog by my side.

Theo's hand grazes my back. It moves slowly, rubbing back and forth. I'm so embarrassed, I can't even offer him thanks or acknowledgment for trying to comfort me. I'm just glad we have time to spare so I can collect myself.

I sit up slowly and open my eyes. I wipe my tears with the sleeve of my yellow cardigan and stare at the smudges on the window. If my mom had witnessed this meltdown, she would probably tell me I need serious help. And I can't help but agree. I can't keep living like this, in constant fear. Pursuing comfort through objects, numbers, rhythms. But I also know I have no choice. Not living with rituals results in meltdowns like the one I'm currently having.

The thought—the possibility of having a normal life makes a few more tears roll down my cheeks. I mourn my freedom. Freedom from my own mind.

I can't live like this.

A few parking spots down, I see Ash sitting in her car. I'm chagrined when I realize I never checked on her this morning. I completely forgot about her, actually. "What happened to Ash last night?" I ask, my voice cracking. "Did you ever find her?" I still can't manage to look at him.

"She was passed out in the loo at your house," he informs me. "I carried her to your bed before I came back and saw you honking."

"*Honking?* You mean throwing up?" I sniff, turning to look at him.

"Mm." He nods.

He took care of Ash for me. And then he came home and took care of me, too. All after three in the morning. He must have been up for hours. Something in my chest expands. "I guess I owe you some sort of explanation." He still hasn't asked why we were drinking like that on a school night.

He chuckles. "You must find me incredibly thick. That's not necessary, little Willow. Although I would like to know who the bloody hell this bloke Daniel is."

It's not his fault the name rips open the hole in my heart that I've finally managed to stitch up. He has no idea what hearing that name does to me.

"I'm sorry," I whisper.

Theo doesn't have a chance to respond, because Ash chooses that moment to tap on my window. Her eyes are dancing, a carefully choreographed routine.

I roll down the window enough to hear her.

Ash's lips are slightly turned up. "Get the fuck out here," she says. "You have so much explaining to do." Ash looks pointedly at Theo behind the wheel.

Theo smirks.

I sigh. "Can we talk about this later? It's almost time to clock in." Not to mention I'm finally starting to feel better.

She smacks the window frame. Her smile expands, and I wonder if she was ever really crying last night. "No, we cannot talk about this later. *Your* drunk ass left *my* drunk ass last night, so you owe me. Come on."

She has me there. I sigh and follow her to her car. She motions for me to get in, and she sits in the driver's seat.

"Did you sleep with him?" she asks as soon as I sit down. Her eagerness is tangible.

"What? Ash, no! I did not sleep with Theo."

Her face falls substantially, but she's not to be deterred. "Oh, come on! He's so hot. Just do it."

I cover my face. "Ash." She has no idea what I've just been through. Or maybe she does and is trying to distract me.

She scoffs. "He practically lives with you. If you don't do it, I will."

I gape at her. She's smiling like she knows she's won. Though what she has to win, I'm not sure.

"Go ahead," I tell her. "I don't care."

But as soon as I picture the two of them together, I feel like I might be sick all over again. The fact that I care bothers me even more than Ash's threats. Perhaps it's because he's my friend from the past, or maybe because he hasn't treated me with caution since finding out about my illness. It's refreshing to be around someone other than Ash who treats me like I'm normal, even after getting to know me.

Ash rolls her eyes. "Uh huh." She gets out of the car to go clock in, and I follow her.

Charlie is sitting at my desk, reminding Theo about his party. "It's on Valentine's Day," he tells him, eyes twinkling. He catches sight of me and gets out of my desk.

Ash smiles at him. "You know I'll be there." She saunters off in the direction of the bathroom. Charlie cocks his head toward her retreating form.

"Are you coming too?" he asks me.

I bite my lip. "I don't know. I'll think about it."

Charlie shakes his head and goes to his desk. I collapse into mine, wishing I had coffee.

Theo pokes me with his pen. "Do you have other plans, little Willow?"

I glance at him. "I don't know. I just want to sleep for the rest of my life." In all honesty, I already know I'm not going to the party Charlie is throwing, but I'm grateful Theo is still speaking to me after what I put him through this morning.

Mrs. Harrison tells us to start working on each other, washing and styling the hair of the person sitting next to us. I glance around, looking for Ash, but she's still in the restroom. Since Theo is sitting at the end of our row, I'm his only desk partner. Our eyes meet, and I want to make up a reason why I can't work with him. But I know that even if Ash comes back right now, she'll be paired with the girl who sits on her other side.

Theo stands. "Shall we?"

We make our way over to the shampoo bowls with the other students, and I wonder, not for the first time, what is taking Ash so long.

"Do you want me to wash your hair first?" I ask Theo tentatively. "Or do you want to do mine?" My hair is an intimidating beast. My thick, waist-length curls cascade in every direction, impossible to tame. They are a visual representation of the inside of my mind.

Theo considers his options before I roll my eyes and push him into the client chair. He looks indignant, but I ignore it. There's a small hose attached to the shampoo bowl, and I start the water. When it's warm, I run it over Theo's hair. I pump shampoo into my palms and rub it together between my hands, letting it emulsify.

In the moments before I touch his scalp, a surge of dread races through me. This is incredibly awkward. Washing a stranger's hair feels like a violation of their personal space. And after the horrible anxiety attack I had in the car, I'd rather do anything but draw Theo's attention to me. But this is precisely what I'm going to be doing for a living, and Theo isn't a stranger. So, I thread my fingers through his hair.

I massage shampoo into his temples, trying to exact the right amount of pressure to make for a relaxing experience. I'm too far away, and water is starting to drip down my arms, so I take a step closer. My cheeks burn, and I wonder if Theo is uncomfortable with my close proximity. "H-how's the pressure?" I ask him.

His eyes flutter and then fall shut. "Brilliant," he breathes. I'm glad his eyes are closed, because when Ash comes back into the main room and sees me washing Theo's hair, I want to join the shampoo suds in their quest down the drain.

"Ashton," Mrs. Harrison says, "you'll be partnering up with me today, since I placed Eva with someone else." The instructor motions Ash forward with a finger, and I try desperately not to laugh. Her expression promises revenge.

I rinse the soap from Theo's hair, and massage in the conditioner. I briefly wonder if he's asleep. He's hardly spoken a word since I began. "So," I say to him. "How are you adjusting to the move?"

Theo peeks at me from behind hooded lids. "All right," he says. "I'm happy to be away from my dad." His voice is low, relaxed. His face betrays no emotion, but I can't imagine he's indifferent to what he just told me. I feel like there's something specific I'm supposed to say, but I come up empty.

"Yeah," is all I manage.

Theo's eyes open a little more. "What about your father?" he asks me. "What was he like?"

I exhale a long breath. "He died of heart disease shortly after he and my mom split up. I don't remember him. I was only a baby."

"I'm sorry," Theo says.

I shrug. "It's fine." My dad's passing hurts my mom so much more than it bothers me. It's hard to miss someone I don't know.

I rinse Theo's hair for the last time, wrapping a towel around his head. He sits up and pulls it off, rubbing the towel through his hair roughly. It's such a guy thing to do. When he looks at me again, some water escapes his hairline and trickles down his face. I reach for another rag and dab at the water. The gesture feels strangely intimate, especially with Theo's gaze on my face.

When the break bell rings, Mrs. Harrison tells us we'll continue after. I still feel nauseous from last night, but I know I need to eat something if I ever want to feel better.

Ash saunters over to me. She smirks at me and Theo. "Let's go get some fucking food." She's speaking to both of us, and it's not a request. "I'll drive."

Eight

I'm forced to sit in the backseat next to Theo because Ash claims her purse needs a seat to itself. I know she's just paying me back for leaving her to work with our instructor. But I don't mind. I'd much rather sit in the back than the front, since I'm not the one driving. I still tap, though, and even imagine us crashing to prevent it from happening.

"God, I'm so hungry," says Ash, huffing when a group of students cross the street in front of us.

I lean my head against the side of the car. "I'm surprised you can even eat after last night." I peek at Theo, but he's staring out his window.

"Yeah, well. I just puked up whatever was left in my stomach. I'm hungry."

We get to the nearest drive-through, and Ash orders a cheeseburger meal. I order a salad. I doubt I can keep anything greasy down right now. Theo orders the same thing as Ash and hands her cash when we get to the window. "Allow me," he says.

"No way," I tell him. "You are *not* paying for all of us."

Ash snorts. "Speak for yourself. He can pay for me if he wants to." She takes his money. Glancing back at me, she winks. "I'm sure I can find some way to pay him back later."

I shake my head, mortified. But Theo remains oblivious to Ash's blatant innuendo and insists it's no problem, that we don't have to repay him. "It's the least I can do," he says. "You've saved us from having to eat that awful cafeteria food by driving us."

"Do you even have a job?" I ask him. He can't possibly, since he hasn't been in California that long, and doesn't have a car to take him anywhere.

"I told you," he says, "I used to work for my dad. That money, plus my inheritance is gathering dust as we speak."

Ash and I are silent. "You have an inheritance?" she asks, sounding like she's never heard of such a concept.

"My grandparents were quite wealthy," he shrugs. "And generous, it seems."

"Damn," Ash sighs. "If you're so rich, why the hell are you in beauty school?" She pays for our food with Theo's money and hands him the change.

"Honestly," he says, "I'm a rather creative person." He crosses his arms behind his head, sounding as if he's enjoying all the attention. "I know I'll be good at it."

I scoff, and he looks at me, wide-eyed. "You're a guy," I

say. "It's not as if doing women's hair is your second nature."

His answering grin is devilish. "No," he murmurs. "But women, in general, aren't a foreign concept to me, little Willow."

My cheeks burn, and I avert my eyes. "Let's just hope you're able to pass the test. From what you've told me, you're a hands-on kind of guy. And from what I know, the written test is entirely academic."

Theo arches a brow. "That should be no problem with your help. You can be academic enough for both of us." He reaches over and pulls one of my curls, straightening and releasing it so it springs back up. I flick his hand in response, and for the moment it feels like we're children again.

"I'm sure you'd be good at lots of things," Ash cuts in. "But why hair? It seems like such a feminine career for a man like you."

I resist the urge to roll my eyes, but Theo answers seriously, pondering Ash's question first.

"My dad was controlling," he says evenly. "He never let me choose my own path. My secondary school elective was theater and I got stuck as the hairdresser. I almost quit then and there, but to my surprise I ended up liking it. I never would have tried otherwise. There's enough of a balance between science and creativity in hair to attract me. If my father ever knew that . . . " Theo laughs, sounding genuinely amused. "As rubbish as it sounds, this is the last possible career path he'd want for me. And that makes me want it all the more."

I stare at him.

Ash laughs. "If only he could see you now. Scrubs and all."

Theo smiles, but his eyes are far away.

When we finally get our food, Ash grabs hers out of the bag before passing it back to us. As soon as I see the salad I ordered, my stomach churns, but after a few bites, I start to feel better. At least I didn't throw up at school, like Ash.

We eat in silence until Ash says, "So, Theo, do you have a girlfriend?"

"No," he says. "I have many."

I raise my eyebrows at him, and his answering smile makes me want to slap him. "Kidding. I only wanted to see Willow's face, and it was worth it."

Ash laughs, and I resolve to dump the quaternary ammonium solution—our utensil sanitizer—on her and Theo as soon as we get back to class.

But as we clock back in, I'm filled with a new sense of dread. It's Theo's turn to wash my hair. Aside from how difficult my hair can be to manage, washing Theo's first has already given me a preview of what lies ahead.

My worries are delayed for a moment while Mrs. Harrison inspects the work of those who went first. She ruffles Theo's hair, messing up the perfect way his soft, black waves fall naturally. "Good job, Willow." She moves on to the next group, and Theo gestures toward the shampoo bowls, a wry smile on his lips.

I sit down, my stomach rolling.

Theo lets the warm water cascade over my scalp. I close my eyes, unable to help but feel relaxed by the warmth. Not a drop gets in my eyes, and I hear him pumping the cucumber-scented shampoo into his hands. When his fingertips touch my skin, every nerve in my body reacts. He massages my head slowly, purposefully. With the perfect amount of pressure. All my worries rinse out of my head, down the drain with the water. The fact that I feel this much pleasure at the hands of Theo is not only surprising to me, but also quite alarming. He's good, just as he said he would be.

I suddenly understand exactly why a woman would want a male hairdresser. Especially an attractive one, whether he's straight or not. To be touched by such a man, be told how pretty she is, and have him *listen* to everything she says—one of the fundamental reasons people like to get their hair done by someone—and all without cheating on her partner. The arrangement could be too tempting to deny.

Theo is exactly the type of guy who would have his books filled to the brim with clients who'd want him for those reasons. They would take one look at him in a salon full of mostly female stylists and note his elegant jaw, his soft and full lips, set in an arrogant smile. His thick, dark hair, begging someone to mess it up. His body, tattooed, flawless, strong. And his eyes. His blue eyes, like windows to the ocean, captivating anyone the moment they fell subject to his gaze.

Theo Tate as a hairstylist has never made more sense. In fact, he'll probably make a killing with his psychology background, since most hairstylists in the industry unintentionally double as therapists for their clients.

Theo traces his thumbs along my temples, making slow circles. I sigh a little without meaning to. When he rinses out the shampoo, I peek through one eye. I can't see his face, but his arm is right in front of me. His sleeves are rolled up, and I see the hard lines of muscle making up his forearms as he flexes with each movement. Watching him work does nothing to slow the racing in my veins, so I let my eyes fall shut again.

"Your hair is so soft," he tells me. His voice is husky, too deep.

"Thank you," I say, my voice cracking slightly. I clear my throat. "So is yours."

He chuckles softly. With him so close, I catch a whiff of his cologne. It smells like it was made for his skin.

I need him to stop washing my hair. I need to get away from him. From his voice and his hands on me and his scent. But as his fingers move across my scalp, I am liquid. I am spilling out of my skin, splashing from the chair to the ground, yet somehow still corporeal enough to feel his touch. And I can't help but think to myself, *this is the most sensual thing I've ever experienced.* I don't even notice when he turns the water off and wraps my hair in a towel. My eyes flutter open, bringing me back to reality.

He steps aside so I can stand up, but my bones have turned to jelly. I can't move. As if he senses my physical state, he reaches for my elbow, helping me to my feet. My cheeks burn with embarrassment, and I don't even know where to look. My eyes refuse to choose somewhere to land. I find my seat while Theo fetches Mrs. Harrison to check his work, and I take the time to gather my bearings.

Tap, tap, tap, tap, tap.

I realize after the fact that I've just performed a ritual. But why? Like Theo said, I should probably start trying to catch myself before it happens, if I'm ever going to prevent it in the future. But this one happened before I could stop myself. I vow, internally, to try to stop myself from performing another today.

Theo comes back with Mrs. Harrison, and she approves his handiwork. I can't let him touch me again today if I want to avoid tapping for comfort, but he's supposed to style my hair next. I make for the bathroom. I add the styling cream myself, making sure each curl is evenly saturated. To make up for the tapping, I use two paper towels instead of my usual three after I wash my hands. It's extremely hard, and it makes me want to rip off my skin and scream aloud, but I do it. I suppress the anxiety coursing through me, because I can't help but notice that this is the appropriate amount of paper towels I should have been using all along.

Something splashes in one of the stalls, and a groan follows. I consider leaving before whoever's in there can come out, but the door opens. It's Ash. Her forehead is covered in sweat, and she wipes her mouth sluggishly.

"Are you okay?" I ask her.

She touches a hand to her stomach. Closes her eyes. "Just lost the lunch Prince William bought us."

"No more drinking for you," I tell her.

She smiles, her eyes still closed. "No promises."

We enter the classroom, and Theo raises an eyebrow at me. "Did you already style your hair?" he asks me. "I'm supposed to do that."

I'm suddenly interested in my shoes. "I just . . . I figured it would be easier this way. You know, since my hair is curly. And you can just say that you did it." Part of this is true, but I mostly just needed some distance from him. It was also the perfect opportunity for me to attempt eliminating one of my rituals in private. I'm still trying not to react to the fact that I used the number two instead of three, but it's itching me like a rash. I hope it's not obvious. I look up at him.

Theo smirks. "While I appreciate your consideration, love," he murmurs, "it's nothing I can't handle."

"Can you two stop flirting for a sec?" Ash rests her head in her arms on the desk. I wonder why she's still feeling so nauseous. Though I was under the impression we drank nearly the same amount last night, I must have had much less than her. "I'm going to be sick."

My cheeks heat. I can't even look at Theo, but he laughs.

"No," Ash grunts. "I'm actually going to be sick." She promptly stumbles out of her chair, running for the shampoo bowls. The entire class watches her retch into one, her body convulsing with each upheaval. I'm instantly at her side, holding her hair back like I know she would do for me, should the situation be reversed. The snickering coming from more than one mouth makes me want to punch whoever thinks this is funny.

Mrs. Harrison scurries over to us, panicking at the possibility of the shampoo drains clogging. "They just aren't meant for this sort of thing," she mutters.

I ignore her, making sure Ash's slumping body doesn't hit the floor. She gives herself over completely to emptying her insides. I don't think she'll even remain upright if I let her go.

"Someone should call her doctor," Mrs. Harrison says. "I'll excuse the hours if she has a note."

I stare at Mrs. Harrison incredulously. We don't get our hours excused for anything. Not even illness. Mrs. Harrison must really want Ash out of here, away from her salon equipment.

I drape Ash's arm over my shoulder and haul her away from the watchful eyes of the classmates we still hardly know.

"Theo," I say. "Can you follow us in my car? I'm going to drive us in *her* car to the hospital, so she has it with her."

He nods, and I practically throw the keys to Mitten Chip at him. He catches them expertly. I drag Ash to the parking lot, but half her weight lifts from my shoulder. Theo has her other side. Together, we get her into the passenger seat of her Mustang. She moans, barely able to lift her head.

"Don't worry," I tell her. "You'll be fine. We're going to the ER."

She moans. Heart racing, I repeat the words again, but this time, to myself instead of her.

Nine

The waiting room has green walls. I remember reading about the subconscious effect colors have on the human brain, once. Apparently green reminds us of health, and that's why a lot of hospitals and medical centers utilize it. But the walls don't make a difference to me. This place is full of illness, of virus, and of disease.

I burn a path in the carpet as I pace back and forth. A lady in the corner of the room blows her nose into a tissue and then fans herself with it. A mom tries to mollify her feverish son, still in his racing car pajamas. There are so many germs here, and the hospital is lying to us, trying to make us feel safe within its confines, where germs are festering and traveling. If the walls weren't green, we would *all* probably be thinking about how easy it is to catch an airborne virus in this place. But thanks to the walls' illusion of good health, it's probably just me.

"Sit down, Willow." Theo watches me pace with his head resting in his hands.

"I can't."

He offers me a face that says *Suit yourself,* and picks up a magazine.

"It's just that," I begin, my thoughts forcing their way out, "this happened because of me. This is all my fault."

Theo frowns into his tabloid, turning the page. "What are you talking about, little Willow?"

"I stopped myself from reacting to a compulsion." I've been replaying the chain of events from school since we arrived. All was well until I went to the bathroom to style my hair and washed my hands. "I used two paper towels instead of three," I tell Theo. I'm unable to keep the weariness from my tone.

He pauses his reading to look at me. "And?"

"I *always* use three. And," I continue, "as soon as that happened, Ash threw up in the shampoo bowls!" I throw my hands in the air for extra emphasis.

Theo laughs at my enthusiasm. "Sit down, love. Please."

I narrow my eyes at him but take a seat in the chair to his right. "Why?"

"You're working up a sweat."

I stare at him. "Do you think she'll be okay?"

"Of course she will. At most, it's probably alcohol poisoning. They'll likely give her fluids."

I nod several times, trying to convince myself that he's right.

The doctor comes out, and I spring to my feet. "Is she okay?" I ask before he's even in front of us.

The doctor adjusts his glasses. "She needs to stay hydrated. Letting her body become too deprived of fluids can be dangerous."

Theo smirks and holds up his hands, as if to say, *I told you so.*

"How far along is she?" the doctor asks. Dr. Evans, according to his name tag.

I frown. "In school? We just started. It's still our first week."

"What?" He blinks at me, and then chuckles. "No, I mean how far along is she in her pregnancy?"

"Her pregnancy?" The words feel foreign on my tongue.

"Her urine sample is positive, but we haven't done a trans-vaginal ultrasound yet."

I stare at him. There must be some kind of mistake. Maybe the doctor accidentally mixed up his patient files or something. I know for a fact Ash gets the Depo-Provera shot every three months, and she would have told me if she was pregnant, the second she found out.

Unless she didn't know.

But I shove the thought down. I'd rather believe there's been a mistake, that she's not really pregnant. Ash and I have plans after graduation. We're going to travel to Europe

—her idea, not mine—and then we're going to open a salon together.

"I don't know how far along she is," I tell Dr. Evans.

We follow the doctor through the large double doors, down the hall that smells like hand sanitizer, and into the room with the bed that holds Ash.

She's sitting up with an IV in her wrist. She has the gall to look annoyed, like she didn't ask to be here in the first place, but her rigid posture eases when she sees us. "Ugh. Willow, thank God. Did the doc say when we can get out of here?"

"After the *ultrasound*," I say, crossing my arms.

Ash breaks our eye contact and shrugs. "I was going to tell you," she says.

So, she knows. She *knew*, and she didn't tell me.

The ultrasound technician holds up a long, hard-looking instrument. "I'll be inserting this ultrasound probe into the vaginal canal, giving us a visual of the baby."

"You know what?" Theo says. "I'll be out there." He gestures toward the door.

I'm tempted to follow him out, but I imagine the terror I would be filled with in Ash's situation. I would want her to stay with me.

Ash makes an uncomfortable sound as the probe enters her. A static-like noise comes from the screen next to us, and several indiscernible lines appear on the screen.

"There you have it," the ultrasound tech tells Ash. "That's your baby. You're measuring at about six weeks."

She points to a blob on the screen, and Ash glances at it briefly before looking away.

The ultrasound technician prints out a picture of the baby for Ash to take home. Ash stuffs it into her purse without looking at it. When the room is empty save for us, Ash removes her hospital gown and puts on the scrubs she was wearing before.

"I'm sorry I didn't tell you," she says flippantly. She shifts around the blanket covering the hospital bed, checking to make sure she hasn't forgotten anything. "I'm getting rid of it anyway, so I figured there was no point."

My eyes widen. "You are?"

"It's no big deal," she tells me, heading for the doors. Theo is on the other side, leaning against the wall and picking his nails. He raises his eyebrows at me when Ash continues walking and talking without pause. "They have these pills you can take that will make it seem like nothing more than a really bad period."

For some reason, I can't imagine it will be that easy for her, physically or emotionally. Ash has always had a maternal side. When her mom got pregnant with her little brothers, she was so excited that she wanted to become their full-time nanny.

"Is the baby Joseph's?" I ask. "Does he know?"

She continues walking, through the waiting room and out into the parking lot, Theo and I trailing behind her. "Yes, it's Joseph's," she says like it should be obvious. She runs a hand through her hair. "And of course he doesn't know. I'm not going to tell him."

I bite my bottom lip, unable to help but feel a pang of sympathy for Joseph. But none of this is up to me, and I probably shouldn't be prodding her in front of Theo. I know Ash, and despite her faux indifference, she's carefully taking in our every reaction to her words.

I lightly touch her shoulder, stopping her before she can get in her car. She turns around and looks at me. Her blond hair is sticking to her face, sweaty and wispy. Her brown eyes are a store after hours when everyone has already gone home. I won't be getting through to her right now.

"I'm going to drop Theo off," I say. "And then I'm coming over."

She shrugs, like it doesn't matter to her either way. But I know Ash desperately wants me to come over so she can tell me everything. The unfiltered version, without the eyes and ears of someone else nearby. She gets in her car and drives away. I hope she's feeling better, that she's not too dizzy or nauseous to take herself home.

I unlock Mitten Chip, and Theo and I climb inside. I'm driving, thank God. No ritual would be able to ease the amount of anxiety I'm experiencing, so I might as well not aggravate myself by sitting in the passenger seat again. I pull out of the parking lot, my mind far away.

Theo sighs. "Are you all right?"

"No. This is all my fault."

"Unless you somehow knocked up your cousin, I don't see how that could possibly be true."

"I stopped, Theo. I stopped one of my rituals. In the bathroom at school. And what happened to Ash is a direct result of that." My voice cracks. I am filled with so much guilt, I don't know how I will bear it.

"I know you're serious," Theo says. "And I know you believe it, but you must know it's not true, Willow. That's mad." His tone is gentle, and for some reason it eases some of my guilt, though only slightly.

My shoulders sag. "I honestly don't know what to think right now."

"Is it really so bad? Your cousin being pregnant?"

"Well, considering she's nineteen years old, not in a serious relationship, and doesn't have her career in order yet . . . I'd say yes. It's pretty bad."

He's silent. My keys jingling in the ignition is the only sound in the car. Theo's cologne wafts through my senses again, somehow reminding me there are other people in the world with other problems. Problems they've somehow managed to overcome. It's a lot to get from a whiff of cologne, but I'm past trying to understand my train of thoughts.

"Would you want to know?" I ask, breaking the silence. "If your on-again, off-again girlfriend was pregnant with your child, would you want her to tell you? Or would you rather her have an abortion? So you'd never . . . you know. So you wouldn't have to deal with any of it." I don't know why, but of all the things contributing to my anxiety, Ash keeping the baby a secret from Joseph bothers me the most. Maybe it's because my own dad wasn't really present in my life, even before he died. And he knew about me. So, if a man actually wants to be in his child's life, I guess I feel like he should have every right.

Theo takes a deep breath. His eyes search the windshield. "Yes. I'd want to know."

After I drop Theo off, I take Iris the Pomeranian and Taco the chihuahua around the block. Iris is my favorite dog, mostly because she closely resembles the one I envision in my happy place: small and fluffy, though she's white instead of black. I take Taco home and sneak Iris a treat before dropping her off, her seventy-year-old owner's hand shaking as she waves goodbye. Then I go straight to Ash's house.

Aunt Christie lives in a development only a few blocks away from ours. She moved to California first, giving my mom even more of an incentive to follow when my dad proposed. Apparently, they never wanted to live farther than a few miles from each other. Unfortunately, Ash's dad died in a car accident when she was in middle school. Aunt Christie remarried after that, but recently divorced, much to the dismay of the twin boys she had with her ex.

Ash's little brothers are fighting when I get inside. Chris

has Dean in a headlock, and Aunt Christie is nowhere to be seen.

"Hey! Stop fighting, you two." I separate them as best I can. They don't even acknowledge me. Though they're my cousins, the large age gap between us prevents them from showing an ounce of interest in me. Dean crosses his arms, and Chris runs to his room.

"Are you ok?" I ask Dean.

"I want chocolate milk," he says, shrugging my hands off his shoulders and opening the fridge.

I sigh and walk to Ash's room. She's lying on her bed, texting, when I come inside. She sees me and sighs, putting her phone down. The chinks in her emotional armor begin to crack, and her eyes become moist.

"Willow," she says, her voice catching. "I don't want to be pregnant."

I sit down on the bed with her, pulling one of her decorative pillows into my lap. Ash's room is messy most of the time, but right now it's neat. A sure sign of how stressed out she is. Her walls are white, accented with teal curtains and an abundance of silver pillows. I play with the tassels attached to the one I'm holding. "I don't want you to be, either," I admit.

She sniffs, and her tears spill over, running down her cheeks. She wipes at them, rolling her eyes at herself.

I lean over the space between us and hug her. Her shoulders shake with her effort to restrain her sobs. But eventually she lets them break free, and I sit with her while she cries. Every ounce of resentment I'd harbored toward her for keeping this a secret melts away, and I'm grateful I listened to my gut. That I came over tonight, so she won't have to be alone.

She pulls away, wiping her eyes again. Her mascara is everywhere, and I briefly consider getting her makeup wipes from the bathroom. But she asks me, "What would you do? If you were me?"

I bite my lip. It's hard for me to imagine being in her shoes. I haven't been intimate with anyone since Daniel. I can't even fathom what it would be like to experience pregnancy. What I would do, or how I would plan my life around such a change is beyond me. I shake my head at her. "I don't know," I admit.

Her lips thin into a line. "You don't think I should have an abortion, though."

I sigh. "That's not for me to decide."

Her eyes flash. "Willow. I want to know what you think. I don't want you to be disappointed in me."

"No matter what you decide, you know I'll support you," I tell her. I rub my hand across my face. "But I guess if it were up to me, I'd want you to tell Joseph and get his opinion. Make the decision together."

She looks away. "I tried. But he's been ignoring my calls since our fight yesterday."

"What were you guys even fighting about?"

She sighs. "I wanted to get back together with him, but

he's been giving me the cold shoulder for dumping him before I went on vacation. And I finally lost it."

I can imagine what Joseph probably thought of Ash's convenient timing for their breakup, but I know for a fact that he's crazy about her. He has been ever since they had their first date at the end of senior year. I wonder how he'd react if he found out what she's hiding.

"Ash," I say. "How long have you known?"

"I found out last night after school. I took a nap, and when I woke up, I got an alert from my period tracking app, telling me I was late. So I took a test." Her voice trails off into a whisper. "It was positive."

"What about your birth control shot?" I ask her. "Aren't you still getting it?"

She purses her lips. "My last appointment was supposed to be the day after I left for Hawaii. But I rescheduled it. I thought it would be fine."

"And you slept with Joseph?" I whisper, afraid her mom or her brothers will hear from outside the door. "Before you left?"

She nods. "The day before." She bites her lip, considering her thoughts. "And lots of times before that."

Despite everything, I snicker. Ash cracks a smile, and together, we start laughing hysterically.

"I'm so fucked," she says, holding her stomach as she cracks up.

This makes us laugh even harder, and before we know

it, Aunt Christie comes in the room. "What on earth is so amusing?" she asks.

"We got food poisoning from our lunch today and Ash threw up in the shampoo bowls," I tell her, still laughing. It's partly true, so I don't feel as bad saying it.

"Food poisoning?" Her eyes narrow. "You seem fine now."

Ash pauses, thinking up a lie instantly. "You know how Willow exaggerates, Mom. We're both fine. I think I just ate too fast."

"Well, maybe take it slow next time, Ashton." She shakes her head and leaves, a small smile on her face. She could be my mom's twin, with her straight blond hair and ocean eyes.

But my words remind me of something. "Ash!" I swat at her. "You drank last night, knowing you were pregnant?"

She looks slightly ashamed. "I know, I know. But I was stressed out! I *needed* one last time. And I was going to get rid of it, anyway."

"Was?" I raise my eyebrows at her.

She shrugs and looks at her lap. "I mean, who knows. We'll see what happens."

Ten

Mrs. Harrison claps her hands together. "Good morning everyone!" She looks around at the class. "Today wraps up our first two weeks of the semester, so I thought it would be nice to do something fun."

Since we only have school Monday through Thursday, the weeks feel like they've flown by too quickly. However, part of the reason I was so excited about American River's cosmetology program is its exclusion of Friday classes.

"Now I wonder what her idea of *fun* could be," Theo murmurs. "A lesson on how to properly clean our tools? A lecture on the most effective active ingredient in sanitizers perhaps?"

I cover my mouth, muffling my giggle.

"We're going to spend the day watching past fashion

show presentations," Mrs. Harrison continues. "If we have time after, I'll let you begin choosing your partners!"

Theo chuckles. "As if people haven't already started partnering up." He leans back in his chair.

Ash turns to me. "I wonder what our theme will be," she says.

I smile. "I hope it's Harry Potter or Disney related."

She shakes her head, but her desk neighbor, Eva, grins at me. "I love Harry Potter," she says. Her voice is raspy and much deeper than I expected. It gives her character. She tucks her highlighted, chin-length hair behind her ear. "Dobby is so cute!"

I lean over Ash's desk. "I know! I love him so much!"

"Are you fucking kidding me," Ash mutters to the air.

Mrs. Harrison connects her laptop to the projector and the video appears on the screen. The class settles down as it starts.

Everyone on the screen is adorned with Roaring Twenties attire. That must have been the theme for their show. As each model is presented, the stylist stands at the podium on a stage while the model showcases her work. The model is the center of attention. Everyone in the audience is watching her.

It terrifies me.

Ash will have to be the model, and I the stylist. Because I will not be brave enough to walk the stage—*runway*, rather—that these girls are strutting down in the video. It simply will not happen.

Ash bounces in her seat beside me. "I'm gonna make you look so *hot!*" she whispers.

I slide down in my chair.

"By the way, I'm going to tell Joseph. That I'm pregnant."

My eyes widen. "Ash, that's great! When?"

"Tomorrow night." She bites her manicured nail. "I'm just so nervous."

"Why?" I ask. "It's a win-win situation. If he's excited, then that's great. But if he's not . . . well, then he'll only be encouraging the plan you were intending to follow in the first place, right?"

Ash purses her lips. "I guess that's true."

I pat her arm. "It will be fine."

"I just wish you could come with me," she huffs.

I look down, feeling slightly chagrined, but she knows better than to ask me to go anywhere extra-curricular with her on a Friday. It just won't happen. "I'm sorry," I say.

Theo's phone vibrates, and I glance at the name of whoever texted him on his screen. I don't mean to; it's a natural instinct. But it catches my attention because the person's name is only represented by a single letter. *E.*

Theo sighs, but promptly responds to the message, hiding his phone underneath the tabletop. I press my lips together. He's not paying attention to the video. What if he misses something important?

"Will you put that thing away?" I say to him through my teeth.

Theo's lips twitch. He sends another message and pockets his phone. "Better?" he asks.

"Pay attention." I turn back to the screen.

My phone vibrates in my pocket. It's a text from Theo. I grit my teeth as I read it.

You pay attention.

I text him back. *I'm trying to.*

Am I distracting you?

I roll my eyes and send him a quick response. *Of course not.*

He laughs, but I refuse to look at him. Instead, I read his next message.

Then why do you care if I'm on my phone?

I don't care!

He begins typing, and I steal a glance at his face. He's grinning full force.

Oh, but you do. You care about everything, little Willow.

I blink so many times, I'm surprised I can see. He must be trying to get a reaction from me, so instead I give him the opposite. I put my phone away and don't look at him again.

The class watches the rest of the video, three more performances. They're all the same. The model displays herself for the entire cosmetology department, in addition to anyone else who buys tickets to the show. With every passing second, I'm even more confident that I would rather be the stylist than the model, even if it means I have to do all the creative work.

When Mrs. Harrison finally flips the lights on and tells us we're free to pick our partners if we're ready, I'm shocked to find Ash asleep with her head on her desk. If she weren't pregnant, I would nudge her awake. I glance at her stomach, still perfectly flat. No signs of pregnancy have altered her body yet, but by the time the fashion show rolls around, she'll probably have a visible bump. Which means if I have a heart at all, I will have to let her be the stylist. Unless Ash *wants* to walk the runway with a baby bump.

The thought of the models on the runway makes my stomach sink. I tap my desk until my anxiety ebbs slightly. Theo raises an eyebrow at me. I shrug innocently.

Charlie marches over to where we're sitting. "Pretty boy," he barks at Theo. "You're my model."

* * *

After class, in the car, Theo hands me three one hundred-dollar bills.

"What the hell?" I ask.

"It's for petrol," he says.

I laugh without humor. "This is way too much. Even a hundred is way too much." I try to hand the cash back to him, but he ignores me, primping himself in the mirror.

"The prices here are outlandish," he states. "I feel robbed *for* you."

I shake my head. "You might as well just save this and buy yourself a car, because I'm not taking it."

Theo grins. "You are taking it, little Willow. And if you saw the amount of money in my trust, you'd know I could buy several cars outright if I wanted to. But I happen to enjoy watching you get flustered behind the wheel. So, take the money."

I stare at him. Unable to think of a response to what he just said, I vow to hide the money in his room later.

"What time are you coming over?" Theo asks.

I start the car. "I'm not."

"Why not?"

"Because I want to be at home." I merge onto the freeway.

He laughs. "But my home is technically part of your home. So wouldn't it be the same thing? Besides, we need to work on ERP if you're going to appease your mum before her deadline."

He has me there. "Fine." I roll my eyes. "I'll come over. But I want to change first." I'm starting to forget what it's like to wear regular clothes.

We pull into the driveway of my house, and I go inside and strip out of my basic navy blue scrubs. I put on some leggings and a T-Shirt and slip my feet into my favorite pair of leather flip-flops.

When I knock on the door to the guest house, Theo answers, wearing black jeans and a white button-up shirt. His cologne hits me as soon as I step through the door, and I have to stop myself from leaning in closer. He looks even more attractive in regular clothes than he does in his scrubs. It almost hurts to look at him.

"Can I ask you a question?" I say. "Why do you even want to work if you have so much money?"

Theo shrugs. "I told you. I'm a highly creative person. If I'm not striving towards something, my life gets bloody boring."

"Ah." I sit on the couch and am instantly reminded of the last time I was here, drunk and confused. The little house is tidy, save for a few boxes cluttered in the corner of the room, and I have to stop myself from organizing them in a way that makes me feel at ease. I bite my lip.

"I saw you tapping in class," Theo says, walking toward me.

I play with my hands. "I'm surprised you noticed, considering your eyes were glued to your phone."

He laughs. "Shall we get started?" He stops right in front of me.

"Sure." I sink deeper into the couch. "Do you still have the list?"

"Why, of course I do, little Willow." He pulls it out of the pocket of his jeans. "And it says here number eleven is contamination. I think we can move on from that, though, after the way you managed your dirty hands at the river."

I think back to that moment, remembering the way those men started hollering at me right after my hands became dirty. The way Theo came back and defended me, how I discovered shortly after that I knew him when I was five.

"We'll continue working on it, but for now let's move on to number ten," Theo says. "Conflict."

I scoff. "You can't just *create* conflict for me to not react to, Theo. I'll know it's fake and it won't work."

He raises his eyebrows. "The same can be said for nine and eight, then. 'Not being in control' and 'not being happy'. If you won't let me create bothersome conflicts or scenarios, it will be up to you not to react when they happen naturally."

I inhale.

"Can you do that?" He fixes me with his intense blue stare.

"Yes," I say softly. "I'll do my best from now on."

"That means no more tapping," he says, scanning the list. "No more smiling into mirrors or imagining things so they won't happen. If you can do that, we can move onto number seven. Objects in an uncomfortable position."

I sigh and nod simultaneously.

Theo takes a pen out of his pocket. "So, let's start with this," he says, setting the pen down on the end table next to me. "Try not to react." He rolls the pen so the clip is resting on the right side.

I meet his gaze. His blue eyes are steady on mine, but my skin feels too tight on my bones, like I'm suffocating in myself. My blood races too quickly for my heart to keep up. "I can't," I whimper. "Theo, I can't."

He sits down next to me on the couch. "But you already are. You haven't tapped once."

I glance at my hands. He's right. But now I'm aware and I'm yearning to tap even more than before. I inhale deeply, and Theo grasps both of my hands together in his, steadying them. I don't move, unable to take my eyes off our joined hands. His skin is warm and shades lighter than mine. The contrast is so blatant.

I can't look at his face. Not with my heart making plans to escape from my chest and the temperature of my body getting too hot for me to endure. Just when I think the anxiety is going to push me over the edge, Theo lets go of my hands and picks up the pen. "Take a few deep breaths," he murmurs. "And then we'll try it again."

It takes six rounds of the same torture for me to finally understand why ERP works. Each time Theo turns the pen the wrong way, he makes me withstand it for longer, with no rituals. And each time it becomes a little bit easier. By no means does the anxiety go away, but it's almost like it gets smaller and smaller, until it becomes like a mosquito bite—still itchy, but no longer a flesh-eating virus.

The triumph of refraining from my compulsion for so long makes me slightly dizzy. I laugh aloud.

"What?" Theo asks.

"I just can't believe it's getting easier. It doesn't make

sense. It should be getting harder, right? But it's not." I can tell I'm rambling now, so I shut my mouth.

Theo smiles slowly. "I told you."

I laugh again. I suddenly want to change the subject because my success is making me uncomfortable. This is a different kind of success than what I'm used to. Masking my anxiety with a ritual doesn't feel quite as clean as this, this nipping in the bud. I shake my head a little, averting my eyes. "What do you like to do in your free time, Theo? You already know I'm a reader. Do you have a hobby?"

"Of course I do, little Willow," he says. "I'm an incredibly talented and creative person, as I've told you many times."

I roll my eyes. "So what's your hobby?"

"I have many." Theo stretches on the couch. "Fixing people's problems, fixing people's hair, painting—"

"Painting?" I interject. "You paint?"

He raises an eyebrow. "Is that so hard to believe?"

I smirk. "I guess not. Anyone can paint. But the question is if you can paint *well*."

Theo displays a wide grin. "All right. I accept your bait. Come and see."

He gets up and I hide my smile as I follow him to his bedroom.

It's clean, and relatively simple. A standard guy's bedroom. His grey flannel comforter I'm familiar with, after sleeping under it not too long ago. It's neatly tucked under his pillows, and I notice a pair of shoes peeking out from under his bed. The walls remain the neutral beige my mom had them painted when the guest house was built for my sick grandma to live in, and I notice that—like me—he doesn't have any pictures hanging on them. Stacks of books are visible from the floor of his closet door, which is slightly ajar. I spy the titles of a few classics on the spines. Of course he would like the classics. His desk is clear, with the exception of an old tin can holding sharpened number two pencils.

I clear my throat. "Well? Are you the next Monet or have you been lying to me?"

He chuckles. "Close your eyes."

I squeeze my lids shut dramatically.

He rustles around his room, mostly near his closet, and my curiosity intensifies. When I hear him come closer to me, I ask, "Can I look now?"

"Yes, little Willow. You can look."

I open my eyes. He's standing next to me, and on his bed are several canvases. Some of them are incomplete, with nothing more than rough pencil markings traversing their smooth surfaces. But others are saturated with color.

I'm immediately drawn to one painting in particular. The urge to touch it is nearly irresistible. The painting is dark on the outsides and light in the center. It takes me a moment to realize it's from the perspective of someone looking through the tiny lock on a door. Through the keyhole, a snowy landscape at dusk is visible. The snow glows like a fiber-optic Christmas tree. The painting makes me feel poignant in a way I can't describe.

"Did . . . did you really paint these?" I whisper. I'm still staring at the canvas.

"I did, little Willow."

I gape at him. "I thought you said this was a *hobby!*"

"It is."

"But they're amazing!"

He shrugs. "I know."

I laugh in spite of his vanity. "Theo, these are beautiful. You could sell them if you wanted to."

He offers me a small smile. "I'm glad you like them. As you said," he points to himself, "the next Monet."

I shake my head at him, and turn back to his art. I study some of the others, all beautiful and unique in their own ways. His use of color makes me never want to look away. All of them include some form of nature, laced with exaggerated elements. One of the paintings depicts a rose with the microscopic silhouette of a human trapped inside the vase holding it.

Another shows a jacuzzi atop a mountain in the middle of a forest. Trees are everywhere, some taller than the mountain itself. Though it's raining in the image, the steam rising above the water makes me long to be there. I shiver, completely awestruck by Theo's artistic talent. He really wasn't lying.

I tear my gaze from his work, against my will. When I

look at him, he's closer than I expect. We lock eyes, and I'm hit by a rush of adrenaline.

I take a step backward, trying to put distance between us. But I can't help but ask him, "Why don't you hang them on the walls?"

He looks around his room. "I don't know," he says. "The paintings are nothing special. And the idea of displaying them seems quite vain, to be honest."

I don't believe him. The attention to detail, the way he captures specific feelings with his paintings, it can't be an accident. I know that he puts more emotion into his work than he's willing to admit. I wonder if growing up with his father made him so blasé. Maybe his dad doesn't approve of his creative talents. "When has vanity ever concerned you?" I say teasingly, earning a wry smile in response.

Theo gets a text, and the mysterious E's name appears on the screen again. I'm about to ask who E is when I realize it would sound nosy. So I bite my tongue and instead say something that's been on my mind since seeing Theo's work. "Your paintings remind me of my happy place."

"Your happy place from your list?" Theo tilts his head sideways. "How so?"

I shake my head. "Your paintings make me feel like I'm somewhere else completely when I look at them," I murmur. "Thinking of my happy place does the same. That's why it helps so much. It's this image I get in my mind. Of myself as a child, lying on my stomach under a tree. It's a flowery spring day, and I'm holding a book. My little black dog is sleeping on the grass beside me while I read." My voice has turned dreamy, and I hold in the happy sigh I want to release. "For whatever reason, it calms me. I think of it as my happy place."

Theo tries not to smile. And fails. "You have a little black dog?" he asks.

"No, but I've always wanted one. Black dogs are always the last to get adopted at the pound, you know. I've always wanted to save one, but my mom never let me."

He laughs, but there's a softness in his expression that wasn't there before. "Is that why you walk dogs?"

"Yep. I like to pretend they're mine."

Theo laughs again just as he gets another text from E. This time, I can't hold my tongue. "Who on earth is E? And why do they keep texting you?"

"That would be the ever-annoying Eliza," Theo sighs. "My ex-girlfriend."

My stomach clenches. "Oh. And you still keep in contact with her?"

Theo shakes his head, distracted by the response he's sending her. "Not on purpose. She can't seem to take the hint."

He rolls the sleeves of his shirt up, and my eyes fall on his tattoos. The *Lucy* one in particular. The tiny handprint with the name in cursive underneath. It's such a sad tattoo, though I can't pinpoint why. It's like his artwork; it makes me feel a very particular way every time I see it. Poignant.

"Has your mum told you yet?" he asks me. I'm startled to find that he's been watching me study his tattoo.

My face heats. "Told me what?"

"What happened to her." Theo's voice is even. "To Lucy."

I feel like a deer in the headlights. I don't know what to say, so I shake my head. "No."

"Eight months before my mum died," he says staring at his paintings on the bed, "she got pregnant. She kept the pregnancy a secret and was planning on leaving my father because she didn't want him to raise another one of her children. Unfortunately, he found out she was going to leave, because her credit was run for a flat in a suburb near London." Theo pauses a moment before continuing. "He beat her bloody, and to stop him she was forced to tell him about the baby. He didn't touch her again until four months later, and my mum lost the child because of it. A girl. Her name was going to be Lucy. She never told anyone what my dad did." He eyes me. "Except your mum, perhaps."

My tongue feels like cotton in my mouth. I don't know what to say. I can't even imagine what it must have been like for Theo, watching his mom suffer abuse, and then losing the sibling he never even had a chance to meet. "Theo," I whisper, "I'm so sorry."

His smile is mirthless. "I'm just glad the bastard is in a different country," he states. He runs his hand through his hair.

"Wait a minute," I say. "You said she lost the baby a few

months before she passed away? Did that have anything to do with ... "

Theo's eyes are hard. "That's what I've been asking myself. Did she take her life because my dad took Lucy's? I don't know. But it's too much of a damn coincidence otherwise. I never told authorities about the situation, because what proof did I have that my dad caused my mum's miscarriage? Her bruises had faded by then."

"Has your dad tried to contact you since you moved here?" I can't help but ask.

Theo sighs. "Every day."

"You can block the jackass," I say, trying to lighten the mood.

Theo smiles, but it falters. "Can I ask you something?" he murmurs.

I nod, ready to tell him anything if it will make him feel better.

He studies my face, like he's trying to decide if he should ask, or possibly working up his nerve. "Who is Daniel?"

My heart sinks. I'm willing to tell him anything, except that. The memory is too painful for me to discuss. I feel ashamed knowing I won't answer him, especially since he just confessed to me what happened to his unborn little sister. To his mom. To him. "No one," I say, hating myself. "Daniel is no one."

Theo doesn't push further for an answer, but I can

sense his disappointment. He changes the subject. "Are you going to the party?"

"Party?"

"That bloke Charlie's back-to-school Valentine's shindig." Theo gathers up his canvases to put them away.

I tilt my head at him. "When is it again?"

"Tomorrow night. We should go together," he says. We lock eyes, causing my heart to flutter.

"Valentine's Day is tomorrow?" I ask, and suddenly recall why I can't go. Theo must have forgotten number four on my list of fears: going out on a Friday. Or maybe he just hasn't made the connection that the party is on a Friday and that's why he's asking me. If I remind him, the conversation will inevitably lead to me going and implementing ERP. Which is not an option.

"Sorry, I can't," I say. "I have . . . chores to do. Lots of them."

Theo narrows his eyes at me. "Is that so, little Willow?"

"That's so, Theo." I widen my eyes, hoping my expression appears innocent. "It's my turn to deep clean, and I can't give my mom another reason to want to kick me out."

He laughs at that. If he knows I'm lying, he doesn't say so. My stomach tightens at the lie, but it's my only option. If there's anything on my list that I'd want to get away with never facing, this would be it.

Eleven

I sleep in Friday morning. Two weeks in, and it already feels odd not to be in the car with Theo or sitting next to Ash at our stations right now.

I eat the breakfast my mom left me on the stove. It's been nice having her cook for me lately, something she never usually makes time for. I wonder if she's been doing it so I won't want to move out. She probably thinks that by cooking for me every day, she'll make me want to stay so badly I'll actually get on meds. She even cut the French toast into little hearts for Valentine's Day.

Nice try, mom.

If I told her right now how I've been using ERP to face my compulsions, it wouldn't be enough for her. I'll need to give her proof by conquering most of my rituals. Once she

148

sees my progress, she won't be able to deny that I've changed.

After taking the dogs around the block, I finish my homework for the rest of the week. It takes hours, and I'm burnt out when I'm done, but I don't have the ability to pace myself with assignments. I'd much rather suffer for one day while I trudge through it all than have to remember to do a little bit of homework every day.

I decide to take a shower after, and when I'm done I make myself comfortable on the couch in the living room. Theo will probably be getting ready for Charlie's party soon. The thought of him there without me makes my stomach heavy with dread. He might even meet a girl there. Not that it matters.

I send Ash a quick text, remembering she's going to tell Joseph she's pregnant. *Good luck tonight.*

She responds instantly. *Thanks, babe. Love you.*

I briefly consider asking her to keep an eye on Theo for me. But I know how that would sound, and I know it's not my business what happens at the party. I've seen the way some of the girls in our class look at him, like he's the hottest guy they've ever seen. And they'll be there tonight, most likely.

I need to distract myself.

I grab my book from my room and sprawl out on the couch. I read for a few hours, breaking only to eat and use the restroom. Those brief pauses, however, lead me to think of Theo, so I quickly reinstate myself in my reading spot. I turn the next page, ready to continue well into the night. The words on the paper consume my imagination, playing out behind my eyes like a movie. A movie directed by my own interpretations, by my own impressions, by the effect the words printed on the paper have on my subconscious.

A swift knock on the door rips me out of the story so abruptly that for a second I forget where I am. In a daze, I open the door.

Theo is here, holding a paper bag. The night sky is set like a stage behind him. Stars peek out from their daytime dormancy like a cluster of white Christmas lights. Theo is dressed for the party, his dark hair neatly styled, framing his bright blue eyes, which are made even more luminous by his black V-neck shirt and dark jeans. His face is freshly shaved of his light stubble.

I blink. "What are you doing here?"

Theo holds up the bag. "I decided to help you with your chores, little Willow," he says with a wry smile. "It's such a shame you're missing the party. But I wouldn't want you to do all this work alone." The challenge in his eyes is blatant. "I've got here some all-purpose cleaner, gloves, and scrubber brushes. I wasn't sure if you had any. Can make a job so much more pleasant if you ask me." When his gaze travels behind me to the couch where my blanket and book are resting, he arches an eyebrow at me. "Aha! I suspected as much."

I begin to stutter a string of gibberish even I can't decipher. "No, I am! I just—"

"Just as I thought." He saunters past me to the couch and holds up my tattered copy of *Harry Potter and the Goblet of Fire*. "And not even a new book. You stood me up to reread one of your old favorites!"

I gape at him. "I did not stand you up!"

"It's the American version, too." He eyes the book with distaste and sets it down to face me. "All right. Out with it, little Willow."

"Out with what?" I can't think straight. I can't even believe he's here right now. I'm completely underdressed, wearing the oversized T-shirt and cotton shorts I changed into after my shower. I'm not even wearing underwear. My hair is a damp and messy forest of curls. I never should have answered the door.

"Why don't you want to go to the party? Ash is there. It can't possibly be that bad, unless you're trying to avoid me."

I scoff. "Avoid you! Don't flatter yourself, Theodore!" But I am trying to avoid him. Or at least, I'm avoiding having to do ERP therapy for such a hopeless situation.

He raises his eyebrows. "Then what is it? I gather you weren't that interested in whether or not Harry wins the Triwizard Tournament, considering the condition your book is in."

"You've read it?" I ask.

"Of course I have." He raises an eyebrow. "Don't change

the subject, love." Despite his apparent intentions to help with chores, he looks dressed to do anything but.

I sigh. "I can't go to the party."

He crosses his arms. "And why not?"

"Because," I say, hoping to somehow avoid telling the truth in case he tries to convince me to face this fear. "I want to read."

Theo narrows his eyes. "Get dressed. We're going to the party together."

I scoff. "Absolutely not."

"You're being completely unreasonable, love."

Dammit. He's really not going to let this go. Exasperated, I blurt, "It's Friday. I don't go out on Fridays. There. I said it. That's the truth."

A moment of startled silence passes, and then his face softens. "Willow. This is a good opportunity." He moves toward me. My heart races with each step he takes. "Don't you want to conquer this?" His voice is soft, his breath tickling my face like a feather.

I look up into his eyes. "Not this one," I whisper. "Not yet."

He squints, ever so slightly. "Is it because of Daniel?"

My chest tightens. I can't speak, so I simply nod.

"Who is he?" Theo's voice is soft. "What happened?"

I think back to that Friday night three years ago, exhaling whatever air is left in my lungs. If I'm ever going to tell Theo what happened, now would make the most sense. I glance at him and look away. I can't meet his gaze while I talk about this. "Daniel was my boyfriend," I whisper.

"Was?"

"Was," I repeat. "Daniel is dead," I say. "He passed away three years ago. We were in high school. It was a Friday night. We went to a party with Ash, and we all had too much to drink."

Theo shakes his head. "Bloody hell." His voice is barely audible. He's giving me his complete and undivided attention.

"Daniel insisted he was sober enough to drive and I was so drunk, I didn't think twice about it. Ash ended up going home with her boyfriend, long before Daniel and I were ready to leave. If we had called her, or her boyfriend, I know they would have come. But we were stupid. We were *wasted.* I got in the passenger seat of Mitten Chip—my car, I mean—and Daniel drove me home." My lips are dry. I wet them, trying to decide how to continue.

I always thought this story would be impossible to tell, but I find myself able somehow. I don't feel like I'm going to cry. I don't have anxiety. If anything, talking about this feels good. I take a deep breath and go on. "On the way, he crashed my car. He wasn't wearing his seatbelt, and he flew right through the windshield."

Theo draws in a low, steady breath. "Were you injured?" he asks, after a long moment.

"No." I shake my head. "Not seriously, anyway. The last thing I remember was the sound of my car hitting something, and of glass shattering. And I remember the feeling of the seatbelt cutting into my skin. When I looked at Daniel, he wasn't there anymore. I passed out after it happened, probably from a mixture of shock and alcohol. I woke up in the hospital, where I heard the news, but at the time I thought it had to have been a dream. Apparently Daniel buckled me in but not himself."

Theo's lips thin. "Is that why you don't like having others drive you?"

I nod. Anxiety courses through me at the very thought of it. "Especially in my own car."

"Well, that makes sense, love." Theo reaches over and touches my hand.

"That's not all," I say, closing my eyes. "When it comes down to it, it's all my fault Daniel died."

Theo is silent for a long moment. "What do you mean?"

I sigh deeply. "When I ride in the passenger seat of a car with someone, there's a ritual I have to perform. It keeps the car from crashing." I open my eyes. Theo doesn't look back at me like I'm crazy. He just listens. So I continue. "But that night, I was having too much fun to care. So, I didn't do it. And if it weren't for that . . . Daniel would still be alive."

Theo releases my hand, and for a moment, I'm afraid he's about to leave. That he's going to make a run for it, because he finally realizes how unstable I actually am. But instead, he takes my face in his hand. His touch is so warm it sends goosebumps down my spine. "I don't for one moment believe that, Willow," he murmurs. "It wasn't your fault. Not at all."

Tears prick my eyes, but I blink them away. "Yes, it was," I tell him firmly. "And because of it, that's the one ritual I will never give up. If I were to ever make my mom completely happy, someone might die in the process."

Theo sighs. I'm glad he's not going to fight me on this, because I'm not going to budge. "While I appreciate you telling me about Daniel," he says, pausing, contemplating. "I still have to ask. You don't have a boyfriend, do you? Currently, that is?"

"No." Despite everything, I laugh and shake my head, ever so slightly. "I have many."

Theo smiles, but it is in no way predatory, or entitled. His grin is almost sad, reminding me of the child he once was, the dark-haired boy I remember. For a moment it's disorienting, but mostly it's comforting.

Theo takes off his shoes. At first I can't figure out what he's doing, but then he stretches out on the couch and I realize he intends to stay.

I frown. "You know you don't have to stay here with me," I tell him. "If you need a ride, you can take Mitten Chip to Charlie's party."

"I don't want to go," he says, lazily. He pats the seat next to him. "Not without you."

My stomach flutters. I can't think of a response, so I sit down next to him. "There's not much to do here, other than read." I say quietly.

Theo laughs. "Believe me, little Willow. I can think of a few things. But I doubt you'd be interested." His eyes turn dark, making me squirm.

"Try me." I raise my eyebrows in challenge.

Theo's eyes spark, and he leans in, stopping when his mouth is at my ear. "Let's watch a movie," he whispers. *"Harry Potter and the Prisoner of Azkaban."*

I can't help it. I laugh so loud I have to cover my mouth. I get up and put it in the DVD player, and then sit back down next to Theo, putting the remote next to me and arranging the blanket on my lap to cover my indecent attire.

"You know," I say. "You really should have called before showing up unannounced like this. I'm not dressed for company."

Theo chuckles. "And given you a chance to pretend to be doing your chores? Not a chance. Besides," he murmurs, looking me over. "I quite like the way you're dressed." Theo's eyes travel slowly up my body and land on my face.

My cheeks burn, but I hold his gaze defiantly, though I want so badly to look away. His eyes are an innocent blue, but they don't fool me. Behind them I can see the mischievous bad boy. The darkness. Eyes really must be a window to the soul because I only see heartache in his. My stomach ties itself into knots. Without my permission, I lean into him slowly until I'm inches away from his face. He exhales, and our breath mingles together and I'm suddenly desperate to taste his mouth, to feel the softness of his lips against mine. I close my eyes, feeling a pleasant yet torturous ache in the pit of my stomach. This friend of mine, this boy from the past, all man now.

The Harry Potter theme song blasts from the speakers on the TV, startling me away from him. I pat around the couch for the remote, realizing I must have sat on it. My butt turned the volume up. Nice. I find the remote under the blanket and turn the volume down, but the pounding of my pulse still rings in my ears.

Theo laughs, sounding slightly breathless. "Bloody hell."

I laugh unsteadily. Our eyes meet, and I'm suddenly embarrassed at what just happened—at what *almost* just happened—so I keep the movie at a volume slightly too loud to allow casual conversation.

Fifteen minutes in, my eyes start getting heavy. Watching movies at night puts me to sleep faster than anything else in the world. It's a curse.

Theo grabs the remote and turns the volume down. "Tired?" he chuckles. "Why don't you close your eyes for a bit?"

I glare at him and sit up. "I'm fine."

"Haven't you seen this nearly a hundred times by now?"

I yawn. "Nearly a hundred and one."

He smirks. "I'll bet you can't stay awake till the end."

"I bet I will." I try not to let my exhaustion show as I shift on the couch, lying my head down on the armrest. Challenge accepted. I might as well get comfortable.

Theo gets a text message, and I glance at his phone.

It's E.

Eliza.

I shift my gaze back to the movie before Theo can realize I saw. A flash of irritation shoots through me in spite of myself. Why doesn't he just tell her to leave him alone?

Thirty minutes later, my eyes are alternating between open and closed. In my half-awake state, I dream up possibilities of what Eliza could possibly look like. Maybe she's blond. Or a redhead. Either way, I'm sure she's pretty like Theo. I stare at the TV screen and try to straighten my exhausted vision.

"Who's your favorite character?" Theo asks a few minutes later.

"Luna Lovegood," I reply huskily. "Even though she's not in this one." I close my eyes, unable to hold them open any longer. I could almost be dreaming right now, or maybe I'm in that strange state in between sleep and consciousness.

"Why is she your favorite?"

"Because," I say, yawning a final time. I'm not sure I'm even making sense at this point. "She's just as sane as I am."

Theo chuckles, or maybe he doesn't. Either way, within seconds, I drift completely to sleep.

"Well this is fucking adorable."

Ash's voice stirs me awake. I blink against the blinding sunlight peeking into the living room and stretch, stifling a groan. A warm pair of hands flexes against my waist.

My eyes widen. Theo is still here. On the couch. With me.

We must have fallen asleep together while watching the movie last night. I blush furiously, hoping to God my mom didn't see us when she came home from work. But she must have. It's bad enough Ash is here, and now my mom is probably going to yell at me for letting Theo sleep over without asking her first, which is so stupid because he practically lives here anyway.

Ash stares at me, triumphant as a blue-ribbon winner, having caught us entangled like a pair of wild vines. Theo's eyes are still shut, and he slides his hands across my waist, up my shirt, and under my back. He makes a sleepy, satisfied sound, and I want to die of embarrassment. Falling into a black hole would work, too.

I smack his shoulder, and he squints at me for a moment before removing his hand from my skin to rub his eyes. Realization hits him, and he stares at me, blinking away the sleep he was embracing not seconds ago. Completely unfazed, he removes his other hand and crosses his arms behind his head.

Ash laughs. "Looks like you two had fun last night."

Theo seems to realize Ash is here for the first time, and his smile turns into a scowl. "Is it a crime to let a man sleep?"

"It is when that man is keeping my morning date from me." She crosses her arms. "It's Saturday. We're getting pedicures, remember?"

I groan, falling back onto the couch.

"Besides," she continues, "it looks like we both have some catching up to do."

* * *

As soon as we're both in my car, Ash pulls out a mirror to fix her makeup.

"I told him," she says without preamble. "We're keeping it." Her voice and expression are positively flippant, as if her news is nothing at all.

It takes me a moment to register what she's talking about. "You told Joseph about the baby? And you guys are keeping it?" My mouth falls open. "Ash, that's amazing!"

She shrugs. "It would have been whatever, either way."

I ignore her indifference. I know she cared all along what Joseph's opinion was, and though I don't know for sure, I think she was hoping he'd want to keep it. "Tell me everything."

She shrugs, applying mascara while I drive. It's a talent of hers I've always been jealous of. "I explained the situation," she says, trying not to smile. "He was surprised but told me he's always wanted to be a dad, so he's excited."

"Ash," I breathe. "That's wonderful. I'm so glad you told him."

She stops applying mascara so she can glare at me. "Don't bullshit me. I know you're not *that* excited."

"We'll just have to change our plans now, I guess," I say. "It's not that big of a deal."

She rolls her eyes. "It's a huge deal, babe. I'm not thrilled about it, either."

I look at her. "So, what are we going to do, then?"

"Well," Ash sighs. "Obviously traveling after we get our licenses is out. But we can still open a salon together."

I give her a withering look. "You don't mean that. Owning a salon is a ton of work, but having a baby is . . . "

She laughs. "Don't be so uptight. We'll be fine."

"I'm not being uptight. I'm being realistic."

She puts her sunglasses on. "Well, stop it."

"Fine."

"Speaking of *fine*, did you sleep with Theo Tate?" Ash grins.

"No!" In the rearview mirror I can see my cheeks have turned an alarming shade of red. "He fell asleep on the couch with me. That's it."

When we get to the nail salon, our technicians have everything ready. The hot water on my feet nearly puts me back to sleep, but Ash's relentless questioning is anything but relaxing.

"For the last time," I say through gritted teeth. "I did not have sex with Theo."

She narrows her eyes at me. "Really." It's not a question.

"Yes, really! I told you. We fell asleep watching the movie. That's it."

The nail technician raises her eyebrows at me.

"She's crazy," I inform her, pointing at Ash.

"Please tell me you at least made out with him." Ash holds two nail polish bottles in her hands, trying to decide which color to pick.

"Nope." I stare at my lap, remembering last night, moments before the movie started. His eyes on mine, turning me to liquid. How the feel of his skin had set me on fire. The ache I'd felt, deep in the pit of my stomach, begging to be relieved. "Nothing happened, Ash."

"You're a fucking nun," she tells me. "He's hot. Eva thinks so too, and she said some of the other girls in class are planning on asking us to switch stations with them so they can sit by him."

"Are they?" My stomach flops. "Is that even allowed?"

Ash turns to face me. She tilts her head sideways, examining me. "At least admit he's hot, so I know I'm not imagining all the eye-fucking."

There's no way I can hide the truth from her, regardless of whether or not I acknowledge it myself. She's known me since I was born. Many times, she's made my own feelings clear to me when I've been unable to recognize them myself.

I imagine Theo, the way he was when we were children. Brave and somehow mocking, yet chivalrous, like the king he pretended to be when we would play make-believe. I think about how he's grown, the way he makes me feel with nothing more than a glance.

I shrug. "I mean, he isn't ugly."

My eyes flicker to Ash, but rather than smug, she looks relieved. "I was starting to think there was something wrong with you," she teases.

"Is that wrong of me to say?" I begin, unsure how to articulate what I'm feeling. "After what happened to Daniel? Is it unfair to him for me to . . . "? I trail off, hoping Ash knows I'm not referring to merely finding Theo attractive.

Ash reaches over and grabs my hand, squeezing lightly. "No, babe. It's not." Her lips thin into a line. "Don't let your guilt over him keep you from living. He would want you to be happy."

Happy.

It feels like such an imaginary concept. So far-fetched. There are times I feel *at ease*, sure. Content, even. But true happiness isn't something I've experienced in what feels like as long as I can remember. To be free, to escape from the confines of my own mentality seems like something that would only make sense in a dream.

"I wish you came to the party last night," Ash sighs.

"Oh, yeah," I say, remembering that she wanted to tell me about it. "Was it fun?"

She turns to me, suddenly animated. "So much fun. Charlie's brother is in a band, and they played. Also, the food was really good."

"You didn't . . . " I'm not even sure if I should ask. "You didn't drink last night, did you?"

She rolls her eyes at me. "I had *one* beer. No big deal."

"Ashton!"

"What? They say one drink is fine!"

"They say one glass of red wine is fine, in the *third trimester!*" I want to tap so badly, to correct the situation. I know it would ease my anxiety. But instead, I take a deep breath and imagine my happy place. Theo was right. Real life conflict, I'm going to have to work through on my own. He's not always going to be here to help me.

Ash scoffs. "Sorry, mom. I'll wait until I'm huge enough to have another drink, then."

My shoulders loosen. "Thank you." I fold my hands across my lap.

"Let's go to the grocery store," Ash says when we've slipped our feet back into our sandals, my toenails white and hers blue. "I need a tuna and olive sandwich, but I don't have the shit to make one."

Twelve

Over the next month, my ERP sessions with Theo become more intense. We work our way halfway up my list, until I'm able to stop reacting to almost half the compulsions I normally would. As Theo said before, the compulsions haven't gone away. They constantly torment me, making me feel like everything around me is about to start falling apart if I don't react with a ritual. But I don't. Not every time, at least.

"You're doing well, little Willow," Theo says around the pen in his mouth, eyeing my list intently. He's sitting on my bed—a tradition of his when we have sessions in my room—and I grit my teeth to backlash my racing adrenaline.

He crosses out several things on my list and I widen my eyes. "What are you doing?"

He glances at me momentarily before returning to the

list, crossing out another item. "We don't need to keep working on these. You know what to do now."

I inhale. "Okay. So what next?"

"It's time to work on the next thing on your list. Number six. Have a look." Theo hands me the list, and I scan it with dread.

6. *Losing time (tapping, arranging objects, anything involving odd numbers)*

"You know," I say. "I'm starting to think maybe we should throw this away. End things here. I've made enough progress."

Theo chuckles darkly. "Not a chance, little Willow. After all the cheat sheets you've given me? That would hardly seem fair. I've got to make sure I deliver on my side of our bargain."

"How am I supposed to face my fear of time passing?" I say, throwing up my hands in exasperation. "It's not like you have a Time-Turner!"

Theo laughs. "You really are a nerd."

I roll my eyes. "Is that supposed to offend me?"

"Not at all." Theo's gaze lingers on mine. "I meant it as a compliment, actually."

I blush and look away, conjuring up my stress over the list again to distract me. "That doesn't change the fact that it's impossible for me to face number six."

Theo leans back on my bed, relaxing on his elbows. "First, let's discuss why you're afraid of time passing."

I take a deep breath. Though I'm used to this process by

now (addressing each item on my list before tackling it) this one seems harder to place. After some thought, I tell him, "I think it comes from me being afraid of dying too soon. I know that sounds stupid. But thinking about the future, or how much time is left, makes me realize it's not going to last forever. That time isn't an endless supply. It's temporary."

Theo's eyes are soft as he listens to me. "That makes perfect sense." He stands up. "It doesn't sound stupid at all. In fact, fear of time is common enough. It's usually caused by fears of uncontrollable situations. Like illness."

I nod. "Pretty much. I don't know how to overcome that, though."

Theo contemplates. "Has anyone close to you ever been ill?"

"My grandmother," I say. "She used to live in our guest house. Actually, my mom had it built just so she could live with us after she had a stroke. But I was young when she died. Probably like six or seven."

"How did you handle her death?" Theo asks.

I try to remember what it was like back then when my grandma was alive. When she passed away, it seemed strange not having her around, like she was ripped out of my world before I was ready to let her go. One day, we had been making paper snowflakes together to decorate her wheelchair with, and the next—she was gone.

"I hated it," I tell Theo. "She had a second stroke, and then that was it. I never saw her again. My mom didn't even let me go to the funeral, so I really never even got to say goodbye."

Theo frowns. "Why couldn't you go to the funeral?"

I shrug. "My mom didn't want me to be traumatized." I stare at the ground. "It's my fault, too. I know where she's buried, and I've never visited her gravesite."

Theo nods slowly. "Little Willow," he says. "It's time for a field-trip."

* * *

There are turkeys wandering the cemetery. Turkeys.

I don't know why the sight of them makes me smile as Theo and I approach the grassy lawn, peppered with tombstones. It's unexpectedly beautiful. I'd been envisioning a thunder-lit sky, dead grass strewn with weeds underneath rotting and cracked plaques. Stoic faces and prying eyes.

But this place is stunning. The grass is better watered than my mom's front lawn. Tall trees are everywhere, offering the perfect balance of life in this place meant to house so much death. But the turkeys are the cherry on top. I cover my mouth but the laugh escapes me. I glance around, horrified. It feels blasphemous to laugh at a cemetery for some reason. "Sorry," I tell Theo, though his expression is amused. "It's just—there are turkeys everywhere."

Theo cocks an eyebrow. "Are they prohibited from

paying their respects to loved ones? After all, Thanksgiving was . . . what? Four months ago?"

My mouth falls open, and I have to cover it with both hands to muffle my unrestrainable laughter. "Oh, god," I say, holding my stomach. "Stop, Theo. You're going to kill me."

Theo grins. "No need to worry, love. There's plenty of space for you here, and the turkeys can keep you company."

I giggle again and swat his arm with my hand. "You're being rude."

He holds his hands up. "You're the one laughing."

He's right. I did start it. I school my features into neutrality as we pass a flock of giant turkeys and search for my grandma's name among the tombstones.

"You haven't the faintest idea where her stone is, have you?" Theo asks, eyeing a tall one with a bouquet of sunflowers beneath it.

"Of course I do," I say. "This is her." Me stumbling upon it is completely coincidental, but there's no way I'm letting Theo know that.

Any lingering humor drains from my body as I take in my grandma's gravesite. Seeing her name etched in italics on the smooth, charcoal marble makes my throat tighten.

Sophie Abrahams. Loving wife, mother and friend.

There are no flowers for her, and I silently curse myself for not bringing any. I blink rapidly. Trying to take quick breaths so I don't cry. But the memory of her stings.

I didn't get to say goodbye.

I don't know why I keep clinging to the memory of making snowflakes with her. As if me seeing her the day before she died had any power in preventing it from occurring. As if taping the stupid paper decorations to her chair helped in any way.

Time still passed.

It only took one day for it to happen.

I look up, and Theo gives me a meaningful glance before walking away.

He's giving me privacy. Privacy to say goodbye.

"Grandma," I say. My voice cracks, so I inhale deeply before continuing. "I know I wasn't at your funeral. And if I could go back in time, I would have come whether Mom wanted me to be there or not." I look over my shoulder, self-conscious, but there is no one else around. Just me, and my grandma's bones beneath the ground. "I think I still imagine you alive," I continue, "because it's hard to think of you any other way. You were so full of life, up until my last moment with you. But then you were stolen from me. *Death* stole you from me before I was ready, stole you before I had a chance to say goodbye." My voice is thick with tears now, and I continue in a whisper. "And I'm afraid it's going to do the same to me someday. But I hadn't realized until now what the silver lining to that would be. I'd get to see you again. Maybe." I wipe my face, and my hands come back wet. "If I ever were to see you again, it would be in death. So maybe it can't be *that* bad. At least I hope it won't be. Until then . . . goodbye, Grandma. I love you."

Theo's footsteps approach behind me, and I wipe my eyes more fervently to prevent him from seeing my visible emotions. He doesn't look at me, only places a small bouquet of flowers, freshly picked, at her grave. Then, without a word, he pulls me against him, my face buried against his chest and his hands stroking my back.

"You did it, little Willow," he murmurs softly. "You said goodbye to her. I'm proud of you."

I sob into his shirt, his words making it all the more real. "I didn't expect to feel this way," I tell him. "I thought I was fine, actually."

I stare at a flock of birds flying above us in a perfect V. Focusing on them helps me swallow back my tears.

"I don't think," he tells me, "that we ever really are."

Thirteen

On Saturday morning, I take the dogs on an extra-long walk. It's late March, and the weather is warming up. A bead of sweat pools at my temple, and Tido pants while we walk, his tongue lolling dramatically out of the side of his mouth.

As I drop the dogs off and make my way up the driveway, a red car parked on the street in front of my house catches my eye. There's a girl sitting in the passenger seat, staring at the guest house. After a moment, she turns the engine off and gets out, causing my stomach to drop. She's gorgeous, with strawberry blond hair, clad in a tight-fitted pair of white jeans and a pink off-the-shoulder top. She's even wearing red heels.

I briefly wonder if it's one of my mom's friends until she walks right up to Theo's front door. When he opens it, I frown and quickly hide behind one of the nearest trees, slowly peeking out from behind it. I don't know why I'm hiding. I live here. But this visit seems clandestine to me and I feel like I'm spying. If Theo saw me, I doubt he'd think my lurking around the front yard is natural.

The girl says something to Theo, and though I can't make out her words, her tone is cheerful. But Theo shakes his head. His voice is low, agitated. I only catch the last thing he says before he lets the girl inside. "Make it fast, Eliza."

Eliza.

Eliza as in E, as in his ex-girlfriend from England? I was wrong; she's even prettier than I thought she would be. There's no reason to be upset, yet I feel myself crumbling, like a cookie left in a pocket for too long. Like a paper full of mistakes.

Before I know it, I'm knocking on the guest house door.

What the hell am I doing?

I consider running, or maybe hiding behind some bushes. But that would be ridiculous. For all Theo knows, I'm completely unaware he has a visitor. He has no reason to think I'm prying.

The door opens, but it isn't Theo who greets me. Eliza's eyebrows fly to her hairline as she looks me over, reducing my self-esteem to the size of a tiny pebble. She's gorgeous. Her eyes are a mixture of green and blue, and her hair is layered neatly, honey blond with hints of red. She's slightly taller than me, and her lips are red as an apple. Eliza opens her mouth to say something, but Theo interrupts her from the other side of the room.

"Who is it?" he asks.

She presses her lips together, opening the door wider and revealing me to Theo. He's wearing the most irritated expression I've ever seen. When he sees me, his face becomes slightly bewildered, like he can't imagine why I would possibly come over at a time like this, and for some reason it makes me angry.

"So, this is the famous ex-girlfriend?" I blurt.

"Willow, what the bloody hell are you doing here?" Theo sighs. "And believe me, she's the last person I was expecting." He flashes his eyes at her.

Eliza scoffs. "Must I be the villain? I'm only here to deliver a message!" Her voice is high, accented the same way as Theo's, and I become jealous all over again.

"Eliza," Theo mutters. "Just go. Please."

"Why?" she asks, genuinely puzzled. "Because of your lady friend?" Eliza gestures toward me.

Theo rubs a hand across his face. "Because what you told me doesn't make a difference. You still slept with my father. You still mean nothing to me. And you still can't take a hint that I don't care to see you again, even on friendly terms."

My mouth falls open as Eliza flinches. "Fine," she says, sounding resigned, and I can't help but feel a stab of sympathy. "I'll see myself out. But please, Theo. Remember what I told you."

Eliza waits, as if hoping for some sort of reaction from him, but he doesn't give her one. She turns to me, a small smile on her lips. "By the way, you're very pretty for a black girl," she says. "You *are* African American, aren't you?"

Though her tone is kind, I stiffen, unable to help but feel completely insulted. What the hell is that supposed to mean? *Pretty for a black girl?* As if I'm some sort of exception, and being black isn't already beautiful on its own? "Yes, I am." I don't bother telling her I'm also half white, and instead say, "You're pretty too. For a white girl."

Theo chuckles, but my words don't seem to have the same effect on her. She takes one last glance at me before opening the front door and shutting it firmly behind her.

Theo exhales deeply as soon as she's gone, yet I feel anything but at ease. "What was that about?" I ask him.

Theo rubs his forehead. "Not now, Willow."

"Why not?" I demand.

"Because," Theo says. "I am not in the mood for a Willow Bates interrogation."

I roll my eyes. "Whatever that is."

Theo sighs. "Fine. Go ahead. Ask me your most pressing question. I can see I'm getting nowhere telling you no."

His words sting, but I consider my question carefully. "Was that true? What you said about her sleeping with your dad?"

"Yes," Theo says darkly. "Can you understand why I might not want to discuss something like that?"

"Not really," I say. "Unless you still have feelings for her."

Theo gives me a withering look. "You can't be serious."

"Why else would it bother you so much that you can't even talk about it?"

Theo steps closer to me. His eyes are blazing, though with what, I can't discern. "I'm not hurt because of *Eliza*," Theo says fiercely. "I was going to break it off with her anyway. What disturbs me is that my father would—as she said—buy sex, not to mention from a girl young enough to be his daughter. One dating his own son, to top it off."

My face burns. "Oh my god. I didn't know." I touch Theo's arm, hard beneath my fingers. To my surprise, he doesn't pull away. "I'm so sorry, Theo."

He stares at me, but his eyes are distant. To bring him back to the present, I ask, "Why were you going to break up with her before that? She seems nice enough, and she's very pretty." Despite the ugly, backhanded compliment she gave me.

Theo scoffs. "Her appearance is nothing to be jealous of and she's the most twisted person I've ever met. Don't let her fool you."

"Of course I'm jealous." The words are hard to admit, and I try to laugh as I say them.

Theo's eyebrows pull together. "And why on earth would you be?" He searches my face. "You're beautiful. Inside *and* out."

My heart stutters, and I try with all my might not to

look away from his gaze. "I still don't understand why she was here in the first place."

Theo's eyes harden. "It doesn't matter."

"Yes, it does," I say. "What message did she have for you? Did it have to do with your dad?"

Theo groans. "Just drop it, Willow. Please."

"Fine." I let my anger flow freely. "Then I'm leaving. Maybe you should catch her before she's gone and tell her to come back." I spin on my heel, ready to leave, but I feel his hand on my elbow.

"That's not fair, Willow," he says.

I turn to face him. Half of me is angry that he's right, but the other half feels wronged that he's keeping her message a secret. Things feel different between us now. As if two days ago, after he visited my grandma's grave with me, some invisible barrier was broken. I have no grounds for jealousy—and yet it's clinging to my blood and flowing through me with every passing second. "Why don't you trust me enough to tell me?"

Theo pinches the bridge of his straight nose. "Will you please just leave it alone?"

"No!" I practically shout.

"Why not?" His face is close to mine now, his eyes demanding.

We're both silent for a long moment. Why can't I let it go? I don't even know the answer. Maybe because if his dad is threatening him, I want to help. But it's more than that. The fact that she was here—Eliza—and there's a secret between her and Theo now that I'm not a part of makes me want to hurl something across the room.

I know the moment Theo somehow reads my thoughts in my expression, and I glance at the wall behind him briefly. He brings his hand up to my chin, forcing me to meet his gaze. His eyes are still hard though the anger has melted away, replaced by something else. "Could it be," he murmurs, "that you care for me more than you'd like to admit?"

My heart races as I stare at him, transfixed. The boy I once knew is still part of him but only a small portion of the man he's become. The man who still treats me like an actual person, despite knowing the darkest corners of my mind.

A strand of Theo's neat hair falls into his eyes, making him look even more devastating. We stare at each other for a moment. I know he's waiting for me to answer.

Instead of saying anything, I grab Theo's shirt in my fists and press my lips against his.

Instantly, he's kissing me back and the feeling that courses through me is so unexpected, I hardly manage to stay upright. My knees threaten to buckle, and I lean into him for support. His hands grip my waist.

I part my lips, gliding my tongue along the edge of his, and the kiss deepens. His mouth moves against mine with urgency and it fills me from head to toe, nearly tearing me apart. There's a frenzy in me I can't suppress.

Theo groans and before I know it we're stumbling

down the hall until we're on his bed, a tangle of limbs and hair and teeth. His weight presses down on me in the most satisfying way.

Theo. You're kissing Theo, my brain screams.

His bed vibrates. I glance next to my head and see Ash's name on my phone. How it ended up out of my pocket and next to me on the bed, I have no idea. But Theo's lips are on my neck, and I shut my eyes again, reveling in the sensation. I can't contain my moans, and they only fuel the fire igniting in Theo, the fire that is now attaching itself to me and spreading through my veins.

My phone vibrates again, but I ignore it. I push Theo and roll on top of him, almost tearing his shirt when I pull it up, over his head, and throw it on the floor with mine. I'm inevitably conscious of the nude bra I'm wearing. I wish I'd chosen to wear something more exciting today. But Theo doesn't seem to mind. He takes me in, and his eyes darken, his pupils expanding. I look at him too—and tremble. His body is a piece of art as fine as his paintings. His fingers trail down my stomach, leaving goosebumps in their wake as they map out every inch of my skin.

When his hands travel lower, the need coursing through me becomes unbearable. "Theo," I whimper.

His fingers pause and he's about to say something when my phone goes off again, irritating me beyond belief. I sigh and get off him to reach for it. It's Ash again. I glance at Theo and hold up a finger. "Let me just answer this," I tell him. Into the phone, I say, "This better be important."

"Willow," Ash breathes. Her voice is frantic, and it's enough to take my mind off Theo for the moment.

"What's wrong?" I ask, suddenly alert.

"It's the baby," she says, her voice cracking. "I'm at the hospital. I think I started my period."

Fourteen

"But what about the pains? Those must point towards a miscarriage." Ash is arguing with the doctor. He assures her they're called round ligament pains, and despite her bleeding, the baby is perfectly healthy. Apparently, women can bleed during pregnancy, and it doesn't necessarily mean anything is wrong. I have no idea how Ash stays so calm all the time. If I were her, I'd constantly think something was wrong with my baby and be even more of a mess than I already am. Maybe she's a mess too, and merely hides it well.

In my urgency to meet Ash at the hospital, I rushed away, leaving Theo shirtless on his bed, offering nothing more than a frantic, unintelligible explanation. I blush, remembering how his hands on my skin, his lips against mine, had almost undone me.

I glance down at myself and notice my shirt is on backward.

Ash scoffs at her doctor. "How the hell am I supposed to know if something is actually wrong, then?"

I try to tune out their conversation. Now that I'm away from Theo, I'm able to think clearly. My heart is still floating, high in the sky, never wanting to come down. I haven't been open to the possibility of a relationship since Daniel. I haven't wanted to give myself a chance to open my heart to anyone else, at risk of hurting them unintentionally with my thoughts. But maybe giving up my rituals isn't as dangerous as I believed. I've been weeding them out slowly, and nothing drastic has happened yet. I have to admit I was worried about Ash, that maybe my lack of tapping, of smiling into mirrors, of sterile hygiene had affected her and the baby. But she's okay. Her baby is fine too.

Perhaps there's a chance I can live a normal life, free of myself, someday in the future.

The only thing standing in my way is my mom. I have no idea if she'll even accept my journey through ERP therapy over taking medication. If she doesn't, I'll have no choice but to move out, and then I can kiss any hope of sanity goodbye. I can't be alone or live with a complete stranger. I just can't. Even the thought of it makes me wish I hadn't been born so I won't have to suffer through it.

The doctor washes his hands after he's completely finished examining Ash. He uses two paper towels. Two. He throws them away crumpled together, hugging and clumped like they're one, but they aren't even balled up into a round shape. I have to literally force myself not to reach into the trash can and pry apart the paper towels he threw away. They're uncomfortable, stuck together like that. The doctor says something to Ash, but all I can think about is the way the paper towels are lying in the garbage can. I need to fix them.

He leaves, and Ash begins to dress herself. "Such bullshit," she mutters.

"What is?" I ask her. "That they want you to take vitamins?" I stand up, completely unable to stop myself from reaching into the garbage can. I take out the wad of paper towels and smooth them out one at a time. Then I add a third one to the stack. I throw them away all over again, myself this time, making sure they're in the correct position.

"What the fuck are you doing?" Ash holds up her hands. "I thought you were working on your compulsions, babe."

"I am." When I finish, I wash my hands and dry them. But the paper towel I use on myself dislodges the others when I throw it away, and I'm forced to repeat the process all over again. "But number seven still bothers me sometimes."

"Number seven?"

"'Objects in an uncomfortable position'," I explain.

Ash comes up from behind me, reaching for the trash in my hands. "Stop."

I move it out of her reach. "*You* stop." Now she has me all messed up. "Sit back down. Seriously."

She sighs but doesn't take a seat. "Just meet me out there when you're done. She heads for the door. "I refuse to watch you play with trash."

I go back home to explain everything to Theo. The sun is about to set, and it's starting to get chilly outside, so I stop at my room first to grab a sweater.

I pause in the doorway when I catch sight of someone in the kitchen. Gus Badgely is sitting at the table.

I wave awkwardly, even though he isn't looking at me. "Long time, no see, Gus."

Gus jumps, clearly startled by my presence. His white polo shirt makes his red hair stand out more than it did the last time I saw him. "Willow!" He stands up and shakes my hand.

I grin at him. "Good to see you."

"Hey—you didn't wipe off my handshake this time." He smiles good-naturedly. "I feel honored. Looks like the meds are kicking in!"

I laugh, despite how much his jab stings. "Actually, I'm not on meds."

He tilts his head to the side. "No? That's not what your mom said."

I resist the urge to roll my eyes. "Actually my mom only *wants* me to take medication. I haven't, nor do I intend to."

Gus frowns and pauses for a long moment. "That's strange," he says slowly. "Because your mom filled a six-month-old prescription for Anafranil with me shortly after . . . the first time I met you." Gus shifts on his feet, as if uncomfortable from recalling that day. "She said it was from your most recent therapy session, and you finally agreed to give the meds a go. Good thing she filled it when she did, because it was close to expiring!"

I stare blankly at Gus. "What do you mean she filled the prescription?"

"Wait a minute." Gus frowns. "You really didn't know? Maybe she forgot to tell you."

My heart races. "I don't think that's something she would forget."

The front door opens and my mom walks in looking harried. Today is her day off, which is the only reason she's awake right now. When she sees Gus standing next to me, she pastes a smile on her face that only I can tell requires quite a bit of effort. "Sweetheart, I thought you were meeting me at the restaurant in half an hour."

Gus grins. "I couldn't wait that long."

My mom's lips thin. She glances at me. "Willow, honey. Did you eat the leftover breakfast I made you this morning? You look too thin."

I don't say anything. I can't trust myself to speak after what Gus told me.

My mom checks the fridge, and when she sees the plastic container she left me with French toast still inside, she sighs. She takes the container out of the fridge and hands it to me. "Please eat it, honey."

I frown. "It's dinnertime. I'll eat it tomorrow morning."

She shakes her head. "No, you'll eat it now. I made it for you and missed out on much-needed sleep because of it." She tries to hand it to me again, but I don't take it.

"I don't want the food right now, Mom."

Her face turns a faint shade of red. "Willow Daphne Bates."

I scoff. "Why do you want me to eat it *right now* so badly?"

Gus's gaze shifts back and forth between the two of us. His easy smile starts to slip.

"Because," my mom says. "I want to make sure you actually eat it."

"Why?" I ask. But as the words come out of my mouth, a wave of horror—of disbelief crashes into me. The reason hits me: why my mom randomly started making me breakfast every morning, when she hadn't done so since I was in middle school. Why she's been saving it for me in clearly labeled containers even when I don't have time to eat.

"Gus told me, mom," I whisper. "He said you filled my Anafranil prescription."

My mom's face whitens. She stares at me, motionless. "I—"

"Have you been putting the meds in my breakfast?" I cover my face with my hands. "Have you, Mom?"

I expect her to immediately deny it. To somehow shake the confidence in the revelation I've just made. In fact, there's nothing I want more than for her to tell me she would never do something like that. I want her to call me crazy, to tell me not to ask such outlandish questions. But she doesn't say anything at all. She just stares at me, gaping and wide-eyed.

She doesn't need to answer.

Her silence is enough.

I shoulder past her and Gus, ignoring my mom's weak attempts at an explanation, and run out the door.

Fifteen

I knock on the door to the guest house, tears tickling my cheeks as they slide down my face. I need to be away from my mom. I can't be in the same room as her right now, or even the same house. In fact, there are only two people I want to talk to right now.

I text Ash, asking if I can come over and stay the night.

Of course, babe, she responds. *What's going on?*

Theo answers the door before I can respond to her, and the moment he sees me, his eyes blaze. He swings the door open and his arms are suddenly around me, tucking me into him and pulling me close. "Willow," he says, his voice bordering on rage. "Are you all right? What happened, love?"

I exhale, but it's invaded by sobs. My body shakes with each silent round of crying.

"Bloody hell, Willow. I'm about to murder someone." Theo's voice is deep, anxious. "Tell me what happened."

"My m-mom has been . . . " I take a deep breath. "She's been putting Anafranil in my breakfast every morning. She's been giving me medication without my consent and I just found out."

Theo's jaw twitches. His eyes are full of denial and barely concealed rage. "That's illegal," he says. "She could be arrested, not to mention lose her nursing license." He runs his hands over his face.

"She wouldn't deny it," I tell him. "I asked her, and she didn't say a word."

Theo swears and stares at the ceiling and then the floor. "God." And then he sits down beside me, pulling me close to his chest. "Are you physically all right? How are you feeling?"

I close my eyes. I don't know how I'll ever be able to trust my mom again, if it's even a possibility. I can't imagine facing her and feeling anything but betrayal, ever again. Our relationship can't possibly be the same after this. It's almost like mourning, thinking about the life I've known for so long, gone in the flash of a truth come to light.

"I feel sick to my stomach," I whisper. "But I don't think it's because of the meds."

Theo tightens his arms around me. "If it weren't for the state you're in right now," he growls, "I would demand to have quite a few words with your mum."

"Please don't leave." I grip his shirt. I just want him to

keep holding me, to let me escape in the comfort of his presence.

Theo gently kisses the top of my head. "I won't."

"What am I supposed to do?" I bury my face in Theo's shirt, and my next words come out slightly muffled. "I can't just go back home and pretend everything is okay. Even if my mom apologizes, it will never be the same between us."

Theo shakes his head as if my concerns are unwarranted. "We'll both move out," he says. "You'll live with me."

My heart skips a beat. Did Theo just ask me to move in with him? I'm not sure I'm ready for such a big step, even if I don't feel safe with my mom. It just seems so . . . sudden. Not to mention the financial repercussions. "But if I move out . . . " I sniff. "My mom won't help me with school anymore. I can't afford to pay for both school and a lease." As much as his suggestion partly sounds like a fantasy to me, I know I can't entertain the idea. This is reality, and it just doesn't make any sense.

Theo's lips form a straight line. "Your tuition is no matter," he says. "Let me pay for it. Or at least let me help."

"No." I shake my head. "There's no way I'm letting you pay for me to go to school. Besides, you won't be in America forever. And once you leave, I'll be alone."

Theo lifts my chin, so I'm forced to meet his eyes. "Then come to London with me after this semester," he says. "We can transfer to a school there. You can take out a loan and live in a dormitory if you really won't let me pay for anything."

My lips part. Going to school in London . . . I don't think anything could possibly sound more exciting. But to drop everything and move to a country I haven't been to since I was five makes my chest tight with worry.

"I can't just leave Ash," I decide. "She's pregnant, and we've always wanted to go to school together." I untangle myself from him and stand up. "In fact, I'm supposed to go to her house tonight. She's waiting for me."

Theo reaches for me again, a small pout on his lips. "Now look who's leaving," he murmurs, placing a feather-light kiss against the edge of my jaw. He presses his lips together, seeming lost in thought. "Will you at least consider my offer?" he asks. "Talk about it with her if you must."

I sigh, searching his face. If I'm going to consider moving to another country with him—the same one his dad lives in—then I need to know everything. I need him to be honest. "Theo," I say. "What was Eliza's message?" Theo's eyebrows pull together when he looks at me, like it hurts for him to think about it. "Please tell me," I whisper.

He pauses for a moment before answering. "My dad wanted me to know that if I open my mouth, I'll pay. And that he'd like for me to come home so he can make sure I stay quiet."

I frown. "Open your mouth? About what?"

Theo holds out his wrist—where the Lucy tattoo is—and stares at me pointedly, as if trying to convey a message without speaking, and I remember what he told me about his mom losing her baby shortly before she committed suicide. How no one else knows his dad abused her, and how that might be the reason she had a miscarriage. If anyone knew the truth, Theo's dad could be implicated.

I nod at Theo to show him I understand, and his shoulders relax. "Thank you for telling me." I thread my fingers through his. "I'll think about your offer," I tell him.

Theo smiles faintly, but it disappears as quickly as it comes. He places a kiss against my hand. "Thank you."

* * *

This is the longest night I've had in a while.

When I finally finish telling Ash everything—including what happened with Eliza but leaving out the part about kissing Theo—she sits speechless on her bed beside me. "What the fuck," she finally says. "I can't believe your mom!"

I stare at her white comforter, my eyes stinging from lack of blinking.

"Hey," she says, nudging me gently. "Are you going to be okay?"

I shrug. "Honestly, Ash? I don't know. I thought I was finally getting rid of my rituals, all on my own. But knowing she's been giving me meds this entire time makes me feel like none of my progress was from my own efforts."

Her lips thin. "Not necessarily. I think it takes a while for those types of meds to kick in."

Part of me doesn't want to hear what she's saying. The part that wants her to tell me there's no point in continuing ERP, especially since I can't go back to living with my mom, to trusting her. The reason I've even been trying to conquer my compulsions was because of her ultimatum: take medication or move out.

She's already given me medication against my will. I might as well move out and go back to the way I'm comfortable being. Consumed by my compulsions.

"Do you have any idea how long this has been going on?" she asks me.

"No," I whisper. "How am I ever supposed to trust her again?"

She bites her bottom lip, absentmindedly. "Okay, I'm going to say something, and I don't want you to get mad."

I face her. "What?"

She takes a deep breath. "I get why you're upset. I'd be fucking pissed if someone tried to pull that shit with me. But what if what your mom did was sort of a blessing in disguise?"

I gape at her. "Ash, what are you talking about? She went behind my back! She tried to *cure* me! Like I'm an illness or something."

She sighs. "You do technically *have* an illness," she reminds me. "And despite how you may feel about medication, you have to admit you really have made progress in such a short amount of time. Nothing bad happened to you either. You didn't have an allergic reaction like you did when you were little."

I blink several times. "Why are you defending her?"

"I'm not," she assures me. "You know I'm always on your side. I'm literally just telling you what I think. And even though you might not want to admit it, you're strong enough to fight your compulsions, with or without medication. If you really want to."

"I guess."

"You *are*." Ash squeezes my hand.

There are no coherent thoughts left in my brain. I can't grasp how I feel about what she's saying. If Ash really thinks my mom was justified in her actions, then I don't know what to do. I thought for sure she of all people would convince me that my mom deserved to be cut out of my life forever.

What she did hurts so badly, in ways I didn't even know I could be hurt. Closing myself off from people is my tried and true defense mechanism against the what-if, against the possibility of getting hurt, against traumatic situations happening—just like this one. But I never thought I was supposed to protect myself from my own mother. I wasn't supposed to get hurt by her, to get so utterly betrayed. And yet, my heart feels like it was dropped on the ground, taped back together, and placed carelessly back inside me.

"So, what?" I ask her. "You think I should just forgive her? Go on like it never happened?"

She laughs mirthlessly. "Fuck no. Make her pay." She

smiles. "But maybe, if you feel like it, consider forgiving her eventually."

"Ash," I say. "If I never found out my mom was medicating me . . . do you think the compulsions would have *gone away*?

She stares at me for a long moment. "I mean, I don't know what it's like to be you. To have OCD. But in my opinion, I doubt the compulsions would ever *go away*."

A knot forms in the back of my throat. I nod at her, trying not to let my face convey my hopelessness.

"But that's not to say," she continues, "that you could never succeed in fighting them."

I swallow. "What do you mean?"

She shakes her head. "I know it's probably really difficult. But you could definitely not perform rituals, if you really, really worked at it. You just have to find other ways to help your anxiety."

I sigh. "Easier said than done."

She nods. "Oh yeah, definitely. But that doesn't mean it can't be done, right?"

And then the realization hits me. Not hard and fast, but slow and creeping, like a shadow being cast on the ground. "I've never actually, truly wanted to give all my rituals up," I admit. "Because I'm afraid of what could happen if I do. I'm terrified of all the things that could go wrong without me controlling them."

"Babe," Ash says. "People live every day without controlling things, and they're fine."

"A lot of them aren't," I point out. "Things go wrong for people constantly. And most of them have no idea why. It's like they're magnets for bad luck and tragedies."

Ash pauses. "So you're saying that nothing ever goes wrong for you? Because you can control everything that happens to you with your thoughts and rituals?"

"I know it sounds ridiculous." I wrap a strand of hair around my index finger, not wanting to see Ash's expression. "But I can't help but believe it."

"Willow, let me ask you something." Ash sounds so thoughtful, it's almost enough to make me glance up at her. "Have you given up your rituals? Cured your OCD, or whatever?"

Though I've managed to refrain from reacting to a few compulsions for a while, I'm nowhere near where I would need to be to consider myself free. Every time I stop myself from performing a tried and true ritual, I'm filled with such anxiety and dread that I make up for it in other ways. Like going to my happy place.

Lying on a spring meadow, under a tree, with a book in my hands. My little black dog sleeping on the grass beside me.

It's getting harder and harder to imagine. Sometimes, the image escapes me completely. It's those days I rely more heavily on my rituals.

"No," I tell her. "I've improved, but I still definitely use rituals."

"Then why," she asks me, "are things going so wrong for you right now?"

I blink at her. My heart races, and I'm afraid. Afraid that she's right. Afraid that she's wrong. Just so completely afraid.

"Because I'm not doing things right," I breathe. "I've given up too many rituals."

"Or maybe," she says, placing her hands on my shoulders. "That's bullshit and you know it. What I don't get is why you even care. Who gives a fuck if everything goes to shit? At least you know you'll be dead someday and you won't have to deal with it anymore."

"Ash," I say, appalled. "Do you really feel that way? I thought you were braver than that."

"And I thought you were braver than *this*." She shakes her head at me. "You're afraid of any little thing in your life going wrong. You're terrified of people dying when death is a part of life. You already lost Daniel. And guess what? You survived. You need to be happy, Willow," she says. "But you also need to be sad. You need to feel loss. Anger. Hurt. Pain. Fear, even. All of those emotions are important because they let you grow and get stronger. There are so many more valid, relevant, important emotions than happiness. And you're depriving yourself by running from them constantly."

I don't even realize I'm crying until I feel air hitting the wetness on my cheeks. "When did you get so wise?" I whisper, a small laugh in my voice.

She smiles at me, but it's a melancholy smile. "Wouldn't

it be so much easier," she says, "to embrace fate, rather than fight it?"

And though I've been fighting fate all my life, with my thoughts, with my rituals, with my compulsions, her words help me realize something.

I'm exhausted.

I'm so tired. Tired of worrying constantly, of trying to protect everyone I care about, myself included, from anything ever going wrong. Ash is right. Emotions are important. Emotions are the keys to doors with locks made just for them. They help us get to a place we could never be without them. They help us grow. They make us wise. And perhaps that's why I constantly feel so naive, because I live in a state of constant worry that my bubble of security will explode. And Ash's point about embracing fate rather than fighting it brings me something I don't expect.

Comfort.

Comfort I'm not prepared to feel.

The exact same type of comfort that performing rituals brings me.

Continuing to live with my mom isn't something I care about anymore, isn't something I could even endure, which means nothing is keeping me from falling back into my compulsions. Yet, there's a new incentive tempting me to resist them. One I wasn't sure I wanted until now. One I was partly afraid of, and still am, though not nearly as much as before. One I'm finally, finally ready to experience.

Freedom.

Ash chuckles. "Your boyfriend keeps texting me."

I raise my eyebrows. "Why?" I don't bother correcting her. It will only make her suspicious, and I honestly don't know if it's not true at this point.

"To make sure you're okay." She holds out her phone so I can read their conversation.

Theo: *How is she? I can't sleep and her phone is turned off. I've already tried calling.*

Ash: *She's fine, Prince Harry. Go to bed.*

Theo: *Thought I was William.*

Ash: *Yeah, but she's really more of a Meghan Markle than a Kate Middleton. So you're Harry now.*

I laugh despite everything, and then remember what he proposed before I left. "Theo thinks I should move out," I blurt. "And live with him."

Ash actually laughs. "That's ridiculous. You're only eighteen. And you hardly know him."

"Actually," I point out, "I've known him since we were kids. But you're right. It *is* ridiculous."

Ash studies me, her eyes narrowing with each passing second. "You want to," she accuses. "Don't you?"

I shrink. "No."

"Don't lie to me. I know you."

I sigh. "Well, I don't really want to be near my mom at the moment. I feel like she practically tried to poison me. And I have to admit, I'm a little nervous his ex-girlfriend knows exactly where I live now. What if she tells Theo's dad where he is, and he comes after Theo?"

Ash interrupts me. "First of all, if that Eliza bitch opens her mouth, I'll shave her hair off myself. Second, you won't make enough money anywhere at part-time minimum wage to support yourself if you move out. We live in California, babe. Not Texas. You should just wait until you finish school to make rash decisions."

"Or finish it in London, like Theo suggested," I say. "It's better than letting him pay for everything like he wants to."

Ash's eyes widen into saucers. "Are you serious? Let him!"

"No way." I frown. "That's not happening. I need to figure this out on my own. This isn't Theo's problem to solve just because he has money."

Ash shrugs. "I would let him, because there's no way you're moving to another freaking country without me."

I laugh. "Don't worry," I tell her. "I know."

She shakes her head. "And would you really feel comfortable moving all that way with Theo Tate?"

I think about all the moments Theo and I have shared that she hasn't been there for. All the times he's caused heat to spread through my body like wildfire with a simple glance. The way he held me in the graveyard while I cried into his shirt. It must seem like I hardly know him—to her.

"Actually," I say hesitantly, "we *have* gotten a lot closer lately."

Ash pauses for a moment, and then her mouth falls open. "Tell me everything."

Sixteen

I wake up the next morning at Ash's house. It's Sunday, and her mom makes us pancakes. I try not to focus on the uncanny resemblance between Aunt Christie and my mom —or between pancakes and French toast—and instead try to focus on Ash's brothers, fighting at the table.

"That's it!" Aunt Christie yells. "Go to your rooms, both of you!"

Chris and Dean frown at each other in accusation, but otherwise obey, marching to their rooms like it's a competition.

Aunt Christie sighs. "I'm going to go talk to them. Enjoy your breakfast."

When Aunt Christie is out of earshot, I turn to Ash. "When are you going to tell your mom you're pregnant?"

The sun is shining through the drapes, illuminating the

room and casting a bright glow on Ash's hair, like a halo. Pregnancy definitely suits her. In fact, the light only adds to the glow she's been sporting these days. She's probably around thirteen or fourteen weeks but she's hardly showing. The small bump her stomach has become is easily hidden by her clothes.

She scrunches her nose with distaste. "I have no fucking clue," she says. "I was hoping to have some sort of commitment from Joseph by now, but apparently that's not happening. It would make telling her so much easier."

"Commitment," I repeat. "Like an engagement ring?" I can't hide the surprise on my face. I'm sure it's audible in my voice, too. Ash and Joseph are on and off so often, it shocks me she might be willing to agree to something so permanent with him.

"Yeah, well," she says, "we are having a baby. We might as well."

I give her a knowing smile. Ash likes to pretend her reasons for doing things are purely practical, when in reality, she's almost always driven by her heart. "Oh, shut up," I tell her. "You love him, and you know it."

She glares at me. "I love him as much as you love Theo Tate."

I roll my eyes, but her words cause my heart to race.

After my talk with Ash last night, I feel confident about my mental health. I'm ready to give up my rituals for good this time. Not for my mom, but for myself. I know it's going to be hard, but I don't care. I'm finally ready to be free of my thoughts, of my compulsions. I couldn't be more sure of myself.

But when it comes to Theo, I'm afraid.

He's going to have to go home eventually. And when that happens, I don't know what I'll do. It would be stupid to get attached to him.

I swallow my last bite of pancake. "Ash?"

"What?"

"Thank you for talking to me last night." I purse my lips. "You really helped me."

She raises her eyebrows. "I thought you didn't need help."

"I didn't," I say. "But I appreciate it anyway."

* * *

When I get home, my mom's car is in the driveway. I consider driving right back to Ash's, but I know I'll have to face her eventually. I can't keep hiding.

I take a deep breath, wanting so badly to think a comforting sequence of odd numbers. But I don't. I can do this without rituals.

The brightness of the day begs me to be in a good mood, yet my nerves are anything but uplifting. The front porch is neatly kept, adorned with clay pots housing forget-me-nots and hydrangeas. My mom must have swept under the welcome mat recently, because there are no more stray twigs scattered around the entryway.

Inside, I don't see her anywhere. She must be in her room, asleep. I could easily postpone talking to her if I want to. I could go to my room and take out a book, and I could read. All day long.

And once the book runs out, I could clean.

But that's something the old Willow would do. The one driven by her anxiety and compulsions.

I stand outside my mom's bedroom door, staring at it, like it's going to open by itself if I wait long enough.

I knock.

Not three times, not five, but twice. It's awful, but I do it.

"Come in," my mom says, and I open the door. She's not trying to sleep like I expect, but folding laundry on her bed, which is made neatly, the sheets and brown duvet pulled tight and tucked underneath the mattress. Her essential oil diffuser is going, filling the space with the scent of lavender. When she sees me, she looks like she has a million things to say but is trying hard to restrain herself. "Hi, my love," is all she utters.

I sit down on the bed, careful not to jostle the piles of folded clothes. "Mom," I say. "I want to start by telling you that you really hurt me." She presses her lips together, allowing me to speak, so I continue. "I can't believe you would go behind my back like that. First, filling my prescription without me knowing, and then sneaking it into my food. You need to stop trying to cure my OCD. Mom," I say, a little breathless. "It's not your problem. It's mine."

She walks over to me, reaching out and smoothing my hair down. When I was little, she used to straighten my hair to make styling it easier for herself. It wasn't until I was a teenager that I learned how to handle and style my natural curls on my own.

"Sweetheart," she whispers. "Of course it's my problem. Everything about you, from your physical well-being, to what's going on inside that head of yours matters to me." Her eyes glisten. "I just want you to be happy."

Happy.

I remember what Ash said about happiness not being the most relevant or important emotion, and again I'm filled with a strange sense of calm. "Mom," I say. "I've decided to give up my rituals. For good." Her eyes widen, hope threatening to show itself in them, but I continue. "But not because of anything you said or did. Because I want to."

She swallows, and her lips quiver, like she can't decide whether to laugh or cry. "Then, you are welcome to continue living here, Willow."

I pause. "To be honest, I'm not sure if I want to, Mom. But I'll keep you posted."

My mom offers me a half smile. Her eyes are far away. "I understand."

"And if you ever give anyone medication without their consent again, I will make sure you lose your nursing license."

I look her hard in the eye and walk out of her room,

before she can say anything else. Behind me, I hear her sharp intake of breath, but I don't turn around to see her expression. I close her bedroom door behind me.

Even though I've said everything I need to, I can't help but still feel unsatisfied. And then I realize my mom never apologized to me. In fact, I bet she wouldn't even take it back if she could. And that hurts almost more than the fact that she did it in the first place.

I need to see Theo. I'm heading straight for the guest house when I'm brought up short by something shiny parked in the driveway.

It's a motorcycle.

I stare at it, unsure if I'm hallucinating, when Theo comes outside. When he sees me, his eyes flood with relief. "Willow."

"What is this?" I ask him, unable to help it. I feel like I've walked into a brick wall.

"How are you?" he murmurs, pulling me into his strong arms. "I was worried about you. You didn't respond to any of my messages."

"I'm fine. I turned off my phone last night so my mom couldn't call." I close my eyes, embracing his warmth and the feeling of being tucked into him like this. And then I remember the shiny piece of machinery eavesdropping on our conversation. I pull away from him reluctantly, gesturing to the bike. "Is this yours?"

He tilts his head at me, momentarily confused.

"That's a motorcycle," I clarify. "Where did it come from?"

"Ah." Theo glares at the bike like it's offended him. "This ruddy thing. It showed up this morning as an anonymous gift. No return address either, so it looks like I'm stuck with it."

I gape. "Someone dropped off a motorcycle for you *as a gift?*"

He nods, shrugging a little. "It appears so." He grabs a tag on one of the handlebars and shows it to me. *To Theo,* it reads in a typed font. *From, Anonymous.*

I laugh uneasily, my mind running through a list of possible admirers who could have given him such an expensive gift without taking credit. "Do you know how to ride one?"

"Of course." He grins. "I used to ride my dad's all the time. Though I rode the tube far more often." When I don't respond, completely shocked and slightly awed, he asks, "Would you like a go?"

"A . . . go?" I've forgotten how to speak.

"Ride with me." He holds his hand out, waiting for me to take it. He arches a brow at me, and I'm filled with so much dread, I'm surprised I'm standing upright. "I mean, you obviously don't have to," he says. "But it would be quite fun. And a step toward number three on your list."

3. Sitting in the passenger seat of a car while someone else drives.

It's finally hitting me this bike is Theo's now. And he

intends to ride it. On the street. Motorcycles are so much more dangerous than cars, which terrify me as it is.

"My mom isn't going to kick me out anymore," I tell him, slightly breathless. "But I still want to do this. I want to stop using rituals, for myself. And then I want to move the hell out of her house."

Theo raises his eyebrows, a slow grin spreading across his lips. "Is that so? Then the obvious choice would be for you to accompany me."

I've managed to stay mostly ritual free today, with the exception of some thoughts. But right now, there is nothing I want to do more than retreat into myself and let my anxiety find an outlet through my rituals. I want to comfort myself by going back to the old Willow, the one I decided to throw away last night. The one constantly holding me back. And for the first time, I realize how hard my resolution is going to be to fulfill.

Riding Theo's new bike with him could be a good way to start. It would be scary. It would definitely give me anxiety. But I could ride with him and try to resist performing any rituals. At the same time, I'm absolutely terrified to ride a two-wheeled death machine with him. I can't think of anything worse at the moment, actually.

So, I do what the old Willow would do. I search for a way to buy myself some time to hyperventilate. "I need to change my clothes first," I say, which is actually true. There's no way I'm getting on that thing unless I'm covered from head to toe. I'd like to avoid getting skinned alive, if possible.

"All right." Theo leans against the closed garage door to wait for me. He picks his nails, oblivious to what's happening inside me.

I go to my room and sit down on the floor. It's mostly clean, with a few things purposefully out of place. To anyone else, it would look pretty normal, but to me, everything is where it is for a reason. Normally, being here would set my anxiety at ease, but knowing what I'm about to do has my heart racing already.

1, 2, 3, 4, 5. Tap, tap, tap, tap, tap.

Thinking the sequence of numbers and tapping calms me instantly, but I'm also pricked with a sting of guilt and shame for having such a weak moment.

I am better than this.

And even though I know it's true, I feel so, so small right now. I need to talk to Ash.

I send her a novel of a text message, explaining exactly what's happening, and how I'm feeling. I hit send, close my eyes, pressing my fingers to my temples. I breathe in and out, trying desperately not to tap as I do, willing myself not to breathe to a particular rhythm.

I don't even realize when Ash comes into my room. How did she get here so quickly? How long have I been sitting here? Her face a fierce mask of disapproval. "Pull yourself together. Are you fucking joking?"

I close my eyes. "I'm scared! I want to be brave, but it's a motorcycle!"

Ash crosses her arms. "Did you mean what you said? About actually trying?"

I nod tightly, my lips thinning into a line.

"Then I don't give a flying fuck if you're scared! Go hop on that bike with that sexy hunk of a man and stop bitching!"

I groan. "Why don't you just go with him?" I'm trying to buy more time to mentally prepare myself and Ash knows it.

She glares at me. "He's not my type. Too regal. Not to mention," she says, considering, "I'm pregnant."

"I know you, and I know you'd give anything to be the one riding on the back of his motorcycle." I'm saying it more to myself than to her, as if voicing aloud Ash's inherent courage will allow me to muster up some of my own.

"Yeah, except if it was me, we'd just lose the motorcycle and get straight to the point of riding."

"Ashton!" I resist the urge to laugh.

She holds her hands up. "Okay, fine! There would be foreplay involved."

I slap a hand on my face. This is what I have to deal with.

"Okay, look, Willow," she begins again. "You really have nothing to be afraid of. I've gone on plenty of rides with guys in my lifetime, with and without motorcycles, and both are really fun." She smiles like her advice is helpful.

I peer up at her, wishing she could just occupy my body and be me for this small bit of time. Why do I have to be the one with anxiety? Why couldn't I have been born brave, headstrong, and carefree? It isn't fair. Life isn't fair.

I don't know why I'm wallowing. I know this, that nothing is fair. So I sit up and take a deep breath. The only way for me to be brave, headstrong, and carefree, is to work toward it. Since I wasn't born with those particular qualities, I'll have to develop them myself.

Seventeen

Theo is still waiting for me outside. I'm honestly surprised he didn't conclude that I'd chickened out.

I'm garbed in a stiff pair of jeans, boots, and a pullover sweater. My hair is in a low braid, draped over my shoulder.

Theo's relief when he sees me is palpable. He gestures to his bike. "Are you ready?"

"To get on this death trap with you? Yes." I nod, quickly. "Yes, I really am. I'm ready."

He studies me, his eyes lingering on mine for a moment too long. "Are you sure?" He brushes my cheek with his finger. "Will you tell me if it's too much for you? I don't want to put you through anything you aren't ready for."

It's like he can read my mind, but I don't know what I'm more nervous about: backing down or getting on that bike. My smile is weak. "I promise."

"All right then." He grabs a helmet from the seat of the bike. Before I know it, he's handing me one as well.

"The bike has two helmets?" I ask him.

"Of course." He frowns. "You didn't think there was any way I'd let you ride without one, did you?" I briefly wonder why whoever gifted him the bike would give him an extra helmet unless it already came with it.

Theo holds up a finger. "A few things to note." He pats the seat of the bike. "I'm all for ladies first, but you'll have to get on after I do, so I can keep the bike steady."

I nod, willing myself to pay close attention. "Okay."

"If for any reason at all you want to stop, just say so," Theo says softly.

I frown. "But how will you hear me? Won't it be too loud?"

"It will be like talking on the phone," he says, tapping a small microphone attached to the helmet. "The helmet has Bluetooth," he explains.

I raise my eyebrows, not willing to admit aloud that I'm impressed. Theo slides the helmet over his face, and swings one leg over the bike with ease. He holds out a hand to help me up, but I hesitate.

"Alright?" his muffled voice asks.

I take a deep breath. I can do this. I take his outstretched hand and hoist myself over the seat, struggling less than I thought I would. With Theo's feet on the ground to balance the bike, it actually doesn't move around too much.

"Ready?" I hear Theo's voice through the electronic device inside the helmet. His tone is so clear, it feels like he's speaking to me inside my head. Though it's slightly unnerving initially, I have to admit it's also comforting. He's right; it does sound like we're talking on the phone.

"Yes," I breathe. "I'm ready."

Theo starts the engine, and I feel the bike come to life beneath me. The reverberation reminds me of a purring cat, a running washer machine. Its steadiness soothes me for some inexplicable reason. The motorcycle makes a sound that one can only describe as a *vroom*.

And then we start moving.

We take off at a speed that makes my stomach drop like a rollercoaster. I keep my eyes shut at first but realize quickly how much that isn't going to help me. When I finally peek, I see a bit of Theo's shoulder and the street blurring below us. Without turning my head too much, I watch my neighborhood fly by, the wind whipping my braid like a victory flag.

But the most surprising part of it all is that I feel like I'm *flying.*

We are flying.

My mouth splits into a grin so wide, it hurts against the restraints of the helmet, and I don't understand why I'm not scared. In fact, I've never felt so exhilarated.

"Care for some music?" Theo asks. "I can connect to my mobile."

"Sure," I say breathlessly.

He presses a button on the helmet, and music begins to play through the speaker in my ear. I recognize the song as *Every Time You Go* by Ellie Goulding. I actually laugh aloud. "You like this song?" I hope he can still hear me despite the music playing.

And then I hear him in my ear, only slightly louder than the song. "Actually, I saw it on your playlist." There's a smile in his voice. "I added it to mine a while back out of curiosity. I thought it might relax you now to hear a song you like."

Now I'm grinning impossibly wider than before. "How did you even . . . " I trail off, deciding I actually don't care how he managed to sneak a peek at my playlist. "Thank you," I say, simply.

We turn out of my neighborhood onto a main road, and while I've been enchanted up to this point, I feel my first surge of unease. There are other drivers to factor into the equation now.

We peel down the street and I try not to scream, certain it will hurt Theo's ears. I tighten my grip around his waist, and my heart rate increases in response. He's so close right now, I'm sure if I weren't wearing a helmet, I would be able to smell his skin, his neck, his cologne. The thought makes me dizzy.

Out of the corner of my eye, I watch the landscape pass me in a way that is completely different from riding in a car. I am not protected by the barrier of a window, a door, a metal frame. It's both liberating and terrifying. I feel as if I could fly off the back of the seat at any moment, up into the air, soaring through the skies like a balloon.

The song changes, and this time it's one I don't recognize. "What band is this?" I ask.

"It's Phoenix," Theo replies. "Do you like it?"

I pause, giving the tune a listen, and find I do like it. "It's not awful," I tell him.

He laughs.

We're about to get on the freeway. I squeeze my eyes shut for a moment and then remember I don't like the way it feels to ride with my eyes closed.

I'm completely out of control. And also, a bit nauseous.

Deep breath, I tell myself. *In and out. But not any specific number of times. You can do this.*

As if he senses my internal struggle, he asks, "Alright?"

"I—I think so," I mutter.

"Let's pull over," he says.

"No," I say quickly. "I'm okay. I'm fine." I take another deep breath, steadying myself. My hands tighten around his waist.

I imagine my happy place. I'm lying in a spring meadow under a tree with a book. My little black dog on the grass beside me. The twittering of little birds all around me. Hummingbirds' wings flapping, bluebirds chirping, robins flying—

Our light turns green, and we enter the freeway ramp. I try not to focus on all the cars surrounding us. All the accidents that happen here. The fast speed mandatory for us to travel at.

Instead, I focus on Theo. His strong, broad shoulders. His British accent. The dark hair hiding under his helmet. His blue eyes piercing through me every time they stare at me. His intoxicating scent.

We take the first exit.

I frown beneath my helmet, wondering why we're slowing down, why we're stopping in a shopping center. When Theo pulls into a parking space and turns off the bike, the absence of the rumble echoes through my body. He gets down, and I worry for a moment it will tip, but he holds it upright with his hand and secures the kickstand.

"What are we doing?" I demand. "Why did we stop?"

He removes his helmet, and stares at me incredulously. "Willow, you clearly were uncomfortable."

I take my helmet off too, showing him my indignation. "I was not!" But I know he can see the lie on my face easily.

He sighs. "If you say you're fine, I believe you. But you can tell me the truth." Theo crosses his arms. "Were you frightened?" he asks me, his tone plain and serious.

I close my eyes. "I wasn't." I don't want to see his face when I admit the truth. "Until we got on the freeway."

He's silent, and when I open my eyes, his expression is gentle. "It's all right, you know," he says. "I think it's brilliant that you enjoyed as much of the ride as you did." He flashes an impossibly white grin.

"Well, we're not done," I inform him. "I want to go again. Highway this time."

He arches a brow. "Are you sure? I'd say you did well enough today."

"I'm sure." My tone is firm, and I'm filled with a calm resolve. I haven't had any deeply intrusive thoughts yet. I try to keep from thinking too in depth about it, for fear that doing so will induce them.

He puts his helmet back on. "All right then, let's go."

The freeway isn't that bad.

It's only scary if I think about it, if I let myself dwell on the reasons why it's dangerous. So instead, I ponder why this is better than riding through town. For one, we don't have to stop at any lights, which rips me out of the very welcome illusion that I'm flying, like a bodiless entity traveling at the speed of light. Like a bird permeating the condensation we call clouds.

We never stop. We fly across the roads, not held back by a single thing, physical, mental, or emotional. I can't believe I find so much meaning, so much depth, so much purpose in the small act of traveling in a new vehicle.

But it's more than that.

I'm finally allowing myself to embrace a situation that's entirely out of my control. The restraints on my mind have loosened, allowing me enough space to crawl out, to set myself free. It's the first and largest step I've ever taken towards escaping the prison I've built around myself.

When we arrive back at my house, it's too soon; I don't want this to end. I want to live on the back of this motorcycle, holding Theo close, all the while hidden from his view. He turns off the bike once we're parked in the driveway. Again, my body feels like it's lacking something without the motorcycle emitting its vibrations through me.

Theo helps me off and removes my helmet. Without the barrier of it, I feel almost naked, strangely vulnerable and exposed. "I think it's safe to say you were brilliant, little Willow." Theo holds the helmet between us. His eyes are hooded, gazing at me in a way that makes my stomach flutter.

"*I* think it's safe to say I deserve a break from ERP tomorrow."

"If you so desire," Theo says, arching a brow. "But then, you won't have an excuse to come and see me."

I laugh. "I wasn't aware I needed one."

"Of course you do. I might get the wrong idea otherwise."

I roll my eyes, unable to conceal my grin. "Goodnight, Theo."

He smiles faintly. "Goodnight, little Willow." When he grabs my face and presses his lips against mine, my knees threaten to buckle. His lips are so soft. I twine my hands in his hair, and Theo grips my waist. The kiss lasts long enough to make my body react, the heat between my legs making me squirm.

When I go inside my house, I lie down on my bed and stare at the ceiling. My thoughts linger on Theo. On how much I wish he was lying next to me. The way his muscles flexed as he worked the bike, and how the feel of him calmed me in my brief moments of nervousness.

For the first time in my entire life since developing obsessive compulsive disorder, I made it through an extremely anxiety-inducing experience—one the old Willow would have never, in a million years, voluntarily placed herself in.

I rode on the back of a motorcycle.

And I didn't perform a single ritual.

Eighteen

"Willow?" My mom knocks on my bedroom door. "May I come in?"

It's been nearly two weeks since I've last spoken to her. Two more weeks of ERP with Theo and progress she can't deny. But it doesn't mean my feelings have simply gone away, or that I'm ready to talk to her.

So far I've been successful in avoiding her, but I know it can't last forever. "Sure." I set down my paperback of *To Kill a Mockingbird*. Since finishing my reread of the Harry Potter series, I needed something to distract me from starting it all over again. "Come in, I guess."

My mom enters my room and sits on my bed. Offering me a weak smile, she smooths my hair down and takes in my face. She wrinkles her nose. "No makeup today?" she asks. "Did you go to school like that?"

I sigh. "What do you need, Mom?"

Her smile wavers. "I just wanted to know if you made your decision yet. If you're moving out or staying here. With me."

I fidget with my hands. "I have, actually."

She holds up a finger. "Before you say it, I want to tell you something."

I raise my eyebrows. "What is it?" Whatever she has to say probably won't influence my decision. I still don't feel like I can trust her. And she hasn't apologized once for what she did.

My mom sniffles, smoothing out my bedding with concentration. "Gus broke up with me."

"He did?" My mouth falls open.

She nods, pressing her lips together so tightly that wrinkles form around them. "He didn't like the idea of me putting those meds in your food. He thought it was wrong."

"Well, it was wrong, Mom."

She doesn't say anything for a long moment. "It's just going to be me here," she says so quietly. "All alone, if you leave me." Her eyes shine.

I lower my gaze. "Maybe you should have thought about that before you did it."

Her eyes flicker to mine. "Does that mean you decided to move?"

I shrug. "I think so."

My mom stands up and crosses her arms. "Where will you go? You don't have any money saved. You don't make enough walking those dogs, and if you leave, I won't pay for school. You really don't have a choice here, Willow."

"No, Mom." I meet her gaze, low and steady. "You don't have a choice."

She shakes her head. "Fine then. Leave. Just like *him*."

Something in my chest falters. "My dad?" I raise my voice. "Just like my dad?"

She glares at me, not even trying to hide the resentment radiating off her. "Yes."

My throat becomes thick with angry tears. "I remind you of him, don't I? And you can't stand it! You think of him when you look at me, and that's why you hate me so much."

My mom looks baffled. "Hate you? Don't be ridiculous, Willow. I love you."

I swallow. "But you see him in me, Mom. Admit it." I hold up my arm and point to it. "And only because I'm black!"

She scoffs. "Well, it isn't your beautiful hazel eyes."

The anger building inside me explodes. "Well, I'm not him! I know you resent me for what he did to you. For cheating and abandoning you while you were pregnant with me, and maybe even for dying before he had a chance to fix things. But you can't turn me into *you* with hurtful words. You have no idea how heavy they are. And ironically, I used to wish I looked just like you so you wouldn't be in pain every time you saw me."

I take a deep breath. I can't believe I'm telling her all

this, but something inside me has finally cracked, like a dam, and the giant lake of feelings I've been holding in is impossible to contain now. I continue. "But if I had to choose now, I would rather be black, like him. He was never here, but at least he never hurt me like you have."

Her face becomes impossibly whiter. She doesn't say another word. Just stares at me like she's never seen me before, like she doesn't even recognize me. And then she turns on her heel and marches out the door, closing it a little too loudly.

My shoulders sag. I sit in silence for a long moment, trying to slow my rapid breathing.

It feels like a giant weight has lifted off my shoulders. But at the same time, I know how badly my words hurt my mom.

I grab my phone and call Theo. I need to hear his voice. His British accent could do wonders on even the most stressed person alive.

He answers on the first ring. "Miss me already? We just had school together."

I melt against my pillows, instantly mollified by his voice. "Come over," I say softly.

"Tonight. I have something for you."

I frown. "For me? What is it?"

I hear the smile in his voice when he says, "Patience, little Willow. I'll bring it to you after your mum goes to work. It has to dry just a bit more."

He hangs up, and I'm left even more confused than

before. But rather than dwell on what the surprise could possibly be, I pass the time reading, occasionally sending Theo emojis and texts. I even pour myself a cup of tea and light a candle.

A few hours pass, and I'm just about to doze off when a knock on my bedroom window breaks me away from my thoughts of sleep. I peek through and see Theo.

I hold up my finger and motion for him to come around to the front door. When I unlock it, we tiptoe through the dark halls, careful not to alert my mom. She'll be leaving for work any minute. As soon as we're both in my bedroom, I close the door and lock the handle. The last thing I need is for my mom to check on me before she leaves.

I smile shyly at him through the dim lighting in my room, his face illuminated by the candlelight. His eyes are mostly pupil, dark with rings of light blue. He looks freshly showered. His hair is still damp, the smell of his aftershave sharp and clean.

I realize for the first time he's carrying a flat square wrapped in tarp. It's about the size of a small laptop. I point to it. "What's that?"

He holds it behind his back. "Your surprise."

"Can I have it?"

"I'll trade it for a kiss."

I nod and wrap my arms around his neck, kissing him softly. Theo grabs my waist with his other hand, bringing me against him. I pull away, unwilling to let him distract me. I can't wait a moment longer for my surprise. I briefly wonder if it actually is a laptop, but then remember he said it needed to dry.

Theo places the square on my bed and waits for me to unwrap it. I remove the tarp, careful not to peek until it's completely off.

When I stare at the square—no, *canvas*—in front of me, I can't breathe.

"I remember you telling me about your happy place." Theo says nonchalantly. "You told me when you have anxiety, it sometimes helps when you imagine it. Yourself lying in a spring meadow with a book. Your little black dog on the grass beside you."

"Theo." My heart is racing. "You—"

"I don't ever want it to become hard for you to visualize. When you can't see it, you rely heavier on your rituals. And when you first told me about it, I thought to myself how lovely it would be to never have to leave the place that makes you feel so at ease. I thought perhaps if you had your happy place with you, to look at and hold in your hands whenever you felt sad or anxious or scared . . . you would never have to leave it. You could stay in it always." All traces of teasing are gone. His voice is so soft, so gentle and I still can't breathe. I can't move. I simply listen to his words and stare at him, transfixed.

I'd thought Theo's paintings invoked specific emotions in me, but things I felt while looking at his previous paintings were nothing, *nothing* compared to this.

I'm staring at myself on the canvas. My face is painted

in shades of light and dark, my expression more peaceful than I've ever seen it in a mirror. I'm wearing a long, fluffy, white dress with a matching hat that ties underneath my chin, my curly hair spilling out around me. I'm lying on my stomach, and my ankles are crossed in the air. There's a book in my hands, and a large willow tree offering me plenty of shade to read. The grass is swaying in the wind, wildflowers sprinkled throughout its body like freckles. Next to me, sleeping soundly, is a tiny black dog.

"Theodore," I choke, not caring that my face is wet with tears. "Are you serious? You painted my happy place?"

His eyebrows pull together. "Did I get it right? You don't exactly look happy right now." He glances down at the canvas.

I reach for the painting and stare at it. I can't stop staring.

It's like he's taken part of my mind and turned it into something tangible. And taken the happy feeling with him too, stitching it inside the wood and plaster and sealing it with the paint.

Fresh tears travel down my cheeks, and I place the picture on my bed behind me, gently, before turning back to him and kissing him with so much force, he's momentarily astonished.

And then he's kissing me back.

His lips part mine and his hands tangle in my hair. I urge myself impossibly closer against him, not an inch of air separating our skin.

I tear at his shirt, pulling it over his head.

"Willow," Theo says. He stops my hands with his own, searching my face. "What—"

"Please," I interrupt him. "Don't try to stop me." I meet his gaze, communicating with my eyes that I want this, to be close to him.

To continue.

Theo releases an unsteady breath and let's go of my hands, placing his own on the sides of my face so he can kiss me again.

I close my eyes as he makes his way from my lips to my neck. My stomach flutters, and the rest of our clothes come off in a rush. With nothing left but skin between us, we're closer than we've ever been before. And yet, it's still not close enough for me.

I grip his shoulders and lie down on the floor, pulling him with me.

Theo's fingers caress my body, heat blazing between us, until my breathing gets heavier. My body stiffens in antici-pation and I move his hand lower, until his fingers are pressed against the most sensitive part of me. "Please," I whisper. "Don't stop."

Theo's eyes darken. "Bloody hell, Willow."

I kiss him again, more deeply this time, and his fingers move intently, making me squirm and gasp for air. I can't get enough. "More," I breathe. "Please."

A wicked gleam lights the darkness in his eyes and he begins kissing a line down my stomach. The carpet is rough under my back, but Theo's lips are impossibly soft. His mouth travels lower and lower, exploring freely and continuing even when I grab his hair with both hands. I gasp. A surge of pleasure like I've never experienced before consumes me until I'm unaware of space and time, of mind and matter. My body trembles and I'm suddenly weak.

I am liquid.

When my heart eventually slows, I open my eyes. Theo grins, clearly satisfied by my reaction. I part my lips, and he takes the opportunity to kiss me again, this time softly, tenderly. I run my hands along Theo's tightly muscled arms, caging me. Our gazes lock for a moment and electricity sizzles between us. "Willow," he says, his voice hardly more than a whisper. "Willow, if you want to stop—"

"No," I say firmly. I feel the weight of my words as I say them, but they ring true.

He exhales and touches his forehead to mine. "Then please tell me you have a condom, since I already know damn well you aren't on the pill."

I can't help but smile. He's right of course. I'm not on the pill. I've never taken it in my life, but I do have a few condoms. I point at my nightstand. "They're in the bottom drawer."

Theo takes one and removes it from its package. The break in our physical touch clears my head and for the briefest moment I'm anxious. But the feeling disappears as soon as it arrives, replaced by frantic anticipation.

Theo. This is Theo.

He kisses me again. I grip his shoulders tightly and lift my hips.

Theo breaks our kiss as our bodies connect and pleasure courses through my entire body. Each continuous movement brings our energy closer and closer to a tipping point. I dig my nails into his back, clinging to him desperately.

In this moment, with my blood rushing beneath Theo's fingertips, with his skin ending where mine begins, with my heart in his hands, I think, *there's no going back now.*

And I don't want to.

My vision transforms into an explosion of stars.

Every nerve in my body intensifies beyond what I can bear. It seems to last forever, and when Theo finally relaxes against me, we lie still together, in a heap on the floor. I have no idea if we lie for seconds or minutes or hours. My arms and legs are wound around him like a tangle of vines and his heart races in my ear, thrumming like a lullaby. As I drift into unconsciousness, I can't help but think that I've never heard anything so perfect.

Nineteen

"Oh my God," Ash says at school the next morning. She's already in her seat by the time I clock in and sit at our table. "You had sex!"

"Keep your voice down!" I glance around, horrified, but luckily no one else is nearby and Theo is headed to the restroom. I stare at Ash, my confusion overpowering my desire to remain discreet. "How do you know? I mean, what makes you think that?" I try to keep my tone hushed.

Her lips pull up into a slight smirk. "It's written all over your face, babe. I just hope it was with Theo. Finally."

My eyes widen, and I try to mask my features into that of a closed book rather than a wide open one.

Theo comes back, taking his seat next to me. Ash's eyes light up, but she's prevented from interrogating him when

Mrs. Harrison starts taking attendance. She passes out sheets of paper—which means we'll be learning something new today—licking her thumb in between each page. Gross.

"We're learning perms today," Mrs. Harrison tells us. "Get your rods from your lockers and follow the instructions I passed out. Come to me if you need help, and I'll be checking your work as you go."

We get our perm rods and set up our mannequin heads. The odor of the perm solution begins to permeate the room. I glance at Ash, thinking about all the chemicals in the solution. It can't possibly be good for the baby—for her to inhale and sometimes touch toxic ingredients.

"Is it okay for you to be around this stuff?" I ask her.

"I don't know, but it fucking reeks," she complains. "I thought I wouldn't have to smell actual shit for like, six more months."

I laugh, and accidentally lose hold of my section of hair. Rolling the perm proves more complicated than expected. It's a challenge to hold the sections of hair between the endpapers without them slipping out, and to roll them onto the rod without the hair sliding out the edges. I realize I'm not the only one struggling when I look around and see most of the other students in the same predicament as me.

Theo, however, has already completed an entire section.

"How are you so good at this?" Ash asks him.

"He's a hands-on kind of guy, remember?" I tell her.

Ash smiles and raises a brow. "You would know, Willow."

One of the girls in our class, Chutney, overhears and I don't miss the venomous glare she shoots me. I don't understand, considering she's never talked to me or Theo before. I swallow and turn to him. "Really though. How are you doing that?"

Theo chuckles. "It's easy, little Willow. I'll show you." He moves behind me, where I'm trying to trap a section of hair between the endpapers. The hair won't stop slipping out.

"First of all," he tells me, "your sections are too large." Theo's voice is husky and deep as he reaches around me from behind to grab my section. "Far too much hair. And you need to get your tissues wetter." He holds a paper-thin slice of hair between his fingers before sandwiching it in the endpapers he's holding, and then soaking them with my water bottle. "There. Now, hold it like this." He grasps my hand and puts the hair in it, moving my fingers into the right position. They stick perfectly. His touch lingers on mine longer than necessary before he moves back to his own mannequin, and Ash smirks at me.

Mrs. Harrison walks around, checking everyone's progress. She stops often, showing the students the correct way to roll the rod, or hold the endpaper. When she gets to our aisle, she checks Theo's work first. "Amazing job," she says, taking off her glasses to look him in the eye. "You really got the hang of this pretty quickly, eh?" She turns to my mannequin. "Not bad, Willow," she says, putting her glasses back on. "Try to keep your sections even, like Theodore's, if you can. You want each curl to come out the same diameter as the rest."

Theo gives me a cocky smile when she leaves, and I squirt perm solution at him.

"*Oi*," he complains. "That burns!"

I laugh, and he sprays me back. It does sting a little, like lemon juice.

"Knock it off you two, or I'll hose you down with water from the shampoo bowls," Ash tells us.

At lunch, Theo and I get coffee—only one, since we don't have an extra cupholder on his motorcycle. Luckily, he buys the biggest size and we manage to ride back to school without spilling it. The sky made up its mind to be foggy today, but the slight wind that tickles my neck is hot. The afternoon crowds of students weave in between cars trying to park, some holding fresh to-go cups of coffee or bags of fast-food.

"Shut the fuck up," Ash says when she sees us in the parking lot.

I let my arms fall from around Theo's waist. "What?" I ask.

"How did you not have a conniption fit on the way here?" she demands. "You're riding that thing with him *again?*"

I shrug. "It's actually kind of fun." Sometimes I forget the progress I'm making isn't obvious to everyone. Every hurdle I face is such an achievement to me, I feel as if I'm constantly wearing triumph on my face like a mask.

Ash gapes at me, but I ignore her, taking Theo's hand and letting him help me down. "You guys are too much," she says. "I'm going to find Joseph."

We drink our coffee on a bench near the cosmetology building, taking turns sipping it.

"I never used to drink so much coffee," Theo tells me, "until I came here."

I cock my head. "What did you get your caffeine from?"

"Mostly black tea. Coffee now and then, I suppose. But you Americans take it to another level."

I laugh. "I can't imagine my life without coffee. It's tangible happiness."

Theo chuckles. "More like energy, if you ask me." He glances at his pocket. "Someone's ringing me." When he takes his phone out, he frowns at the screen, and then turns it around to show me who's calling. *Dad.*

I raise my eyebrows. "Are you going to answer it?"

"Of course not." Theo ignores the call. "I never do."

"What if it's important?" I ask.

Theo shakes his head. "He's only calling to demand I come back home, I'm sure."

Theo's phone rings again, and this time Eliza is calling. "Answer it," I suggest.

Theo sighs and brings his phone to his ear. "What on earth do you want, Eliza?" Theo's tone is clipped. She says something back to him, and his face remains unreadable. Bored. "I don't care," he states before promptly hanging up.

I lean forward. "What did she say?"

Theo sighs. "That my dad is sending me a warning. If I don't return home tomorrow, that is."

I raise my eyebrows. "A warning? What kind of warning?"

Theo shrugs. "I've no idea. Nor do I believe him."

My thoughts are a flutter of chaos as I try to glean what could possibly happen, what Rob could do from England to warn Theo. Would he do something that could actually harm him?

Breathe, I tell myself. *Don't tap. Just breathe.*

The bell rings, signaling the end of our break. Most of our class is nearby, and they come inside promptly, not wanting to be late. Theo and I clock in last, just after Raymond and Charlie.

"I'm a little worried Ash isn't back yet," I tell Theo, scanning the classroom for her face.

Theo frowns and tugs on one of my curls. "Don't worry, little Willow. I'm sure she's done snogging Joseph and will be back any moment."

I nod at his words, and then realize belatedly that I've started tapping.

I stop.

"You can do this," I whisper to myself.

To prevent Ash from being late, I should keep tapping. I should rearrange my station, or count.

No more.

Instead, I take a deep breath and think of my happy place.

Theo and I take a seat, and Mrs. Harrison informs us the rest of the day will be dedicated to working on our fashion show models. Since I'm Ash's model, this means that I'll be playing mannequin all day when she gets back. And so will Theo as Charlie's model.

Eva leans across Ash's empty desk to tell me something. "Your cousin is here."

I turn around and see Ash rushing inside. She grabs her timesheet just as the bell rings.

"Oh, come on," she whines to Mrs. Harrison. "You saw me come in on time. Can I please not lose fifteen minutes?"

The instructor clicks her tongue. "The rules exist for a reason."

Ash rolls her eyes and flips off Mrs. Harrison after she turns around. When she sits down next to me, she whispers, "Why didn't you clock me in?"

I stare at her incredulously. "Seriously? How was I supposed to know you were even coming back? If you didn't show, I could have gotten sent home for the day."

She flips her hair. "Fine."

Theo leans over. "Why were you late?" he asks her.

"I was hardly late!" She pauses. "And I might have been making out with Joseph. So what?"

Theo smirks at me. "Told you."

Charlie makes his way over to our table. His hair is in freshly gelled spikes, his leather jacket dressing up his scrubs a bit. He smells like cigarettes and expensive cologne.

"What are you thinking for Willow's hair?" he asks Ash. "For Theo I know what I'm doing."

Ash leans forward in her desk, her voice animated. "Curls galore, which obviously won't be hard. And look what I found on Pinterest."

Charlie studies Ash's phone, and the two begin comparing costume ideas.

"I can't believe this semester will be done in a little over a month," I say quietly to Theo.

He glances at me. "I know. And then I'll be returning home to London."

His words make my body feel like it's been submerged in ice water. I stare at my hands. "I wish you could just stay."

His expression softens. "I know. But I'm not an American citizen, Willow. I have to go back home."

"But don't you have a student visa? Can't you at least stay until you get your cosmetology license?" I don't know why I'm suddenly panicking. I knew this was coming. Theo even offered to let me come with him, but instead, I chose to stay in California so I can be near Ash. To move out and find an over-priced apartment. To live alone. I don't have a right to complain.

"I could come back," he says. "But I still need to return home between semesters."

Tap, tap, tap, tap, tap.

The ritual happens before I can stop it. I don't even mean to do it, but it happens anyway. And Theo notices. He laces his fingers through mine, rubbing his thumb against my skin.

I swallow, hard. The thought of him being so far . . . in London. It's terrifying. I don't even realize I'm about to cry until he sighs and touches my face.

"Willow . . . what's the matter?" He rubs his thumb against my cheek, and for some reason, it calms me. I swallow back my tears, willing myself not to cry.

"I just didn't expect to feel this way when it comes to you leaving," I say, clearing my throat.

Theo searches my face. "I'm still here," he says. "I'm not leaving yet."

Ash and Charlie approach our tables from the other side of the room. I didn't even notice they left.

"We grabbed some styling products from the lab," Ash tells me. "You guys are going to look so fucking hot."

"What's the theme for the show, again?" I ask her, trying to sound normal. Theo drops his hand from my face, and I blink to clear my eyes. We were assigned our theme a few weeks ago, but with everything that's been on my mind, I haven't been as focused on school as I should be.

"Victorian era," Charlie says, hardly able to mask the excitement in his tone. He claps his hands together. "Such fun."

We make our way to the shampoo bowls, and Ash washes my hair and combs through it with ease. We've grown up together playing beauty salon all our lives. She knows how to handle my mane.

But when I sit down at her station, she starts adding perm rods throughout my hair. I give her a quizzical expression. "Isn't this a little counterproductive? I already have curly hair."

She rolls her eyes. "I know, babe. But these are going to give you *different* curls. More defined, controllable curls that will do what I want them to."

I smirk. "Sounds like wishful thinking."

Theo is getting his make-up done by Charlie, and I try not to laugh at his obvious discomfort when Charlie lines his eye with a dark pencil.

"I just don't see why this is necessary, mate," he complains.

Charlie shushes him. "This will make your features more visible from the stage," he assures Theo.

Mrs. Harrison observes each pair as she makes her way around, row by row. When she gets to Charlie and Theo, she visibly swoons. "You look like the cover of a naughty romance novel, Theodore," she informs him. He glances at me helplessly, and the laugh I've been trying to contain bursts from my lips.

"So what the fuck is up with you guys?" Ash asks me, her tone quiet enough that only I can hear. "Have you had sex or not? Because you were riding that bike like you wished it were him."

I blush furiously. "Oh, my—"

"Don't even try to deny it," she interrupts. She has her no-bullshit look on her face, made even more severe by her bun hairstyle and red lipstick.

I purse my lips and remain silent, which is basically all the confirmation she needs. Her knowing smile tells me as much.

Ash continues working on my hair, seeming satisfied when the perm rods manipulate my hair into a more defined texture. She practices several up-dos, gives me a full face of makeup, and even does my nails.

Hours later, my legs feel numb from sitting. Theo walks to my station after Mrs. Harrison deems his look complete.

"I can't wait to wash off this rubbish," he states, gesturing at his face. I have to admit, he does look extra hot with all the makeup on.

"Ow," Ash mutters from behind me. I tear my eyes away from Theo. Ash touches her lower stomach.

"Are you okay?" I ask.

She grimaces. "I think so." She takes a deep breath. "Ah! Oh my God. Ow!" Ash shrieks, and every eye in the class is suddenly on her.

Mrs. Harrison frowns in our direction. "Are you okay over there?"

Ash is panting now, holding her stomach with desperation. "I think I need to go to the hospital," she whimpers. "It feels like I'm going into labor."

Twenty

"Again?" Eva asks, rushing over to us. "Your baby legit has it out for you."

"Let's go see your doctor," I tell Ash. "I'll go with you. I'll drive you in your car." I'm already gathering her things, and Theo helps Ash out of her chair.

"Are you going with them?" Eva asks Theo, sounding dismayed.

"Yes," Theo says at the same time that I say, "No."

"Just stay here," I tell him.

"Like hell," Theo says.

I shake my head. "You don't need to lose the hours, and you'll probably end up having to leave the room anyway."

Theo's lips form a tight line, but he nods after a moment and then kisses me on the lips, right there in the middle of the classroom. My cheeks burn. If I weren't so worried about Ash and her baby's well-being, I would be both embarrassed and flattered in this moment.

"I'm taking her to her doctor," I tell Mrs. Harrison. "She isn't feeling well."

Mrs. Harrison nods, her eyes tight. "I can't excuse the hours this time."

"That's fine," I say, but my stomach drops. There goes my spotless record. I'll just have to find a way to make up the hours somehow. There's no way I'm making Ash go alone for the sake of perfect attendance.

We rush out the doors and through the parking lot. I glance briefly at Theo's bike parked a couple spots down.

Ash groans, doubling over, and I try not to panic.

Ash is not in pain because of me, I tell myself. *It has nothing to do with my lack of rituals.*

I get in the driver's side, contemplating.

But what if it is my fault?

I stare at the rearview mirror, and decide this small, insignificant ritual couldn't hurt. If anything, maybe it will somehow make the situation better. I smile at my reflection in the mirror.

1 second, 2 seconds, 3 seconds.

And sigh with relief and regret.

When we get to the hospital Ash is admitted right away, even though the waiting room is packed with people who got there first. The doctor asks her a million questions while prepping her for an ultrasound.

"How far along are you?" he asks calmly.

She shakes her head in exasperation. "I don't know. Something-teen weeks."

He squirts gel onto her stomach and spreads it around like butter with a tiny handheld instrument. The same familiar noise from before sounds from the monitor. The doctor squints into the screen. "What does the pain feel like?"

Ash grits her teeth. "Like someone driving a knife through my—" She breaks off as another contraction seizes her. She takes a deep breath when it's over and says, calmly, "Like period cramps, times a thousand."

"Any blood?" the doctor asks, unfazed.

"No."

His lips thin into a line as he continues examining the screen. "Your baby looks healthy. Measuring sixteen weeks. Good size, healthy heartbeat . . . " He raises his eyebrows. "Would you like to know the gender?"

I smile in excitement, but Ash doesn't react even slightly. "Why am I in pain then, if everything is fine?"

The doctor removes his glasses. "It's likely you were experiencing Braxton-Hicks contractions. Completely normal."

"They didn't feel fucking normal. If childbirth is anything like that, I want to be sedated."

"You can always opt for an epidural," he informs her.

"Fuck that," she says. "Just numb me. Cut me open."

The doctor laughs. "Are you sure about the gender? It's pretty clear . . . "

I look to Ash, not bothering to hide my anticipation. "You should have a gender-reveal party," I say. "It would be so fun!"

Ash snorts. "Yeah, okay. Sure thing. I'll just look for a checklist on Pinterest."

"Can you write it down?" I ask the doctor. "In case she changes her mind?"

He nods. "Absolutely." He hands it to me as Ash gets dressed. The paper in my hand begs me to open it, but I can't ruin the surprise. I'll just have to wait and find out—at the party she *will* be having—with everyone else.

When we're free to go, Ash insists on driving, now that she knows her baby is in perfect health. But of course I refuse to sit in the passenger seat. I get behind the wheel despite Ash's protestations.

"I can't believe you don't care to know the sex," I say and start the car.

She shrugs. "I think it's a boy. But it doesn't matter to me either way. Speaking of sex, how was it with Theo last night?"

I blink furiously. "I don't know what you're talking about."

She arches an eyebrow at me. "If you don't tell me, I'll just ask him."

The blood drains from my face. "Okay, fine!" I sigh, remembering the feel of his skin against mine, the way the urgent longing in the pit of my stomach was finally met with delicious satisfaction. The way it felt to fall asleep in his arms, his even breathing the perfect soundtrack to the best night's sleep I ever could have imagined. His soft lips against my face, my neck, my body. "It was . . . amazing," I whisper.

She grins. "Better than Daniel?"

My heart sinks, her words a needle against my bubble of happiness. Daniel. I hadn't been thinking about him. He didn't cross my mind once while I'd been with Theo. The shame instantly drowns me, guilt weighing my heart down until it sinks to the pit of my stomach. But the guilt isn't for Daniel. I don't feel like I've betrayed him by moving on. The guilt is my own, for not feeling any remorse at doing so.

"I'm so sorry." Her smile vanishes at my expression. She holds up a hand. "I didn't mean to say that. It just came out, I swear."

We sit in silence for the rest of the car ride. I drive us to my house, parking along the curb.

"I'm sorry, babe," she says again, her voice pleading. "I'm such an insensitive bitch."

"No, you're not," I say, taking a deep breath. "It's okay."

Her eyes search my face, as if the truth is hidden there. "Want to read together?"

"Sure," I say, meaning it. I need to take my mind off what she said. "Let's go inside."

I haven't decorated my bedroom walls in years.

Every time I've tried, my anxiety is triggered by the slightest asymmetry of a picture on the wall, whether it's not centered on the wall itself, or tilted to the side. It's never been worth it to me, having to deal with something trivial like a decoration causing my anxiety to spiral out of control. Not to mention, I've never loved a piece of artwork enough to care.

Until now.

Hung in the center of the wall opposite my bed is the painting. The one Theo made of my happy place. My eyes gravitate toward it as soon as I step into my bedroom.

So do Ash's.

"What is *that?*" she says. "Is that you?" She points to the girl in the painting. Her nose is practically touching it, and I resist the urge to tell her to back away.

"Theo made it for me," I tell her. "It's my happy place."

She spins around, turning to face me. Her eyes are wide. "Theo *painted* that?" she asks. "For you? *Of* you?"

I nod.

She presses a hand to her mouth. "No wonder you let him in your pants."

I shake my head, annoyed, though she's clearly joking. "It's so much more than that, Ash. I . . . " I trail off, unable to find any words adequate or satisfactory enough to express the feelings coursing through me. I finally settle on, "I love him."

"Are you serious?" She raises her eyebrows. "Wow.

That's . . . wow." She bites her lip, pondering my confession. "Have you told him?" she asks. "Does he love you?"

I blink at her, realizing I haven't told him how I feel, and I have no idea if he even loves me back. Perhaps I'm just a meaningless fling to him. Just a girl he screwed that semester he spent in California. The possibility makes my chest feel like a wad of wet clay being squeezed in someone's fist. "I don't know."

Ash bites her lip. "Babe, I've been thinking that maybe you should go to London."

"What are you talking about?" I gape at her.

"It's just that . . . " Ash sighs. "I might need to end up taking next semester off to pop out this kid." She touches her stomach. "And if that's the case, I'll only be a season behind you. You should go to school with Theo and all the other Brits when I take that time off."

I shake my head at her slowly. "I'm not going to school without you. This is *our* dream. Not mine alone."

"You're being a dumbass," she informs me. "If our roles were reversed, I would go without you."

"You would not."

"Hell yeah, I would," she says. "Especially if a hot British guy like Theo invited me. Live a little. Let your hair down."

I scoff. "My hair *is* down."

She rolls her eyes. "Seriously, babe." Ash grabs my hand and squeezes it. Her dark eyes shine, a hint of melancholy longing behind their surface. "Do it. Do it for the both of us."

A knot forms in the back of my throat. "It wouldn't be the same without you."

"It's never going to be the same again, anyway," she says. "Not after this baby is born."

I stare at the ground, blinking back the tears threatening to present themselves. "I'll get right on that," I say bitterly. "As soon as he gets here, I'll just tell Theo I love him and that he has a new roommate."

Ash smiles faintly and looks at the time on her phone. "That's in like an hour. Want to read till then?"

I nod, scooting onto one side of my bed so she can take the other. *To Kill a Mockingbird* provides a necessary distraction from the idea of going to school without Ash, and from her earlier comment about Daniel. I don't ever want to compare Theo to Daniel. It's taken years for me to stop feeling depressed about what happened to him, but he would want me to be happy, I think. I know he would at least want me to try.

The time runs away from us, as it always does when I'm immersed in a book. This one in particular is one of the few I've ever related to. Not many people like me are in books, so it's always a surprise when I come across one. It's like an acknowledgement that I exist, somewhere out there in the world; that perhaps, just maybe, I'm not completely alone.

Even if the representation isn't a positive one, at least it's there. I read the part of the story that makes my heart pound with conviction, with true empathy:

"Jem," I asked, "what's a mixed child?"
"Half white, half colored. You've seen 'em, Scout. You
know that red-kinkyheaded one that delivers for the
drugstore. He's half white. They're real sad."
"Sad, how come?"
"They don't belong anywhere. Colored folks won't have
'em because they're half white; white folks won't have
'em cause they're colored, so they're just inbetweens,
don't belong anywhere. But Mr. Dolphus, now, they say
he's shipped two of his up north. They don't mind 'em up
north. Yonder's one of 'em."

I close the book, my thoughts in a frenzy.
They're just in-betweens, don't belong anywhere.

I used to reread this part of the story over and over, if only to know I wasn't alone in my feelings of not fitting in. But when I read it this time, it doesn't quite pack the same punch. Something is different now, and I can't figure out what it is. Maybe it has to do with me blowing up on my mom, because since that moment, I've felt so much lighter inside.

I stare at the book, trying to understand, when it hits me.

I don't feel like I don't belong anymore.

And not because I've chosen to be black or to be white,

like I used to feel the need to do. It would be impossible to choose one because I'll never fit either label. I'm not white. I'm not black.

I'm both.

And I do belong. In a category completely separate from my mom's and from my dad's . . . I'm just right.

I'm me. I'm Willow.

The thought makes me smile.

I glance at Ash, expecting her to ask me why I'm randomly smiling like a crazy person, but she's fast asleep, her phone facedown on her chest and her mouth open.

When I glance at my phone, I realize it's nearly five. Theo should be home by now. In fact, he probably got home over an hour ago. I try not to feel offended that he hasn't called me or come over yet.

I head outside, expecting to see Theo's motorcycle parked in the driveway. But it's not there. I frown, wondering where he could have gone. I try to recall him telling me about any plans he had after school, any prior engagements, appointments, or errands, but I come up empty.

I call him twice, but his phone goes straight to voicemail. My heart pounds in my chest, my worry starting to get the best of me. I'm just about to try calling him again, when my mom's picture flashes across the screen of my phone. I answer her call. "Mom?"

"Willow," she breathes, "You have to come to the hospital."

"Excuse me?" I frown. "I just came back from the hospital . . . " I groan internally at my slip-up, hoping she doesn't question me any further. Ash hasn't announced her pregnancy to our family, and she'll kill me if I end up being the one to spill the beans first.

"Oh," she says, her relief palpable. "You've been to see Theo, then? That was fast. I didn't even see you come in."

"Theo?" I shake my head, even though my mom can't see me. "What do you mean Theo?"

"Theo's here at the hospital," she explains slowly, like I'm a child who can't keep up.

"What is he doing there?" I ask, my heart threatening to escape from my chest. Maybe he went straight there after school, thinking Ash and I hadn't left yet. There has to be a good reason why he's there, because there's no way, *no way—*

"Willow," my mom says, her voice frantic. Her tone causes my adrenaline to run a marathon in my veins. "Theodore is hurt. There was an accident and he went unconscious. I was getting my nails done when the hospital called me. I'm his emergency contact."

"What happened?" I don't know how my mom hears me, because my voice is so quiet, I can't even hear it myself. "Mom, *what happened?*"

"Apparently he got in an accident while he was driving home," she says, her voice thick. My mom pauses for a long moment, and I don't dare speak. "You need to come see him, Willow."

Twenty-One

I'm back at the hospital for the second time today, this time the one my mom works at. I pace the waiting room, trying with all my might not to curl up into a ball in a corner and count. Over and over again. I try not to tap. I try not to crumble from the inside out. The rituals that flit through my mind present themselves so readily, as if to say, *Here we are. The cure to fix everything that's happening right now.*

If there has ever been a time my compulsions felt justified, it's now. Right now. Here, at the hospital, with Theo's life on the line. Situations precisely like this one are what I try to prevent with my magical thinking.

This is my fear.

Someone I love, dying.

I don't know how I'll bear it a second time.

I cover my mouth with my hands, my face crumpling.

My entire body shakes with sobs as I fall to my knees. People might be staring. They might not be. Either way, I don't care right now.

Theo. Theodore William Tate.

My mom's words from two separate occasions play in my head.

Rob is not a good man. And Theo was raised by him.

Apparently he got in an accident while he was driving home. You need to come see him, Willow.

A frustrated scream escapes me, echoing throughout the entire waiting room. A woman stares with wide eyes and ushers her daughter behind her back, shielding me from her child's view. I don't care.

This can't be happening.

I don't know why I haven't started counting yet. What more do I have to lose? At least if I try, there might be a chance he'll be okay. I don't know how I'm supposed abandon my rituals when I need them so badly right now.

I start counting to five.

1, 2, 3, 4 . . .

And stop mid-count, breathing heavily.

Theo wouldn't want this. He'd want me to be strong, even if it meant letting him . . .

Letting him die.

I shut my eyes impossibly tighter. That's the worst-case scenario. I have no idea of his condition yet. For all I know, he could be fine. I open my eyes and search for a seat, refusing to meet the eyes of anyone around me. I find an isolated chair and sit down.

What was the promise I made myself? I can't even remember it right now. All I can think about is Theo. His piercing blue eyes. His comforting scent, his irresistible voice. His teasing smile. How safe I feel in his arms. Him as a child, falling out of his tree house and breaking his arm. The way he held me and let me cry over my grandma into his shirt. Him painting my happy place.

My happy place.

I close my eyes and try to imagine it exactly how Theo painted it.

Me, in my white dress. Reading underneath a tree. A willow tree. A spring meadow beneath me. My little black dog by my side.

In, out. In, out. I breathe deeply. Not to any specific rhythm or pattern. Not tapping in time to my breaths. I just breathe.

In, out. In, out.

I go to my happy place and try to see what the Willow in the painting sees. I become her.

There is a warm breeze shifting the grass around, sending the pages of my book into a flutter. What am I reading? Perhaps *Harry Potter and the Half-Blood Prince.*

My dog is snoring. It's adorable. What's her name again? Luna. Her name is Luna.

In, out.

The tree makes a rustling sound as its leaves scurry in

the air. The scent of roses mixed with daisies wafts into my nose. Lavender, too.

Breathe, I tell myself. *No rituals. Just you, in your happy place.*

"Willow."

In, out.

"Willow, sweetie."

I open my eyes.

It's my mom, wearing jeans and a black knit sweater. As soon as I see her, I spring to my feet. "How is he?" I ask. My voice sounds terribly hoarse. "How's Theo?" *Is he alive,* is what I want to ask. It's what I need to know, but I can't make the words come out.

"He has a broken shoulder," she explains. "And a concussion." She grabs my hand. Her eyes are red-rimmed, but dry. She's not wearing any makeup, and her blond hair is in a ponytail. "No fractures or bleeding. He was unbelievably lucky. It's going to be okay."

I don't dare to breathe. "You mean . . . he's alive? He's going to live?"

My mom blinks in surprise. "Live?" She squeezes my shoulder, her touch tender. "Yes. Of course, honey."

I almost fall to my knees. "Can I see him?" I ask, my voice desperate. "Please?"

My mom sighs deeply. "He's been asking for you for almost an hour. Why else do you think I called?"

I laugh, and it makes me feel lighter. However I felt about my mom now seems insignificant. Not gone or irrelevant, but smaller somehow. At least she was here with Theo until I could come. She leads me to his room, and motions for me to go inside. "I'm going home to try to get some sleep," she says. "I'll be back for my shift later tonight."

I open the door. Theo is lying in the hospital bed, his right shoulder in a sling and covered in fresh gauze and bandages. His face is slightly swollen, and the shadows of bruises threaten to soon make their appearance more blatant. His eyes are closed, but when I take a few steps into the room, he opens them and looks around.

Our gazes meet, and I try to speak, but my throat tightens, preventing words from coming out and air from getting in.

He smiles faintly. "God, it's so good to see you."

"Theo," I breathe. "What happened?"

He takes a deep breath, wincing in pain. "My bike stopped working." Theo grimaces. "I crashed." His voice is slower than normal, and a bit heavier, like it takes energy for him to speak.

My stomach drops. "What? What do you mean it stopped working?"

"The engine." Theo tilts his head to the side. "I think it may have been tampered with. A new motorbike like that should run perfectly. But it wasn't working after school. I didn't make it very far before it stopped going and a car that wasn't paying close attention hit me."

"What?" My vision goes red. "Who would have messed with it?" I shake my head slowly, processing it all. And then it dawns on me. The way the bike showed up so randomly, so unexpectedly on his doorstep. How it was addressed to him anonymously, not long after Eliza visited him.

How Eliza said Rob was sending Theo a warning if he didn't come home.

I don't care, Theo had said.

"It was Eliza," I say, half in a daze. "Eliza tampered with your bike. That was your dad's warning for not coming home." I shake my head. "In fact, I bet she's the anonymous admirer who left it to you in the first place."

Theo chuckles darkly and it's anything but humorous. "I told you she's twisted." He closes his eyes and lets his head fall back gently into the pillow. "That bitch. If you'd been on that bloody thing with me when this happened—"

I shake my head impatiently. "Don't. I'm just glad you're okay," I whisper. "I should have let you come with us."

"What, because of all this?" He gestures to his shoulder with his free hand. "This is merely a scratch, love. Nothing that can't be fixed."

I take in his shoulder, his bruised face. His movements weighed down and heavy from his concussion. I swallow back my tears. "I'm so sorry."

His eyes soften. "Please don't tell me you're blaming yourself for this."

"If you hadn't been alone," I say. "If I'd been there with you, I could have . . . I don't know. I could have somehow prevented it from happening." The words sound ridiculous as I say them, even to me.

"But I'm quite alive, aren't I? And you didn't have to do a thing." He rubs my hand with his thumb, leaving goosebumps in his wake.

"Yes," I breathe. "You're alive." But he could have died today, and I could have lost him, just like Daniel. Yet somehow he survived and I didn't help at all. In fact, the only rituals I performed today were tapping and smiling at myself in a mirror. Based on what I've always believed my rituals could do if I followed the rules correctly, those two minor rituals couldn't have saved him. Theo shouldn't be alive.

But he is.

And it's that revelation, more than anything else, that waters the seed of hope planted within me. Perhaps now it will finally be able to grow into something more substantial, like trust. Or maybe even faith.

Twenty-Two

It's been a week of healing in the hospital for Theo, and when I get to his room after school, I kiss him lightly on the lips. I'm gentle, even though it's only his shoulder that's still healing. Most of his bruises are starting to fade, the cut on his lower lip practically gone, too.

"Eva got sent home today," I tell him. "For wearing leggings instead of her scrub bottoms. Again."

Theo rolls his eyes. "How hard is it to wear the bloody uniform?"

"And apparently Raymond wants to be Charlie's new partner for the fashion show, since Eva is his model and keeps getting sent home." I smile. "Don't worry. Charlie's loyalties lie with you."

"Not to mention, I have much better bone structure than Raymond."

I nod, trying not to smile. "True."

Theo searches my face. "And you? How are you doing?"

"I miss you. School sucks without you."

"I do make things more interesting," Theo grins. "But at least you have Ash. It can't be that bad."

"It's not the same." I lean over and kiss him again, gently, still afraid to hurt him. But Theo pulls me on top of him and deepens the kiss. Before a nurse can walk in, I pull away, back to a standing position. "She's having a gender reveal party."

Theo frowns. "What? Who?"

I can't help but laugh at his bewilderment. "Ash. She's going to find out the gender after all. I can't wait to see what it is. I think it's a girl."

Theo stares at my mouth. "Right. Me too," he says, sounding very much like he couldn't care less about gender reveal parties at the moment. He pulls me against him again and presses his lips to the side of my neck. His hands travel underneath my scrub top, tickling my lower back.

I can't help the little sigh that escapes me, and Theo's lips pursue my skin more fervently. My hair surrounds us like a dark curtain, straight today per Ash's request. When Theo's desire becomes even more physically apparent, I say, "We have to stop. Someone could walk in right now."

"Always so responsible, little Willow." Theo taps my nose. "I can't get you to break the rules, just this once?"

"Don't worry. As soon as you're released, I'll show you exactly how much I missed you."

"Is that so?" Theo growls. "And what if I can't wait that long?"

I swallow and get up before he can unravel my willpower. "Too bad."

"Well, then," Theo says folding his good arm behind his head. "I feel better already. Someone should fetch the nurse."

I give him a withering look. "Just do your homework. Take your painkillers. Get lots of sleep." I grab a pen off the nurse's tray. "Here. You're not going to be allowed to come back to school next week unless all of this is complete."

Theo eyes the homework with disdain. "Rubbish. Mrs. Harrison is all mouth and no trousers."

I snort. "You and your British phrases."

"You'd hear a lot more of them if you came to London with me."

"Won't things just get worse with your dad when you go back?" I ask. "You'll be closer to him, after all."

"You needn't worry too hard, love. I can handle him."

The nurse opens the door and glances at me. "All right, time for this young man to get some rest before we discharge him tomorrow."

"I want her to stay," Theo protests.

I smile at the nurse. "No problem." As soon as she leaves, I give Theo a stern look. "Do your homework."

"Send me naughty photos."

I laugh. "Only if you behave and listen to the nurse. Rest is the best medicine, after all."

"No one likes a know-it-all, little Willow," Theo says.

"Except you," I say before closing the door behind me.

* * *

Theo takes my advice and does his homework before the week is up. Most of it, anyway.

Mrs. Harrison checks it meticulously, as if one small error is all the reason she needs to tell him he can't come back. His situation is unique, because he's only here for one semester. Typically, students who miss more than their allowed number of hours have to drop out and resume the following semester.

But as Theo said, Mrs. Harrison turns out to be all mouth and no trousers.

Over the next two weeks, Ash manages to perfect my final look for the fashion show. We practice it at my house on Friday morning the week before the show.

The only thing I haven't seen yet is my costume, because Ash is still working on it. "I just need to make a few alterations," she tells me. "I'll probably be done by Monday."

"I would offer to help," I say, "but I have no idea how to do alterations."

"That's fine, because you're the model, not the stylist. Leave the styling to me." Ash tugs on my hair as she pins it into place. "Look. You're done. What do you think?"

I glance at my reflection. "I look very Victorian," I state.

She rolls her eyes. "Whatever. At least we're following the theme." She starts taking the hairstyle down. "Where's your car, by the way? I didn't see it out front when I got here."

"I let Theo take it to the school counselor. He's transferring his credits to the school he's going to in London next semester."

Even though the problem with his bike was corrected quickly—frozen peas and carrots in the engine left by Eliza, who claimed not to know a thing—he still doesn't trust it. It would be easy for her to mess with it again, unnoticed.

Ash shakes her head. "I can't believe you're not going with him. I mean, he's here for what? One more week? And then he'll be gone. Thousands of miles away."

"Thank you, Ash." I purse my lips. "That really helps, you know."

She shrugs. "Sorry, but it's true."

I sigh. She's right. Theo will be gone soon, and I still haven't found a new place to live. Everything is too expensive. At this point I might as well just stay with my mom. I don't trust her, but I have nowhere else to go. Now I know what she's capable of, so I'll just have to be more cautious. It seems foolish to move out and live on my own.

My phone vibrates with a text message. It's Theo. *Can Ash drop you off at the river? I have something for you.*

The river. The same place we realized we knew each other since childhood. Before his dad tried to hurt me, and we couldn't see each other again.

Until now.

"Can you take me to the river?" I ask Ash, once my hair is free of its confines. "Theo wants me to meet him."

Her eyes widen. "But—" she breaks off, seeming to rethink her words. "Actually, never mind. Sure!"

I frown at her but follow her out to the driveway. I get in the backseat and look out the window while she drives me. The sun is out, the month of May bringing hydrangeas and an assortment of other bright perennials to the gardens of nearly every house on my street. The ride doesn't take long, and Ash parks next to Mitten Chip at the American River.

"Should I wait here?" she asks.

"No," I say. "I'll ride back with Theo, thanks."

"Okay." She looks me over, a small smile forming on her lips before I go.

Theo is waiting for me, leaning on a tree near the entrance of the trail that leads to the river. He's wearing jeans and a white shirt, and his hair is a dark mass of waves. As soon as he looks at me, I feel the shock of his bright blue eyes slice through me. I don't think I'll ever get used to it.

"Hi." I walk over to him. "What's going on?"

He gestures toward the trail. "Let's go sit down by the water, little Willow."

My stomach tenses as I take in the tightness in his eyes. "Okay."

We walk along the trail leading to the river, the knee-high grass tickling my ankles. We find some large rocks to sit on far enough from the water to keep our feet dry.

Theo turns to me. He's silent for a long moment before he finally speaks. "I have to leave for London tomorrow."

My stomach does a flip. I stare at him, unable to form words, and shake my head slowly. "What do you mean?"

"My dad." Theo sighs. He watches the ripples in the water, the light on the surface reflecting in his eyes. "Apparently he's going to pay me a visit."

I frown. "He's bluffing. He won't really come."

Theo's lips thin. "But he could. And if he's serious, I don't want him anywhere near you. I've already told your mother what's happening, and she agrees I should leave as soon as possible."

"But you can't," I choke. "The fashion show is next week, and the semester is almost over!" I don't know why this is the first thing that comes to my mind, and I cringe at how ridiculous it sounds as I say it. The fashion show doesn't matter. Not when Theo is being threatened by his dad. Not when it means he'll have to leave tomorrow, back to London, and I might never see him again.

Breathe. I gasp in a huff of air.

Theo reaches into the pocket of his jeans. "I want you to come with me," he tells me. He pulls out a white rectangle of paper. It's a plane ticket. He hands it to me, and our gazes meet. "I already have a flat in Surrey. My dad has no idea.

We could attend the London School of Beauty next semester together."

My throat tightens. There's nothing but my own fear keeping me from saying yes, from going with him to England, from not having to say goodbye.

But my fear is a powerful beast. One I have yet to tame. "I can't," I whisper. "Theo, I can't."

Theo's brow wrinkles. "Why not?"

"I just can't." I stand up and face the water. Maybe if I stare at it long enough, Theo won't have to leave. Someone will come forward and prove what a monster Rob is, and he'll get arrested. His threats will cease. None of this will have to happen for one more week.

But what will I do then?

"Willow." Theo stands up and turns me around to face him. His gaze is steady, even. "I love you."

Those three words. They fill my heart and break it at the same time. He has no idea what those words do to me. "You hardly know me, Theo," I say, my voice barely louder than a whisper. I stare at the ground.

"Rubbish." Theo brings my face back to his, forcing me to meet his gaze. "I've known you all my life."

My eyes become moist. My heart is racing, too fast for my mind to keep up. I want to tell him he's crazy. "Why?" I shake my head.

"Why?" Theo laughs humorlessly. "Are you thick? You're the girl who stood up for me when no one else had before, to my unfortunate excuse of a father. You have the bravest heart of anyone I know, though you'd like to think you're a coward. You care about everything, especially the things that don't matter to most people. You're beautiful inside and out. You're the only true mate I've ever had. Of course I love you."

My throat burns when I swallow. I can't stop hope from rising up inside me, yet I feel the need to squash it down. "But I'm crazy. I have OCD. Doesn't that bother you? I practically killed my last boyfriend." I cringe at the stream of stupidity flowing from my mouth. My heart can't believe what he's saying is the truth, and I'm waiting for him to take it back. I need to remind him of all the reasons he shouldn't love me. To double check that he knows them in case he needs to change his mind.

"And yet here I am." Theo wipes my face with his thumb. I didn't realize I was crying. "I don't give a damn what you think, or what anyone else does for that matter. You didn't kill Daniel. Yes, you have OCD, but that's part of you. It's part of what makes you Willow. You're not mad."

I sigh. "But it ruins my life and the lives of those around me. It controls me no matter how hard I try to fight it."

Theo frowns and tilts his head. "Willow, do you even know what bloody day it is?"

"What do you mean?" I sniff.

"You really have no idea." Theo stares at me, astonished. "Here we are, Willow. At the American River, on a Friday. You went out with me on a Friday."

I blink at him, completely motionless. I recall the way

Ash looked at me when I asked her to give me a ride here, as if she couldn't believe what she was hearing. Her small smile before I got out of the car, completely unaware. "What?" I check the date on my phone to see if he's telling the truth, and he is. It's Friday. I'm not home, and it's Friday.

My face feels numb. I don't know how this very significant day of the week somehow escaped my notice. I don't know how it wasn't the first thing I thought of when Theo asked me to meet him here. But most of all, I don't know how or why I'm not completely riddled with anxiety.

There's no panic. I don't feel compelled to perform a ritual.

I feel . . . fine.

My mouth splits into a grin so wide, I actually start to laugh. "How—what?" I say, not understanding the sensation I'm experiencing. "How am I okay with this right now?"

Theo presses his lips together. "Because you're getting used to the feeling of not reacting to a compulsion. And now you've conquered number four on your list."

My brows lift together. "I can't believe it."

"You'd better." Theo gives me a half smile. "I can't tell you how proud I am, little Willow."

I stare at the plane ticket Theo bought me. "Can I think about this overnight?" I ask him. "Coming to Surrey with you, that is."

Theo searches my face. "Of course." He kisses my forehead and we take the trail back to the parking lot where my car is waiting. We get inside, and I think again about today being Friday while I drive. I went out on a Friday.

I went out on a Friday.

And everything is okay.

Twenty-Three

As soon as we get to Theo's house, I glance around, taking in the boxes housing some of his things. I had no idea he already started packing. It makes everything feel more real.

His bed is still set up, so I sit on it. I glance around his room and briefly wonder when I started thinking of this place as Theo's instead of my grandma's. His clothes are strewn all over the place, some of them hanging out of boxes, and others all over the floor.

Theo gets a text message, and he nods at the screen. "I found someone who wants to buy my bike."

My eyes widen. "You're selling it?"

"Well, I can't very well take it with me, love," he says. "Apparently this person can meet right now. It's probably a good idea, since I'm leaving tomorrow." Theo glances around the house and swears. "And I'm still not packed."

I laugh. "Don't worry. I'll stay here and help you pack while you go sell your motorcycle."

Theo looks relieved. "Thank you, love."

"If they decide to buy it, let me know and I'll come pick you up."

He kisses me before he leaves, and I'm left alone in his little house. I check my face in the mirror, cringing at my hair. It's a mess after Ash worked on it, so I take a moment to braid it loosely, not needing a hair tie to secure it because of its texture.

Someone knocks on the front door.

Who on earth could that be?

I swing it open, expecting to see Theo, possibly coming back to get something he forgot, but instead am greeted by a man who looks to be middle aged. He's in decent shape, with graying dark hair and pale blue eyes. I don't recognize him as someone I've met before, though there is something oddly familiar about his eyes. They're a shade similar to Theo's, but where his are warm and comforting, this man's are the coldest I've seen in a while. The day has transformed into early night behind him, the lampposts illuminated and casting their poles into long shadows beneath them.

I'm staring at the man, stupefied, and still unsure what to say. He speaks before I have a chance. "Do I have the wrong address?"

"That . . . depends," I say, clearing my throat against my unease. "Who are you looking for?"

"Does this house belong to Charlize Bates?" He asks slowly, as if I'm a child.

I frown. "She's not a Bates anymore." This guy must have known my mom when she was still married to my dad, otherwise he would have used her maiden name, Abrahams.

The man looks me over, as if determining whether I'm important or not. Something changes in his expression, only leaving me even more confused. "Are you her daughter?" he asks. "Willow?"

My heart races. For some reason my stomach is on edge even though he's given me no reason to be afraid. If this man is a friend of my mom's, I should probably let him in, or call her to let her know he's looking for her. "Yes," I say quietly. "I'm Willow. And who are you?"

The man smiles, but it's anything but kind. "Now tell me something, Willow. How can it be that you don't remember me, when I know exactly who you are?"

I stare, completely at a loss for words. This man's voice is so strange, wavering between sounding normal and sounding faintly accented, like he's either trying to hide where he's from, or is starting to take on the accent of a place he's recently moved to. As I study him, a slow smile spreads across his face.

And I suddenly remember exactly who he is.

It's been so long, I'm surprised at my own memory. I don't say a word. And apparently I don't have to.

"That's right," he says, nodding. "It's me. Rob Tate."
This man is Theo's father.

Twenty-Four

See, the thing is," Rob says. He eyes me up and down, like he's taking in every detail of my appearance. "I recall you owing me an apology." He nods, a good-natured smile on his face, and it gives me chills. Rob is wearing a burgundy button-down shirt and a pair of business slacks. He's handsome now but must have been absolutely striking in his youth. Yet, there's something inherently repulsive about him, as if he's let his tendency for being a vile human being taint any appeal left in him.

I force myself to meet his gaze. I will not let him see I'm afraid. I won't let him catch onto any inkling of cowardice I have, especially since Theo isn't here. From what I know of Rob, he has no qualms with violence. He beat Mildred so badly when she was pregnant that she lost her baby. And Theo's never said so outright, but I have a gut feeling he too was a victim of his dad's heavy hand. The thought of Rob hurting Theo makes me stand up straighter, anger flaring in my blood.

"And why is that?" I snap. I let the venom I feel towards this man flow freely. If I'm lucky, it will poison him. "Because unlike everyone else you interact with, I refuse to take your shit?"

Rob's eyes harden, turning to ice within seconds. I feel like I'm standing on it, the thin ice of his eyes that's about to crack, plunging me into the cold depths beneath the surface. "Careful." His voice is low, dangerous. "You don't want to talk to me like that."

"What are you even doing here?" I ask, wanting nothing more than for him to leave. I send a quick text to Theo without glancing at my phone, trying to hide the motion as well as I can. A single word and nothing more.

Help.

"I'm looking for my son. Perhaps you've seen him," says Rob.

"Sorry. He isn't here. I'm not sure why you thought he would be." I swallow, regretting sending that text and hoping to God Theo doesn't come bursting in. Maybe if I can convince Rob he was never here, he'll leave and look for him somewhere else. I try to slam the door in Rob's face, but he catches the frame in his hand. He throws the front door wide open and steps inside the house.

"Elizabeth already told me everything. She'd do anything for money. Even me," Rob says between his teeth.

"You lying little bitch." He moves a step closer, and as badly as I want to, I don't step back in response.

"He *was* here," I improvise, "but he left already. Last week, I think. I'm not sure where he went."

Before I even know it's coming, Rob's hand whips out and slaps my cheek with so much force, I stagger back. The flash of pain is belated but once it hits, my entire face is on fire. "His things are still here!" he shouts, making me jump. "There are pictures of him and my wife on the wall! Don't you lie to me!" Rob grabs my wrists in each of his hands, forcing me back against the wall. My heart feels like it's about to fail. I'm panting, unable to hide how much his blow hurt, or how much I'm trying to hold it together in front of him.

"Leave me alone," I say, my voice half a sob. "Fuck off, you disgusting prick."

Something inside Rob snaps, and part of me wonders if I'm the first person in his entire life to talk to him like this. He snarls at me—actually snarls. "You've always been such a little bitch," he growls. "Never knowing your place. I should have shown it to you when you mouthed off to me in my own house. I would have, if your mother hadn't stopped me. But now, you're going to learn to respect me." His voice is calm, deadly, as if holding back every ounce of anger he has toward everyone, only so he can release it on me at the right time.

I spit in his face. "Burn in hell."

Rob throws me onto the ground and kicks me in the stomach.

I can't breathe.

It feels like my lungs have burst.

He takes both of my wrists in one of his hands, and my long, braided hair in the other, and drags me down the hall to Theo's bedroom. I'm crying, sobbing, screaming for help, when he throws me on the bed and covers my mouth with one of his hands.

No, no, no, no, no.

Rob roughly begins to remove his belt, and for the moment, I'm five again, back in his horrendously wrong yellow bedroom.

I gag against his hand and bite down on his finger as hard as I possibly can. He roars, pulling his hand away from my mouth for a split second, and I use that tiny window of time to scream as loud as I possibly can. I expect to feel his hand clamp back down hard on my mouth, but instead, Rob is ripped right off me.

I hear the sound of flesh meeting bone, hard. I scramble up quickly to see two men in a heap on the floor. One of them is Theo, and his fist is pounding into Rob's skull, hard and fast as lightning.

I blink, unable to believe what I'm seeing, as Rob's face starts bleeding and Theo's blows don't cease. Rather, they come harder and harder, aimed at Rob's nose, his jaw, his gut, his throat. Rob is helpless beneath his son, clearly unprepared to be attacked at this moment. Theo is leaner than his dad, and taller. Despite Rob being thicker, his age and out-of-shape body are clearly against him.

But if Theo doesn't stop now, he's going to kill his dad.

And sick as the man is, I can't let him do it.

"Theo!" I scream, and he looks at me. The distraction costs him though, and Rob throws Theo off him and puts him in a chokehold.

I scream when Rob tightens his arm around Theo's neck, causing Theo to gasp for air and claw at his dad's arm.

My heart races. I grab the lamp off the table next to Theo's bed and smash Rob over the head with it. Rob falls to the ground, allowing Theo to breathe.

Theo grabs the lamp and smashes it against his dad's face until blood stains the carpet.

I wail and cover my eyes.

Rob begins to lose consciousness, but Theo starts kicking his dad's bloody, weakened body. It takes me a moment to react. "Theo." My voice sounds as breathless as I feel. "Theo, stop!"

Theo kicks his dad's head in succession, each time sounding wetter and more sickening. I grab Theo's arm and he stops instantly, broken from whatever murderous trance he's in.

I grab his face, forcing his eyes to meet mine, and he reaches for me, pulling me against him. I feel the flex of his hard muscles as he wraps his arms around me. His breathing is hitched and labored, and he holds me like this for the longest of moments.

My sobs fill the room, and I press my mouth against Theo's chest to mask them.

I try to breathe. I untangle myself from Theo and sit down on the bed I was forced onto only moments ago. My hands won't stop shaking. Theo holds them in his, steadying them, and takes a good look at me.

"You're hurt. Did he—"

"No." I cut him off before his imagination can get carried away. "I'm fine."

Theo exhales, but his eyes are dark with rage. He reaches up to touch my cheek, and by instinct I flinch. His fingers hover over my skin. "He hit you," Theo growls. "That bastard." His expression turns murderous as he looks at his father, nothing more than a bloody, unconscious heap, and I grip his hand before he can actually kill him.

"I'm fine," I lie. "Really."

"We should call the police," Theo says, sounding resigned.

Suddenly it all hits me, what just happened, that Rob physically attacked me. That he would have continued to hurt me—in whatever way he wanted. The knowledge is crippling, so much so that I can hardly see straight. I can't help it when I start crying, shaking uncontrollably. Theo pulls me against him, rubbing my back hesitantly, like he's not sure I want to be touched. But I crave his touch so much right now. I want to erase the feeling of Rob's violent hands on my skin. I bury myself further into Theo's embrace. "Don't tell my mom what you saw," I whimper against his chest. "What your dad was going to do."

"Why?"

"Please," I repeat, sounding like a child, even to my own ears. "Don't tell my mom. She'll blame you."

Rob is not a good man. And Theo was raised by him.

"Willow," Theo says roughly. "You've been badly hurt. Stop thinking about me."

I shudder.

"Come here." Theo pulls me into a standing position and takes me to the couch. "I don't want you anywhere near him right now," he says when I'm sitting down, wrapped in a blanket. I have to admit, I do feel a little better now that I can't see Rob's mangled face anymore.

"Is he . . . dead?" My voice sounds so small.

Theo's eyes meet mine, and in them, there is so much darkness, so much pain. "I hope so."

* * *

I wake up in Theo's bed to an assortment of voices emanating from the living room. I have no idea how I got back in his bed, but I'm willing to bet Theo carried me here. I rub my eyes and kick off his comforter, tiptoeing out of the room. I peek around the corner.

The cops are here, asking Theo questions. Ash and my

mom are here too, their backs facing me and hiding me from Theo and the officers' view.

"How did you get him off her again?" my mom asks, sounding incredulous.

"I removed him," Theo says, leveling his gaze at my mom. "With my hands. Like I said before."

My mom crosses her arms, like she doesn't trust Theo. It's almost enough for me to walk out there and defend him, but I want to see what happens next without her knowing I'm watching. I can practically feel the judgement radiating off her, just like I knew it would. It's like the words she's thinking are audible. *This is your fault. If I hadn't taken you in, this wouldn't have happened.* And then I hear the words she said aloud to me months ago, the words I haven't been able to get out of my head since she spoke them.

As much as I care about Mildred's son, be careful around him, Willow. Rob is not a good man. And Theo was raised by him.

But my mom had it all wrong. By being such a bad man, Rob taught Theo exactly what kind of man to avoid becoming. Theo is nothing like his dad. Theo is good and kind and brave. And no matter how long Rob spent raising him, Theo refused to let him taint the good in him.

"I can't be here right now," my mom says. "I can't process what's happening. I'm going outside to get some air."

"You're just going to leave?" Ash snaps. "Your daughter

was physically attacked and you're leaving because it's too much for you?"

"Please," the officer cuts in. "Let's everyone calm down."

"Bloody hell. Enough of this endless questioning. You can arrest me or not," Theo says. "I don't care. He was trying to force himself on Willow, and I stopped him before he could. Even if I killed him, I would do it again a million times over."

The officer shifts on his feet. "I know the victim is resting, but it's time to question her. We really need to hear her side of the story."

"Don't wake her." Ash crosses her arms. "She's in shock."

I come out from around the corner. "It was self-defense," I state. "Like Theo already said."

The entire room faces me, wide-eyed. Theo moves toward me. "Willow—" he begins, but I hold up a hand.

"I'll tell you whatever you need to know," I say to the officer.

* * *

The paramedics took Rob away and fixed Theo's shoulder in a sling while I was sleeping. Apparently it hadn't healed enough to withstand the force of the beating he gave his dad.

When the cops are eventually satisfied with how my

story lines up with Theo's, I go back to his room to lie down while they finish talking to him.

I shut my eyes, willing unconsciousness to take hold of me again, but it doesn't. It's time to face reality, and it's much too soon.

Footsteps sound down the hall and Ash opens the door, wordlessly crawling into Theo's bed with me. She combs my hair back into a braid with her fingers, and I shake silently with sobs. I can't stop shaking. My tremors are so violent my teeth start chattering.

Ash wraps her arms around mine, shushing me gently. But I can't calm myself.

I shiver. "Th-Theo—"

"He'll be fine," says Ash. "Trust me. The cops are just being redundant. Everything you said was the truth, right? And you didn't leave anything out?" I nod to the best of my ability. "Then it will be fine."

"You don't know that." I clear my throat against the thickness clouding it.

"Yes, I do."

The door opens again, and this time it's Theo. I reach for him, and he walks to the bed, taking me into the circle of his good arm immediately. Ash gets up, giving my hair a final pat. "I'll be out there, babe. I want to talk to your mom and see if she's okay. I think I was a little hard on her." To Theo, she says, "I'm glad she has you. I'm going to have someone else to baby soon enough." She seems to touch her stomach without realizing it, and then shuts the door quietly as she leaves.

Theo carefully gets into his bed with me, pulling the covers over us both. I rest my face against his chest, my slow tears blurring my vision. "Is your dad going to be okay?" I ask. My voice sounds so small, even to my own ears.

"Apparently he's in a coma," Theo says. "I don't know if he still has a fighting chance."

"You're not going to jail, are you?"

Theo rubs my hair the same way Ash did moments ago. "I don't think so. From what I understand, the damage I did to him is considered self-defense, since I was protecting you. But if I were to go to jail, I wouldn't give a damn. No one puts their hands on you like that and lives to tell the tale."

My heart throbs. I lean away from Theo's chest to look at him. My eyes fill with tears. "I need to tell you something," I say.

"What?" His brows pull together in concern.

I take a deep breath. "I love you."

Theo's eyes linger on mine. In them, I can see something breaking, like the last barrier between us, the final protective wall around his heart. "I love you, too." He touches my face. "Is that what you needed to tell me?"

"Yes. Theodore," I say. "I love you. I love you so much, and I've never even told you."

Theo is motionless for a moment. Then he presses his forehead against mine. I can hear his unsteady breaths with him so close. He kisses me softly, first on the mouth, and then on each eyelid, making me close them.

"I'm sorry," he whispers against my mouth. "I'm so sorry this happened."

"Don't be." I blink past the moisture clouding my vision. "At first I thought this happened because I went out on a Friday. But even so, everything is going to be okay. You stopped your dad just in time. It's almost like I used a ritual."

"But if I hadn't—" Theo breaks off, unable to finish his sentence. "If I'd been too late, if my father had actually hurt you the way he'd intended . . . the thought brings me such fury I can't see straight."

I lightly touch his face. "But you did. And since your dad can't hurt anyone now . . . " I bite my lip. "Does that mean you won't leave tomorrow?"

Theo nuzzles his face into my hair. "I won't go anywhere until I have to, little Willow. I'll stay right here with you."

I smile, even though I know he can't see it. And I'm glad, because it isn't a happy smile. This moment, comforting as it is to be lying next to Theo, can't last. And as it passes, I mourn it. I long for it before it's even gone.

Twenty-Five

Ash sleeps over the night before the fashion show.

I haven't slept alone since Rob attacked me, and even though I've been relishing in having Theo next to me when I fall asleep, Ash is a welcome change. Pretty soon, she's going to be a mom. I won't be able to spend as much time with her as I'm used to once her baby comes, so I want to soak up as much as I can.

The fashion show is the best distraction I could have hoped for. Focusing on it has given my mind something else to turn over, other than Rob Tate.

I dress plainly in the morning—leggings and a T-shirt. I won't need to wear my dress until it's time for the show. Ash is decked out in black from head to toe. She claims this will keep her from interfering with the illusion my style creates. "It will be like I'm invisible," she tells me. I have more than a small feeling she's partly referring to her baby belly, which has become a firm bump, small, but finally noticeable.

Theo knocks on my bedroom door, peeking inside at me and Ash. Our gazes lock, causing a flurry in my stomach. "Morning," he says.

I smile at him. "Hi."

Ash yawns. "You two give me morning sickness."

Theo chuckles. "I just wanted to ask what the car situation is this morning, love. Who are you driving?"

My first reaction is to tell Theo to meet us at school in my car, but the words don't come out. It seems like a step backward to insist on avoiding the passenger seat, after everything I've endured. After all, I agreed to do this. To give up all my rituals. And last week, I faced number four on my list. I went out on a Friday. So why am I still holding on to number three?

"I think," I say, hardly believing my own ears. "I'd like you to drive *me* to school today, Theo."

Theo arches an eyebrow at me.

"I swear," Ash says. "If this magical thinking crap of yours turns out to be true, and you choose today—the morning of the fashion show—to do this and we end up losing because of it, I'll drive you off a cliff myself."

Theo cocks his head. "I hear pregnancy hormones make women do dangerous things sometimes. You may want to have your levels checked."

Ash flips Theo off. "Don't make me hurt you. Joseph

already told me how cute my belly is, and I practically stabbed him in the eye."

"You should have done it," Theo suggests. "As a reminder not to make such ghastly remarks in the future."

Ash smirks. "Don't tempt me with a good time."

I huff. "Guys, as fun as this is, we really need to get going. Otherwise we're going to be late."

"Oh, no," Ash says blandly, falling back onto my bed. "There goes my perfect attendance record."

I glare at her. "We'll see you there." I toss Theo my keys from my bedside table. "Now, let's go. Before I change my mind."

Theo grins.

We walk to my car and I take several deep breaths before getting in the passenger seat. *You survived Rob,* I tell myself. *You'll survive this too. And so will Theo.*

As Theo drives, I stare out the window, trying to imagine us on his motorcycle, how the wind in my hair made me feel like I was flying. How completely free I felt.

It's not the same, being in the car, but I try my best. I hold my fingers still to keep myself from tapping, despite the mambo my heart is doing.

"Alright?" Theo asks me.

"Nothing," I say. "It's great." My cheeks burn. What did I just say? It doesn't matter. Not when my blood is rushing like a river, when my nerves are roaring in my ears.

Theo laughs. "What do you mean nothing? Are you all right, little Willow? Or shall I pull over?"

I hope I don't say anything else that will make him question my ability to process human conversation. I close my eyes and think of my happy place. I don't answer him until my adrenaline stops making me dizzy.

When I open my eyes, I think about the way it felt, waking up in the hospital and being told Daniel was dead. How I'd thought if only, if only I'd been able to do a ritual to stop it from happening. How I swore in that moment I would never let anything like it happen again.

I glance at Theo, and he looks away from the road to meet my gaze with concern etched in his blue eyes. For a brief moment, panic seizes me, and I almost tell him to stop driving. But then I remember what Ash told me.

Wouldn't it be so much easier to embrace fate, rather than fight it?

I shake the nerves off my body—literally shake them off. My body trembles with my efforts, and Theo's brows pull together.

"Yes," I tell Theo. "I'm okay."

Theo parks us at school, and we sit silently in the car for a moment.

I did it.

I actually did it.

I rode in the passenger seat of a car without performing a ritual.

"You know," I say, half in a daze, "I should have brought my list with me. Crossing this off would have been really satisfying."

Theo's mouth twitches as he tries to fight off a smile. "I was hoping this would go smoothly, because I had the exact same thought." He reaches into his back pocket and takes out a folded piece of paper.

My list.

My eyes widen. "You brought it?"

Theo holds it out to me. "I brought it. Cross it off, little Willow."

I can hardly believe my eyes. I can't believe Theo had the foresight to bring my list with him today. Did he grab it before or after I said I wanted him to drive? I have no idea, but it doesn't even matter, because this moment is magical.

I unfold the paper and reach for the pen in my glove compartment.

I cross it off.

"You know," I say. "I think number two deserves to be crossed off as well. After my mom put me on meds, and nothing bad happened . . . I don't know. I really thought I would've had an allergic reaction. But I didn't. And that made me feel a little bit better." I cross number two off, too. And I stare at the list.

WILLOW'S TOP 11 COMPULSIONS/FEARS THAT COME TO MIND
(IN DESCENDING ORDER)—
AND THEIR RITUALS:

11. ~~Contamination (washing the contaminated area repeatedly)~~

10. ~~Conflict (tapping and imagining the worst-case scenario so it doesn't happen)~~

9. ~~Not being in control (tapping, or finding little things to control to prove I am in control)~~

8. ~~Not being happy (most of my rituals, like smiling at my reflection, serve as a way to prevent this from happening; if I find myself unhappy, I will sometimes think of my happy place)~~

7. ~~Objects in an "uncomfortable" position or in the wrong place (readjusting the object repeatedly)~~

6. ~~Losing time (tapping, arranging objects, anything involving odd numbers)~~

5. ~~Even numbers (tapping my fingers an odd amount of times)~~

4. ~~Going out on a Friday (there is no ritual for this because I would NEVER do it)~~

3. ~~Sitting in the passenger seat of a car while someone else drives (see above parenthetical comment)~~

2. ~~Taking medicine (forcing myself to vomit until all the medicine has been expelled. But again, taking medicine is not something I would ever do unless my life depended on it)~~

1. The idea of a loved one dying (the last time this happened, all my rituals were collectively exacerbated)

"I don't think I'll ever really get over number one," I whisper.

"And I think," says Theo, "that is completely fine. Completely normal, if there's such a thing. As long as you don't let it control you or your decisions."

I stare at him, a small smile intruding my face. "I won't." I lean across the middle console and kiss Theo. "Thank you. Thank you for everything."

Theo shakes his head slightly. "It was all you, little Willow." He threads his fingers through my hair, gripping the back of my neck, and brings my face back to his. His lips are warm and soft against mine, and the stubble on his face grazes my cheek. I part my lips, and his tongue slides against mine. I press myself as close as I can to him, with the limited space my car allows, but it's not enough for him. He grabs me from my seat, pulling me onto his lap so I'm straddling him. In this position I can feel every part of him, where his body aches to meet mine, and I sigh with longing.

The tips of Theo's fingers graze my waist and then slide up my back, tickling my skin. My breathing grows heavy, and I'm about to suggest driving back home when Ash knocks on the car window.

"Seriously, you guys," she says through the glass. "I'm going to hurl."

* * *

When we enter the building to clock in, the entire interior of our classroom is decorated in gold balloons and streamers. The desks have been rearranged, making room for a pop-up dressing room in one corner and a large table filled with extra supplies for our stylists to use. Since half of us are stylists, and the other half models, the amount of stations has been equally divided.

Ash sits me down, getting to work immediately. She's practiced on me enough for this morning to go smoothly. I washed my hair last night, mostly to make things easier for her right now. All she has to do is place a few perm rods along the base of my neck and around the front of my hairline. The rest of my hair is to be styled into an intricate updo. When the rods come out, soft curls will strategically frame my face. I also get to wear the no-makeup makeup look, something I'm particularly happy about. Minimal makeup will save us time we could be spending on my hair, which is much more difficult.

And then there's my dress. Ash finished all her alterations, and the garment fit me like a second skin when I tried it on. It reminds me of something a character from a Jane Austen novel would wear. I have to admit, I feel a little bit like a princess in it.

Charlie has already set up his station, and I'm dismayed to find the one he chose is across the room from us. Now I won't be able to sit with Theo while we get ready.

The show is at five this evening, which means it will be a long while before I'm allowed to get back into my leggings and go home. I sigh and settle into my seat while Ash begins detangling my heavy curls.

"I'm so nervous," she says quietly.

"Why? You're not the one who has to walk across the stage in front of everyone." But to my surprise, I'm not dreading it as much as I thought I would. Not to mention, as soon as all this fashion show business is over, we'll be eligible to start working on actual clients.

"I might puke," Ash informs me. "I'll bring a bucket, just in case."

I laugh. "You have nothing to be nervous about."

She scoffs. "Are you kidding me? If we don't get at least third place, we won't win a spot in the boutique next semester! Of course I'm stressed."

I scoff. "Ash, the boutique is just a glorified mini-salon. It's overrated."

She puts her hands on her hips. "It's sectioned off from everyone else, you get to wear normal clothes, and you have first dibs on all the clients! It's absolutely not overrated!" She tugs on my hair, and I grit my teeth, trying not to complain.

From across the room, my gaze locks with Theo's. I want to sit next to him, to spend every second I can with him before he goes back to England. To his new flat in Surrey.

The thought of him leaving stabs a hole in my chest. How will we talk to each other every day, especially with a time-zone difference? How will it feel to spend weeks without the feel of his arms around me, without him living so close? I sigh, trying to remember that I can technically go and visit him whenever I want, if I so desire. If I can afford to.

"Hey," Eva says to Ash. "Can I borrow some bobby pins?"

Ash glances at Raymond in the chair next to mine and gives Eva a saccharine smile, though I can see the irritation behind it. Raymond has hair as long as mine, and we need almost every hairpin in our inventory for the updo I'm supposed to wear. "I mean, I guess?" She says to Eva. "You couldn't remember to bring your own? Just go grab some from the supply table."

Eva scoffs. "You know what? Whatever. Forget it."

I grab the pins, handing them to Raymond. "No, it's fine," I say. "Just make sure you leave exactly nineteen for us, please." Not because it's an odd number, but because that's how many we end up using each time. I've been counting.

Eva raises her eyebrows. "You know what? Just forget it. It's fine." She purses her lips, and adds under her breath, "You'd think with her pregnancy-brain, she'd cut me some slack."

Ash inhales, clearly fighting the urge to snap a retort back. She meets my eyes in the mirror as if to say, *This is for you. I'm biting my tongue for you.*

I fight a smile.

Hours later—when my butt is sore from sitting, my hair

is styled and dry, and my almost invisible makeup has been applied—Ash tells me it's time to change into my dress. We've been waiting until the last minute, afraid any refreshments I eat might accidentally fall onto it and stain it.

There's only thirty minutes left until the show starts, and the nerves that have been tormenting Ash seem to have escaped her, choosing a new victim in me. My palms are sweating, and my stomach feels like I drank an entire pitcher of flat soda.

Nearly all the models are ready, some of them already dressed in their nineteenth-century attire. Others are holding cups of fruit punch and plates of cupcakes, chattering in excitement about possibly winning a spot in the boutique. Only two or three stylists are running behind, still hard at work and sweating with the effort to finish on time. Pity slices through me, but I stay where I am. I would offer to help if it weren't for them being Ash's competition.

Ash and I enter one of the makeshift dressing rooms, and she gets to work on my corset. I enjoy my last full breaths of air as she tightens it into impossibility, constricting my lungs. Ash has me step into the hoop skirt. She pulls the long-sleeved, full-skirt dress over my head, careful not to let any part of the pale pink garment touch my hair or face. She adjusts it here and there, tying the white sash, and once I'm suited to her liking, we slide open the curtain.

I don my white wrist-length gloves as we walk out, gathering up my skirts so I don't trip, but somehow don't lift them high enough. I stumble, about to lose my footing when a strong hand grips my elbow, holding me upright. I look up into Theo's face.

He stares at me, locking me in place. A thrill shoot through my body.

"You look beautiful," he says. "Absolutely stunning."

"Thank you," I whisper, realizing for the first time that he too is already dressed. He's wearing a long-sleeved shirt under a vest and a pair of dark trousers. His boots are fastened with buttons and hooks, and a silk necktie the exact shade of his blue eyes graces his neck. His dark hair falls gracefully against his forehead. My knees suddenly feel weak again. He is so perfect it makes me want to cry. "You look like a true English gentleman."

"Don't worry," Ash says from beside me, a smile in her voice. "You'll have plenty of time to rip those clothes off each other later." She pulls me forward, and we make our way out of the cosmetology building, heading for the back entrance to the drama theater. "Remember," Ash tells me. "Smile. Don't trip. Spin slowly, so that everyone can see the back of your hair, and curtsy at the very end."

I swallow. "Anything else?"

"Yes," she says. "Get me into that damn boutique. I can't find maternity scrubs anywhere."

We enter the drama building through the back, and I'm surprised to find we're one of the last pairs to arrive. We're supposed to walk the stage in order of group number, which is assigned alphabetically by the stylist's last name. Since Ash's last name is Majors, we'll be the sixth pair in line. Theo's turn won't come until later, since Charlie's last name is Samuels.

I search the room for Theo, willing him to materialize out of thin air. I'm starting to feel more anxious with each passing second.

"I'll be right back," says Ash. "I'm going to use the restroom really quick." She rushes out the side door. If she's not back in time for our turn, they're going to have to skip us. Because there's no way I'm doing this without her.

On my way to get in line, I see my reflection in a floor length mirror propped against one of the walls, and my breath catches. Ash has truly worked some kind of magic. The way my curls gracefully graze my forehead and jaw make my reflection almost unrecognizable. My eyes stand out in my face, the green flecks made more prominent against the brown somehow. My lips are full and pink, and the dress itself is a piece of art as fine as a jewel. I can't honestly say I would have made such a diligent stylist, had our roles been reversed.

Ash will win a spot in that boutique. I will somehow make it happen for her, if it's the last thing I do. For working so hard, for ensuring I don't make a fool of myself. For always being such an amazing cousin and best friend. She deserves it.

With my determination comes fear, as always. The

thought of not winning makes my heart sink, but there's no way for me to guarantee such a thing.

Except to perform a ritual, a small part of my brain tells me.

My breath catches. I never want to go back to that mentality, but since I've managed to mostly eliminate reacting to compulsions from my daily life, it's hard to see the harm in one tiny ritual.

I don't have long to decide, because the sound of the music starts, and Mrs. Harrison enters the backstage room. "Get in line, everyone!" She moves her hands in the direction of the stage. "And be quiet back here. We don't want the mics picking up anything extra."

I look around the room for Theo again just as he opens the back door and comes inside after Charlie. I catch his eye, and he immediately walks over to me.

"Thank God," I say, about to unleash my worries.

"I—"

"Places!" Mrs. Harrison somehow both shouts and whispers.

Theo touches my cheek. "Don't worry, little Willow. I'm right here." He kisses me and gives my hand a firm squeeze. "You'll be brilliant."

"Ready, babe?" Ash says, appearing back from the restroom. I nod, and she pulls some oil blotting strips from her apron, dabbing at my nose. She smiles. "You look perfect. Let's do this!"

An employee from the cosmetology department gives

the audience her introduction, thanking them for coming, and explains that the funds gained from the ticket sales will go towards bettering our department and supplying products for the students.

The first pair to go onstage is Jess Anderson and her model Cami. Their obvious confidence as Cami struts onto the stage makes my stomach swim. Cami's ruby red gown is adorned with sequins, cut low and showing off her sharp collarbones.

What if I fall? What if Ash pukes? What if—

"Babe," Ash whispers. "Pay attention." She gestures in front of us.

The line moves forward. I shuffle ahead, careful not to trip on my skirts.

It's disorienting to not be able to see what's going on behind the curtain. We can all hear the claps and cheers of the crowd, the Victorian drawing-room music playlist going, and the sound of Cami's heels as she struts up and down the stage. I wish I could see what she's doing. How she's walking, if she looks nervous, if she trips and falls.

Breathe, I tell myself. *You'll be fine.*

I still have time to tap. Doing so could guarantee everything will go according to plan. But I'm worried if I tap, I'll fall back into the trap of relying on my rituals to solve all my problems.

My heart races when the next pair goes, and then the one after that, and when I'm the next one in line, I feel like I'm about to faint or turn inside out or crumble into dust.

Lola and Peyton have finished, which means it's our turn. Mrs. Harrison signals for us to get onstage, and I swallow my nerves, lifting the ends of my skirts again, as high as I can get them.

We step out from behind the curtain.

At first, I'm blinded by the spotlight pointed directly in my eyes. I blink a few times, seeing the light even from behind closed lids. I'm worried I'll somehow end up walking straight off the stage but remember that there's green fluorescent tape signaling where we're supposed to stop walking.

I take a few wobbly steps forward. Steady myself. Continue.

The announcer's voice sounds from the speakers. "Stylist Ashton Majors has modeled Willow Bates after a mid-century, high-status lady of age." She continues, explaining Ash's inspiration behind the style, but I'm no longer listening. I'm too focused on breathing, which is even harder for me now, thanks to my corset. I concentrate on keeping my footing even, and on not falling flat on my face.

When I reach the part of the stage closest to the audience, I pause. Spin slowly, just like Ash told me to. Smile. Walk back—and remember her last request. I curtsy. The crowd applauds, and my smile is genuine when we make our exit backstage.

"You did so good," Ash tells me. "I'm so proud of you." She squeezes me.

I exhale loudly. "Thanks."

The next pair is called forward, and Mrs. Harrison tells us we can watch the rest of the show from any leftover empty seats in the audience, if we like.

"You go ahead," Ash says to me. "I'm going to take a nap in my car."

I laugh, sure she's joking, but then I remember she's pregnant and probably completely serious. "Okay," I tell her. "I'll text you when the winners are about to be announced."

I head for the exit, stopping when Theo reaches out from his spot in line, his arm snaking around my waist. "You did amazing, love," he whispers in my ear, sending chills over my entire body.

I give him a quizzical smile. "How do you know?" I ask.

He smirks. "I watched you. Snuck out of the queue when Mrs. Harrison was preoccupied. You were brilliant."

I laugh, simultaneously surprised and embarrassed. "Why did you do that? You could have gotten in trouble." I smack his chest, wincing a little when my finger hits a hard button on his vest.

"I don't care." His eyes are on my lips, and before I can react, he's kissing me. His lips are hard against mine, and I break away when Charlie coughs.

"Lipstick isn't part of his look, princess," he says.

"I wanted to use a ritual so badly," I whisper to Theo, ignoring Charlie.

His eyes show only a hint of alarm. "Did you?"

"I was close," I say. "But I didn't."

It's been weeks of refraining from reacting to my compulsions, weeks I've felt so at ease. There are times it's hard. Like tonight. My urge to find an outlet to my anxiety still hasn't disappeared. Part of me thinks it never will. I'm not sure if anxiety is something that can be simply cured, but what I do know is I am strong. I'm more determined than I was yesterday, and my mental strength will only continue to grow. Every time I refrain from reacting to my OCD, I only build that muscle. And the fashion show just so happened to be one of those instances.

Theo's eyes search my face, and I can tell he wants to ask if I'm okay. But instead he says, "Well, I'm proud of you. And I would still be even if you used a ritual. All that matters is that you keep growing."

I smile. "Thank you. Now I'm going to go find a spot to sit in the audience so I can watch you strut that stage."

Theo smirks, and I leave him there to ponder that information with Charlie. I hope he feels just as nervous as I did, now that he knows I'll be watching him, too. But knowing him, it probably doesn't even faze him.

I find a secluded seat in the back row of the theater. As I watch the next group perform, I realize it doesn't matter if Ash and I place tonight. If we don't, whether it's because I didn't use a ritual, or because fate decided we shouldn't, it will be okay.

I've finally accepted that I don't need to be in control of my life. It's a liberating feeling, letting go of the wheel, letting it spin in whichever direction it chooses. Even if it causes me to crash, even if it results in my end, I don't want to interfere. I don't want the pressure of deciding what little details are going to influence the major events in my story.

I'd much rather sit back, relax, and watch.

Epilogue

This is the first gender reveal party I've ever been to.

For someone who claims she doesn't care what gender her baby is, Ash had an especially difficult time deciding how she wanted the big reveal to happen. Between cutting a cake, popping a balloon, hitting a baseball open to reveal colored dust inside, it really doesn't matter. In the end, the result will be the same: pink or blue. Girl or boy.

Ash hasn't gone with any of these methods. She's decided to reveal her baby's gender by shooting Joseph with a paintball gun. All day, everyone has been complimenting her on her creativity. Personally, I think she just enjoys hurting him.

All her guests are wearing pink or blue to represent what they believe the sex of her baby is. I don't understand why pink and blue are the only acceptable options. My favorite color is blue, and I'm a girl. Whoever assigned color to gender, of all things, I'd like to have a conversation with.

Nevertheless, I'm sitting on a party bench in her backyard, mingling with guests and wearing blue, not because it's my favorite, but because I think Ash is having a boy. I cheated, basing my guess off hers, because they say the mother's intuition is always right.

I'm deep in a conversation with Aunt Christie about how she knew all along Ash was pregnant.

"I was just waiting for her to tell me herself," she says.

I'm not sure why she's insistent on telling this story. I was there when Ash told her mom the news. To say she was surprised would be an understatement. Aunt Christie wouldn't speak to Ash for two days.

Although the baby's gender has been apparent to Ash's doctor for weeks, Ash wanted to have the party at the end of the semester, as a way of celebrating the end of us being freshman stylists. Not only that, but I think she's also hoping for another chance to rub our second-place victory in the fashion show in everyone else's face. She keeps expressing her excitement to show off her new clothes when she and I are in the boutique after she has the baby. I think I'm supposed to be thrilled, but instead, I'm trying not to mourn.

Theo's flight home leaves tomorrow.

This is my last day with him.

I'm not paying attention to what Aunt Christie is saying anymore, instead searching the backyard for Theo. He's leaning against the wall of the house, talking to Joseph. He glances up at me, as if sensing my gaze. My cheeks heat as his eyes trail my body, sending desire burning through my veins.

"You really do care about him," My mom says, causing me to start. I hadn't heard her approaching, but I nod stiffly. Things between us still haven't returned to normal. I'm not sure they ever will, either.

"I do."

My mom sighs and smooths my hair back, away from my face and down my back. "I love you, Willow."

I meet her eyes. "I love you, too."

She smiles, but it looks sad, like she knows there's a barrier between us now, a wall meant to separate us for an infinite amount of time.

"I'm sorry for the things I've done," she says softly. "I didn't mean to hurt you."

I stare at her, in complete shock at her apology. She did it. She actually said sorry.

"Thank you for apologizing." My lips quiver. I don't know if I want to smile or burst into tears.

My mom stares back, and for the first time, it seems like she might not be seeing anyone other than me. Like the resentment she's never been able to let go of is finally starting to fade.

My mom walks away, and I watch her retreat toward a

group of older adults. When I eventually glance back at Theo, he breaks away from his conversation and comes my way. He wraps his arm around my waist, leaning close to whisper into my ear. "All right?"

I nod. "All right."

"Good," he says. "How long until the big reveal? It's hot, and I'm dying to get out of these clothes."

"You're wearing a tank top and shorts," I point out. "It can't be that bad."

"It feels like summer already." Theo scowls.

He's right. It's still technically spring, but the heat is particularly malicious today. My hair is currently straight, and I'm regretting it with every passing second. It hangs even heavier than usual, impossibly long and getting in my face. My neck is sweating, causing the hair touching it to revert back to its curly texture.

"Hey guys," Charlie says, walking over to us, a blue drink in his hand. "Tell Eva it's not a girl. Ashton is carrying too low."

I blink, trying to bring myself back to the present, but Theo answers smoothly to an approaching Eva, "You're mad if you think it's a girl. She's clearly having a mini Joe."

Eva rolls her eyes. "No way. Team pink!"

I'm about to tell them all I could care less what the outcome of this party is when Ash joins our group, looking gorgeous in a long blue dress. Her blond hair is in an elegant French twist. "Having fun?" she asks Charlie and

Eva. "Because we're about to start the next game." She holds up a ball of yarn and scissors. "Everyone has to cut a string of yarn the length they think the circumference of my belly is. The winner gets a prize."

Charlie seizes the yarn and scissors, using Eva's frame to measure. When it's my turn, I take my time trying to cut a piece of yarn the right length, and hand the thread to Theo. He snips off a shorter piece than mine.

"My turn!" Chutney takes the yarn and scissors.

Everyone takes turn cutting off a string, most people using someone else's waist as a guide, others completely winging it.

When Ash goes around measuring everyone's yarn, she stops at Theo's. "We have a winner!"

"You have to be joking," I mutter.

Theo grins and holds up his yarn. "I've got an eye for this sort of thing, little Willow. No need to be jealous."

Ash hands him a mason jar full of candy. "Here's your prize, Prince Harry. Try not to brag too much."

Theo opens the jar and eats a few pieces of candy before handing it to me.

Ash cups her hands around her mouth. "That was the final game, everyone. Now it's time!" Ash makes her way to the center of the backyard and her mom carefully hands her a paint-ball gun equipped with either pink or blue paintballs. Joseph is wearing all white and has a protective mask on, due to what he claims is Ash's poor aim.

"Okay, everyone." Ash pretends to cock her gun. "Start the countdown!"

"TEN! NINE! EIGHT!" Everyone is shouting together as a group. "FIVE, FOUR, THREE, TWO, ONE!"

Ash completely unloads the gun, splattering ball after ball onto Joseph. His entire body is covered in paint.

And it's pink.

A girl.

Ash is having a baby girl.

I cover my mouth, and the guests start clapping and cheering. Joseph looks down at himself for the first time, and to my surprise, starts jumping up and down. He lifts Ash off the ground, swinging her around in a circle, hugging her to him. Her eyes are moist, her smile practically causing her face to glow. She doesn't even seem upset that he's hugging her while completely covered in paint, surely ruining her dress, and my heart swells with happiness for her.

But I guess her intuition was wrong after all.

Ash goes around hugging everyone at the party, and when she gets to me, the paint from her dress smears onto mine.

But it doesn't even matter.

* * *

When almost everyone has gone home, Ash turns on the outdoor lights. There's been music playing since the party started, but it was almost impossible to hear with everyone talking and enjoying the party. Now, with only a few stragglers left, it's hard to ignore, especially when a slower song begins to play.

"My parents are leaving," Joseph tells Ash. "They want us to walk them out."

"Okay," she says. "Coming."

I plop down next to Theo on the couch he's sitting on and reach for his hand. "I'm going to miss you," I whisper. "So much."

He kisses my forehead, tenderly. "Don't think about that right now," he says.

"It's hard not to."

"We'll both just have to find distractions to keep us busy," he murmurs. "Until we can see each other next."

I give him a melancholy smile. "Like what?"

"Like," he says. "Reading. And Painting. And video chatting with one another on our phones. And . . . " he trails off, his eyes shining. He swallows, and his throat bobs. "Dance with me?"

I frown at him. "You can't be serious."

His expression tells me he's completely serious. "Come on, love. Don't be shy."

I scoff. "No."

"This is my favorite song of all time. Are you really going to deny me, little Willow?"

"*My Cherie Amor* by Stevie Wonder is your favorite song of all time?"

Instead of answering, Theo takes my hand and pulls me into a standing position.

Into the center of the yard.

I shake my head, but he wraps his arms around my waist, pulling me flush against him. We begin swaying to the song, and my nerves ebb slightly.

"Okay," I say, burying my face in his chest. "I guess this isn't so bad." The canopy of white lights hangs above our heads like stars, illuminating our dancing shadows against the concrete. The light breeze rustling Ash's plastic table-cloths is warm. A symphony of insects chirps softly from the grass.

He pulls me against him. "No, it's not. It's quite the opposite, in fact." He kisses my hair.

This is a place as happy as the one he painted for me. I could stand here in this moment forever.

And that's when it hits me.

There's no reason for me to stay in America.

Ash already told me I should go, that we can start back up at American River after she has the baby and I come back from London. Me staying here is just another form of me falling victim to my fears. And I've already come this far. "Theo."

"Hm?"

"When does that plane ticket expire?"

"Plane ticket?" He frowns at me. "I don't believe it does. Otherwise I'll buy you a new one."

I take a deep breath. "How do you feel about having a plane buddy for your flight tomorrow? And a desk buddy at your new school?" I bite my lip.

Theo searches my face, as if trying to find hints of bluffing. He doesn't say a word, doesn't breathe, as if doing so will somehow change my mind.

"I'm coming with you," I clarify.

Theo doesn't grin like I expect, but instead swallows hard. His bright blue eyes are shining like a mirror, and I can see my silhouette in them, staring back at me. "Really?"

"I mean, I haven't packed anything. But—"

Theo lifts me and spins me around in a circle. "You don't need anything. I'll buy you anything you want."

I laugh and shake my head. "I don't want you to do that."

"Then I'll have all your things shipped." Theo's smile finally appears. It's brilliant. Beautiful. "All that matters is you're coming with me and I won't have to be without you."

I lean forward and kiss him. He tightens his arms around me.

I could worry about what the future holds. I could ruminate on whether or not our relationship will last. Whether or not something terrible will happen because of my last-minute change of plans.

But if I recall correctly, *he* was once a last-minute change of plans.

Anything could happen. Good or bad. Amazing or

horrific, even. But what matters is that none of it will be because of me.

Because I'm trying this new thing where I live life one day at a time. In the moment.

As carefree as I possibly can.

ACKNOWLEDGMENTS

I really hope I don't forget anyone.

I have so many people to thank, but first, I'm going to start with Ashley Briggs. My cousin and best friend, the person this book is dedicated to. Without you, this story would have been a laughable mess and never would have seen the light of day. Thank you for being the first person to read this book, for reading every single draft, for giving me brutal (and hilarious) feedback, for the endless, hours-long phone calls, for letting me hog our conversations to get your input, and for your endless enthusiasm and belief in this book. You're amazing. I love you.

Next, my son Oliver. You're too young to read at the time that I'm writing this, but I want you to know how much I appreciate you sacrificing some of our play time to let me write, and for enduring my scattered brain constantly. Your smile lights up my life every day, and I'm so blessed to have you.

Thank you to my husband, Michael, my best friend, for always believing in me and supporting everything I want to do. Your high expectations for me keep me going, and so does your love and patience. I'm so grateful we get to do this crazy thing called life together. Love you.

Thank you to my mom for never denying me a book my entire childhood, and for being an Aries with me when I needed someone to understand my indecisiveness, creativity, and spontaneity. The other signs wish they were as cool as us.

Thank you to Breanna Holquin, Nicole Donnelly, Emma Duarte, Tiffany Donovan, Nyesha S. Cammack, and Oriana Castillo Akers for being my beta readers, fellow book club members, and genuine friends. You guys are the best, and I love you so incredibly much.

Thank you to Dr. Suzanne Jones, Dr. Grageda, and Dr. Carlton Oler for the helpful info and encouragement that I'm not dying (and also for being amazing people).

Thank you to all the teachers who have contributed toward my love for reading and writing, namely Glenda Mora and Kimberly Smith, Tobie Schweizer, Barbara Finkle, Jason Tarshis, Ms. LeRoux, and Ms. Riley.

Thanks Gilbert Ramirez for being the best cosmetology instructor, and Samantha Dunaway for taking a chance on me during our first day, even though you were definitely cooler than me, and to Ana Rico for talking books with me when we should have been working on clients. And Laura Gonzales, Lauren Ramos, Alyssa Diaz, and everyone else for making that time as fun as it was.

Thank you Claire Darling for all the London info. You're my favorite.

Thanks Wade Poezyn for letting me pick your brain about South Africa, and Haley Scott, my lovely cousin for planting the seed I needed to realize my inner strength.

Thank you to my parents, step-parents, and siblings, Zach Akers, Elijah Akers, and Taylor Rowan. If you guys made it this far, that means you actually read the book, and I feel truly honored. Thank you all for always respecting my writing time, always encouraging and inspiring me, and for being such good motivators.

Thank you to Kelly Meagher for reading the first book I ever wrote. I hope you read this one, too, and enjoy it as much as my first.

Thank you Nikita Reinhard Akers for all the help and different perspectives you've offered me during this process. Love you so much.

Thanks to Murphy Rae and Ashley Quick for designing the most beautiful cover I've ever laid eyes on.

Thank you Lillian Schneider and Alyssa Garcia.

Special thanks to Marissa Taylor. Your help and insight were truly invaluable. I'm so grateful for how above and beyond you went to make this book what it is during edits. Thank you for loving this story so much, and for having such enthusiasm for it before even reading it. You are awesome.

And finally, thank *you*. You, the one holding this book. Thank you for sticking with me till the end, for embarking on Willow's crazy journey with me, and for reading the words I poured my heart and insanity into. I hope my words made you smile, laugh, and feel happy inside. I hope they made you feel like there's someone else in the world who understands what it's like to feel out of place.

Thank you so much for reading, for caring, and for being you.

ABOUT THE AUTHOR

Whitney Amazeen's love for reading started in third grade and has been going strong ever since. As a result, Whitney has evolved into a full-fledged daydreamer with more stories in her head than she can count. When she's not immersed in a novel, Whitney spends the majority of her time writing down stories about characters in her head who demand to be heard. Whitney lives in California with her husband and son, and can often be found drinking tea, hoping for foggy weather, and obsessing over fictional characters. Whitney is a Ravenclaw.

For more books and updates, visit:
www.WhitneyAmazeen.com

For more information on OCD, anxiety, and mental health, please visit National Alliance on Mental Illness (NAMI.org) and The Anxiety and Depression Association of America at (ADAA.org).

9